I MARRIED A BEAST

Prime Mating Agency

REGINE ABEL

CONTENTS

I MARRIED A BEAST

He is the Beast of her dreams.

Belle prayed for the day she would meet her Beast. As a proud monster lover, she signs up with the Prime Mating Agency for a chance to be paired with an exotic alien. The one she's matched with exceeds her wildest fantasies. With four eyes to better see her, four arms to better hold her, and a rumbling voice that curls her toes, Bayron is the perfect mix of cinnamon roll personality sprinkled with a hefty dose of grumpy to make her melt.

Bayron wasn't looking for a mate when a PMA agent convinced him to marry, and with a human at that. He's still baffled about why he agreed. Compared to a Zamorian female, Belle is delicate, disturbingly eager, and nothing like the submissive female he'd always assumed he wanted. And yet, her boldness, straightforwardness, and eternal enthusiasm stir a possessiveness in him that cannot be denied.

But as events of his past clash with their future, will they be able to overcome their cultural differences, or will adversity tear them apart?

DEDICATION

To those who acknowledge there are always two sides to a coin and who approach conflicts with an open mind. However valid your truth is, it may not be someone else's. Only if we honestly communicate and actively listen can we understand where the other is coming from and find a common ground. If we simply take a second look at a situation through the lens of the other person, we'll often realize how wrong our assumptions were.

To those who do not judge a book by its cover.

CHAPTER 1
ANNABELLE

I shifted in the comfortable, cushioned chair of the waiting area, putting a stop to my restless fidgeting. If not for the irritated glances from the other candidates sharing the space with me, I wouldn't even notice I was doing it. How did I end up with those annoying nervous ticks? No clue. Between absentmindedly tapping my foot, shaking my leg, or scratching at the arm of my chair, I'd pretty much pissed off everyone.

God knew it wasn't on purpose. But no words could describe the insane level of my current excitement. The Prime Mating Agency's founder and principal agent had finally come back to Earth. Saying I was fangirling over Kayog Voln was the understatement of the millennium. I'd been following the work of his agency even more religiously than the most devout—if not fanatical—believer.

On Earth, you couldn't walk two meters without bumping into some intergalactic matchmaking agency. However, there was only one PMA. All the others boasted how they could find us the handsomest, wealthiest, and loveliest alien mate. Aside from that being boring, half the matches ended up in a divorce. For its part, the PMA not only had a perfect score with ensuring the couple would live happily ever after, it specialized in pairings with primitive, and often 'monstrous' aliens.

And I was a proud monster lover.

Humans and the other aliens who normally visited Earth were fine enough but nowhere near as exotic to satisfy my unusual tastes. Frankly, the lack of enthusiasm displayed by the other women and the couple of men in the room was not only offensive to me, but was also seriously starting to piss me off. In their minds, they were *settling* for the lesser dating pool out of desperation. The fools didn't realize how freaking awesome primitive aliens were. Who needed a pompous, advanced alien anyway?

When the consultation room's door opened, my heart nearly jumped out of my chest. I held my breath, hoping. However, Kayog's voice resonated, calling a different person's name. My shoulders slouched, and I kicked myself for the spot I'd chosen to sit that kept me from getting a good eyeful of my hero. Sure, I'd seen him plenty of times in pictures, but in the flesh held a unique magic. If not for the fact that he was already happily married, and at least twice my age, I wouldn't have minded flirting with him.

Although bird folks didn't feature high on my preference list, I wouldn't spit on them. Temerns like Kayog were a rather attractive species. They reminded me of a humanoid version of Earth's birds of paradise—not to be confused with the flower of the same name—especially in his case, as he had the matching golden feathers, maroon wings, and long, fluffy white tail of those birds. The other Temerns came in various colors, his stunning mate having the same white feathers with dark specks as a snow owl.

I still couldn't believe I was only minutes away from meeting Kayog. Hopefully, I wouldn't start squealing like a schoolgirl, further annoying the other candidates. Members of his species were extremely powerful empaths who worked as moderators for various planetary governments and most of the biggest corporations, especially the United Planets Organization. You couldn't bullshit them. They would sense the minute you held ill intentions or were being deceptive. It also allowed them to know beyond a doubt when two people were soulmates.

An exasperated huff made me realize my wretched foot had started tapping again. I stopped, casting a sheepish look at the woman, who didn't appear in any way mollified by my honest apology. I shrugged and let my mind wander some more.

I needed to keep my expectations in check. While Kayog's matches were always perfect, they didn't necessarily happen overnight. Some candidates waited months, even years, before he found their soulmate. I didn't want to contemplate that possibility.

Twice already, I'd missed Kayog's visit to Earth. The first time, I'd been doing the final exam to obtain my art degree. Despite my best efforts, when I finally arrived, he was already gone. The second time, I'd got injured wakeboarding. This time, I all but wrapped myself in bubble wrap and parked my reckless butt at home to make sure nothing would prevent me from being here today.

I perked up at the door opening again, but this time wide enough that I finally got a glimpse of my hero as soon as the previous candidate walked out. His silver gaze zeroed in on me. My eyes widened, and my jaw dropped with disbelief when he nodded and gestured for me to come.

I squealed.

He chuckled while I all but ran towards him under the judgmental glares of the other people waiting. I couldn't have cared less. Right this instant, I had zero fucks to give about who had issues with my enthusiasm. I could barely breathe as I came to a stop in front of him. Damn, that Temern was taller than I expected, at least 6'2 to my 5'6. Eyes as wide as saucers, I walked past him when he waved me in, still chuckling.

I barely paid attention to the rather barren room of the UPO office that had been put at the PMA's disposal for this visit. I made a beeline for the chair across the table that served as a desk and all but let myself fall into it to get off my wobbly legs. My reaction was a little absurd and rather embarrassing, considering the Temern could feel every single one of my emotions.

Kayog walked past the large window to our right as he circled around the wide table to sit across from me.

"Hello, Ms....?"

"Parker," I responded instinctively. "Annabelle Parker."

But even as I spoke the words, a confused frown settled on my forehead.

Despite the stiffness of his beak, I could visibly see his smile broaden.

"It wasn't your turn yet, but the depth of your enthusiasm was much too strong to further ignore. I could hardly concentrate on the other candidates. And my curiosity got the best of me."

My cheeks felt on the verge of combusting with embarrassment. "I'm so very sorry!" I said, mortified.

He laughed and shook his head. "Please, do not be. It is quite refreshing to have someone so happy to see me. Candidates are often depressed, dejected, and in need of a lot of convincing."

"Oh, no convincing needed here. You're my freaking hero!" Once more, I winced while he burst out laughing, although I didn't miss the sliver of shyness on his face. "Ugh, as you can see, I have very few filters, and my wretched mouth tends to run away with me."

"You are absolutely lovely, Ms. Parker. But please tell me that I may call you by your first name. It would honor me if you would do the same with me."

"You bet! Kayog..." I added with a nervous giggle.

Smile lines creased at the edge of his silver eyes as he gazed upon me with something akin to paternal amusement. He was just as awesome as I had hoped he would be.

"So, my dear Annabelle, what can I do for you?" he asked, his fingers flying over the keyboard in front of him, no doubt to bring up my file on the holographic monitor slightly to his right.

I nervously tucked a strand of hair behind my ear before clasping my hands on my lap. "Well, I've read everything about you and your perfect matches. And I'm praying that you can perform the same miracle for me."

"That is always my goal," Kayog said gently. "What are you looking for?"

"I'd like a beast of a mate: the biggest and weirdest alien you can find me," I said, the pitch of my voice going up a notch as excitement crept in. "I'm looking for scales, fur, even feathers," I added, waving a hand at him.

His eyebrows shot up in a mix of amusement and disbelief. "*Even* feathers?" he echoed.

I flinched, feeling myself blush once again. "I'm sorry, I didn't mean it in a derogatory fashion," I said sheepishly.

"I know," he said softly. "I can feel your emotions. But do go on. This is fascinating."

I grinned and nodded. "Tentacles are cool. Horns, tail, claws, bring them on. Fangs would be great, especially if he's a biter. Oh, and grumpy!! Grumpy is sexy as all hell. *BUT* he needs to be cuddly."

He gave me an unreadable look. "Grumpy but cuddly?" The tone of his voice hinted at the fact that he found me bizarre.

Which I was…

I nodded. "Mm hmm. Super intimidating would be wonderful, although he should be a teddy bear with me. I would like him to be nice, but it's okay if he's a jerk to everyone else. He doesn't need to be wealthy, to have advanced technology, or any of that material stuff. As long as we have a non-leaking roof over our heads, don't starve, and don't live in terror, we're good."

Kayog shifted his wings before leaning back against his seat, an amazed expression on his face. "Wow, I wish all my candidates were like you! You make it so much easier. Human females usually request the exact opposite. Which forces me to ask: why do you want a *weird* alien?"

"Because I'm a proud monster fu... errr monster lover," I said shamelessly.

"A *monster lover*?!" he asked, stunned. "That's a first."

I grinned. "It sounds a little crude and maybe even pejorative, but it's not meant that way *at all*. Women like me simply love the unusual... by human standards."

"I fully support people with an open mind. If you want '*weird* by human standards' I can more than fulfill your needs," Kayog said with an odd spark in his silver eyes, instantly putting all my senses on high alert.

I narrowed my eyes at him while his long and slender fingers flew over his keyboard.

"Have you ever heard of an Ogron?" Kayog asked, his gaze glued to his holographic monitor as he continued typing.

"No," I replied, leaning forward with curiosity.

"They definitely fit the *unusual* category. They're peaceful, very social, although not very talkative."

I frowned, taken aback by that comment. "Social but not talkative? That sounds contradictory."

He smiled. "Ogrons like being in the presence of others, but not necessarily to make small talk. They have multiple dwellings, which can be construed as odd as they have few offspring. They love nature, good food, and playing in the water. They also have a very steep libido."

My face heated, and I squirmed on my seat at the knowing smile the Temern cast my way as he spoke those words. I wasn't a sex-starved maniac, but with the right partner, I wouldn't be shy about sating my appetites.

I shrugged, trying to appear nonchalant, even though my posturing couldn't fool his empathic abilities. "I'm sure I can handle it. But what do they look like? I've never heard of them."

"You'll be happy to hear that they do not fit human beauty standards. Ogrons don't have limbs in the traditional sense, but they instantly grow or retract tentacles as needed."

I perked up further, an excited grin stretching my lips. "Tentacles? What else?"

"Here, let me show you."

He pushed a 3D holographic projector in the center of the desk between us and pressed a key on his keyboard. The image of the unholy love child of a blobfish and a giant, shell-less escargot materialized over the projector. My jaw dropped in complete horror.

"A SLIME?!" I exclaimed.

He tilted his head to the side, studying my features with an impassive expression. "While I can see how you could draw such a parallel, they would take great offense at being called that. Although it doesn't seem likely, they're perfectly compatible with humans. For coupling, they grow appendages as needed. They eat their food raw through slow digestion, so special arrangements would need to be made to accommodate your nutritional needs. The one major downside—although a temporary one—is their extremely strong body odor. It's quite nauseating, really. But within a couple of weeks, your sense of smell will be all but gone, so it will no longer be a problem."

I blinked, unable to believe what I'd just heard. "That's going to be a hard pass for me. I… uh… That's a bit too far up the weird spectrum."

"Right. Ogrons are indeed difficult to match. Let's look at someone less extreme in terms of physical differences. Hmm, how about a Drapus?" he asked, typing a few instructions on his keyboard to display the new being.

Although that new unknown-to-me alien species constituted a notable improvement on the Ogron, it still qualified as a hell no! This time, I could have sworn a star-nosed mole had a baby with a purple kangaroo on steroids. His muscular chest was quite impressive, but I couldn't picture myself kissing that funky face.

"Don't answer," Kayog said, his fingers typing some more. "Judging by the barrage of emotions emanating from you, this poor Drapus doesn't meet your approval. Let's go with something a bit more humanoid in appearance. What about this Xigov?"

The Xigov in question resembled a bipedal mole rat with a sick, yellowish skin. I stared at his 3D hologram, speechless. How the fuck was Kayog getting it so wrong? I glanced at him in disbelief, looking for a nice way to ask him if he'd smoked something questionable this morning. But my distress gave way to shock when I finally spotted the teasing glimmer in his eyes.

"Oh, my God! You're making fun of me!"

"Me? I would never do such a thing!" His exaggerated innocent look gave him away.

"You brat! You totally had me going!" I said, unsure if I wanted to laugh or be outraged.

His feathery shoulders shook from his silent laughter as he gave me a semi-sheepish look. "Okay, maybe I was teasing you a little. But hey, you said you wanted a mate *as weird as possible.*"

I scrunched my face at him, which only made him chuckle more. "Right. But within reason," I amended.

"That's better. Often, when people express their wishes, they say what they *think* they want, but reality couldn't be further from it. You must understand what you *really* want. So tell me, Annabelle, what are you really looking for?"

I straightened my shoulders, took a deep breath, and this time gave it some serious thought, beyond the monster lover fantasy. It shamed me to admit that, for all my bluster about being all hot and bothered by monsters, deep down I still wanted him to qualify as attractive in his otherness.

"I genuinely would like someone with an exotic appearance, but yes, not too extreme. I want a badass alpha, who is intimidating as hell, and yet who makes me feel safe and protected. I want to be Belle to my Beast."

"A-ha! Now we're getting somewhere," Kayog said with approval. "Annabelle… I bet you've been called Belle or Bella quite a few times."

I smiled shyly and nodded. "Belle is my nickname."

"Do you like to read?"

"Yes, but not as much as she did. I'm an artist. I enjoy drawing and painting unusual things and people."

He tilted his head to the side in that strange way birds often did. "How are you with danger?"

"Depends on what you call danger. I love thrilling things and practice quite a few extreme sports, although not the most-insane ones. I like the 'lighter' sports like zorbing, scuba diving, wakeboarding, surfing, hang gliding, skydiving and base jumping, and the occasional cliff diving."

He stared at me, looking genuinely impressed. "I had not expected that. But no snowboarding or free climbing?"

I shook my head vehemently. "Nope! As much as I like wakeboarding, I have zero tolerance for the cold. Therefore, no snowboarding or skiing for me. Free climbing always tempted me, but it would wreck my hands and fingers. I need them to be fully functional as an artist."

"Fair enough. That means no ice elementals or yetis for you."

"Are there such aliens?" I asked, genuinely curious.

"There's absolutely everything out there, my dear."

I nodded slowly. While I wouldn't have minded a fluffy yeti to cuddle with, I really didn't want to freeze my tail off.

"But getting back to your question, if by danger you mean things like putting myself in a dangerous situation that would require me to fight or anything like that, it's a pass, unless I have someone there protecting my tush."

"All right. Would you marry a criminal?"

I recoiled at that sudden switch. "Err… That really depends

on the crime he committed, whether he made amends, and if he's truly remorseful."

He nodded but didn't comment further. "You said you wanted an alpha male. Do you consider yourself submissive?"

I blinked, getting whiplash from yet another switch. "Not really, but I like dominant males."

"Are you high maintenance?"

I narrowed my eyes at him but played along. "No. I've never been rich, so I never developed a taste for luxury. As long as I have a warm place to call home, enough food not to go hungry, and basic creature comforts, I'm good."

"How about traveling to odd, out-of-the-way places?"

This time, my blossoming suspicion properly took root. "I'm fine with that. I'm an artist. I will find inspiration anywhere. Odd places will only make my muse's toes curl. Why those very specific questions? Do you have someone in mind?"

"Actually, I do!"

"Really?!" I exclaimed, straightening in my chair before giving him a suspicious look. "Are you pulling my leg again?"

He chuckled and shook his head. "No teasing this time. He has no scales, no horns, no fur, no fangs, and no tail."

Each of his words increasingly doused my enthusiasm. "Does he have feathers at least?" I asked, clinging to hope.

He gave me an apologetic look. "No feathers either." My shoulders slumped, and he snorted with amusement. "However, he's 7' tall, with muscles for days and the strength of twenty men. He's quite grumpy and super dominant."

"Okay," I said cautiously, my interest timidly rekindling.

"He also has tusks, four eyes, and four arms."

"Nice! Now we're talking! Why did you keep the best for last? I'm starting to think you like torturing me!"

Kayog chuckled and shook his head, a mischievous expression settling on his feathery face. "No, my dear Belle. Only you can tell me if what I've actually kept for last is the best or not."

My back stiffened as I eyed him warily. "What? Please don't say he's slimy."

The Temern burst out laughing. "No. There is no slime or mucus whatsoever on him. But males of his species are doubly endowed."

He let the words hang between us while their meaning made their way through my brain. My jaw dropped, and his shoulders shook again from unrepressed hilarity.

"He's got two peens?" I exclaimed.

Kayog slowly nodded, making no effort to hide his amusement. "Is that a problem for you?"

I swallowed hard. Past the initial shock, the idea itself didn't actually traumatize me. But my dirty mind had immediately pondered at the size of that male's peen when Kayog had mentioned he was a 7' tall mountain of muscles. My concerns about handling his likely massive schlong just got doubled.

Still, when Kayog pulled up his 3D image, I instantly started drooling at the magnificent beast it displayed.

"Dang, that was unexpected. But I'm sure we'll figure it out," I said, lifting my chin defiantly. "When do I get to meet him?"

Kayog raised his palms in an arresting gesture while laughing. "Whoa! Not so fast. I still have to talk to him about you."

A wave of worry crashed over me. Of course, Kayog needed to get him on board with marrying a human. What if he wasn't into my type?

"Are we a match?"

Kayog's reassuring smile lifted some of the weight that had suddenly settled on my shoulders. "Yes. I strongly believe so. One conversation with him will confirm it. Just so you know, I've never made a match with a Zamorian. They are not primitive by Prime Directive standards. They have achieved interstellar travel on their own, but we still deem their culture quite barbaric. The UPO supports their species in the program as it hopes marriages with off-worlders will help change their mentalities."

Worry crept back in. "So why have you never paired a Zamorian before? Is it because of their mentality?"

He smiled and shook his head. "No. It's merely because none of them has ever signed up for the program."

I recoiled. "What are you saying?" I glanced at the hologram of the magnificent male I'd love to claim as mine and gestured at it. "*He* has not signed up to be paired? Could he already be married?"

"He has not signed up, but I know he's unmated. Do not fret, Belle. My job is to convince people in unlikely pairings that they are meant for each other. As for the Zamorians' mentality, they can be quite ruthless, they love to brawl, they're extremely dominant, super possessive, and always need to win at all costs."

"All I'm hearing is 'sexy, sexy, sexy, super sexy, and I can cure him of that."

Kayog burst out laughing. "You are adorable, Belle. Very well. Leave it to me. I will get you your Beast."

CHAPTER 2
BAYRON

A human… I'd been paired with a human. Still struggling to come to terms with this fact, I once more glared at Kayog. As with all previous times, my displeasure only prompted him to grin, amused by my annoyance. Any minute now, the female's transport ship would dock with the space station where we were waiting for her.

Why, in Khivolt's name, did I consent to this?!

Except the Hunter God had nothing to do with my decision. I'd just allowed the Temern to sway me with his soothing voice, silver-tongued arguments, and flawless track record. And it was indeed flawless. While I had not actively been looking for a mate, I couldn't deny that having someone to share my life with could be nice.

But a human?

They were a capable enough species and, judging by the hologram Kayog had sent me of Annabelle, my soon-to-be-mate was rather attractive. However, human females tended to be quite willful, with sharp tongues, and obnoxious attitudes.

I'd always expected my soulmate would be a quiet, demure, submissive, and obedient female willing to follow me anywhere my hunts took me. When I stated as much to Kayog, he smiled with an aggravating smugness and said that, like with Annabelle, what I thought I wanted and what I truly wanted were completely different things. As if he knew better than I did what I really wanted.

The last time I'd butted heads with a human female had almost gotten me executed on Trangor. Sure, I hadn't been entirely guilt-free in that drama, but despite what others said, I hadn't cheated. It was a competition in which I'd only cleverly stretched the rules. After all, second place belonged to the first of all the other losers.

The same unpleasant mix of shame, anger, and remorse surged through me as the thought of how my actions during the first Great Hunt of Trangor had totally derailed the life of Serena Bello flooded my mind. She, too, had almost gotten executed for trying to clean up the mess I'd involuntarily created. I didn't want to think of what kind of tragedy might have occurred without her sacrifice. As much as my people took pride in our ruthlessness, having the blood of females and younglings on my hands wasn't something I ever aspired to.

The clanking sound of the large doors of the docking bay parting to let in the shuttle carrying Annabelle saved me from dwelling further on these unpleasant musings. A large shuttle flew through the energy field protecting the integrity of the space station before settling down on the landing pad number four, next to which Kayog and I had been waiting.

"Nervous?" Kayog asked teasingly when the shuttle's ramp descended, and its doors parted.

I emitted an outraged grunt before giving him a dark sideways glance. "Nervous about meeting a female? Hardly. I'm a Zamorian Hunter!"

His silver eyes twinkled with amusement. "What you are is a male about to meet his soulmate for the first time. It's okay to be nervous. But I'll pretend you're not."

I bared my teeth at him as a million ways in which I could painfully pluck his lustrous feathers to take him down a notch filled my thoughts. Although he couldn't read minds, his empathic abilities betrayed my less-than-charitable wishes aimed at him. Far from being intimidated, the Temern chuckled.

He was insufferable, and yet, he held my utmost respect. I'd still pluck him though, if only to see the look on his face.

An endless swarm of people of all species descended from the shuttle. A few of the other people, who had also been standing—or sitting—in the waiting area with us, were waving at some newcomers.

For all my bluster, and although I wouldn't qualify it as nervousness, a restless anticipation laced with a sliver of worry were steadily growing inside me. And then, I finally saw her. Simultaneously, Kayog waved a hand at her. She responded in kind, a huge grin lighting up her face.

To my pleasant surprise, she looked even more attractive in person. It wasn't so much her features. Although nice enough, she didn't possess what would pass as traditional human beauty. And yet, there was an undeniable aura about her. Her long, golden blond hair cascaded in bouncy waves around her pixie face. Big, stunning blue eyes peered at me with blatant curiosity from behind an undisciplined lock of her hair. She had a small, snubbed nose, and fairly thin lips compared to mine. Her face wasn't heavily painted, as with some human females. The only makeup of her face appeared to be darkened eyelashes and some natural-colored gloss on her lips.

I gazed approvingly at the pleasant curves of her body. I'd dreaded a bag of bones some human females tended to be. It was a good thing too, as she otherwise looked rather small and frag- ile. My hands needed far more than toothpicks to hold on to. The frilly white dress she wore swayed around her long legs. I didn't know the style of that outfit, but it evoked a sense of peace, nature, and freedom that I rather liked.

Annabelle sauntered down the ramp with an enthusiasm I didn't quite know how to interpret. While I approved of her absence of skittishness, such bold determination didn't mesh with the submissive personality I was hoping for.

However, a human working in the docking bay drew my attention away from my soon-to-be-mate. Muscular and reasonably handsome, the mid-thirties man was leveling his gray eyes with far too much interest on my female. That displeased me enough, but he had to push it further when she failed to notice him. He deliberately banged a tool on the metal frame of one of the containers on the hover cart before him. As he'd hoped, the noise caught Annabelle's ears. She looked in his direction, and he immediately flashed her an unmistakable seductive smile.

My female blinked, apparently taken aback at first by his flirty behavior. To my relief, her shock gave way to embarrassment rather than reciprocal interest. I realized I'd bared my teeth and was growling menacingly at the male when they both turned to look at me with stunned expressions. The male blanched and raised his hands in an appeasing gesture when I took a threatening step in his direction. The whole time, I bunched the muscles of my four arms and puffed my chest to make myself look even bigger.

"Sorry, man," the human said. "I didn't know this was your girl. I meant no disrespect."

Without waiting for my response, the male set his hover cart in motion and fled without casting another glance at Annabelle. But even as I took pleasure in watching him scamper off, a sliver of worry entered my mind. If she was like the few human females I'd interacted with—most of them Hunters—she'd start giving me lip about how she could have handled it herself, how she could fight her own battles and didn't need me to babysit her.

As if a true male like me would stand by while a pretender would try to usurp what's mine!

I cast a glance at Annabelle, bracing for pinched lips and an outraged demeanor in response to my actions. To my shock, she stared at me wide-eyed; her pressed lips failing miserably to hide her grin, and an air of wonder on her delicate features.

Kayog's chuckle had me glaring at him. "I told you she was your perfect match."

The annoying bird was deriving far too much pleasure poking at me. And, like an idiot, I kept taking the bait. But not this time. I turned my gaze back to Annabelle as she closed the distance between us.

She stopped barely a meter in front of me, her hands clasped around the handle of the small bag she held before her. Head bent back, she looked up at me with an air of pure awe that deeply unsettled me. Based on her delicate appearance, I'd expected the fear and worry I normally inspired in others. Not the eager fascination she displayed.

"Hello, Master Voln," Annabelle said in a surprisingly agreeable voice. Slightly throaty and sensuous, it held some melodic undertones.

I blinked, wondering for a second if she thought *me* to be Kayog Voln, as she had spoken those words with her eyes locked on me.

"Hello, Belle," the Temern replied. "You look lovely in this bohemian dress. Don't you agree, Bayron?"

My head jerked between them, my brain trying to catch up with what was going on.

"Belle?" I asked, kicking myself as soon as the word left my mouth. I should have concurred with the compliment first and questioned other things later.

"It's my nickname," Annabelle responded in his stead, in a soft voice. "It's what friends and loved ones call me."

"Do you wish me to call you Belle, then?" I grumbled, feeling inexplicably nervous around her.

"Sure! Belle or anything else you think would suit me well," she added.

"Belle… Belle suits you," I replied, my voice harsher than I meant to—a reflex that often kicked in to hide my embarrassment or uneasiness.

"Thank you! And thanks for sending that annoying man scampering off," she replied.

I grunted, not knowing how else to answer. To my relief, my grumpiness didn't seem to displease her, quite the opposite. She beamed at me and continued to stare at my face with that eagerness that was seriously starting to destabilize me.

"Well, since you've informally introduced yourselves to each other, let me do the formal presentations. Annabelle, meet your betrothed, Bayrohnziyiek Skortheatis. Bayron, meet your bride, Annabelle Parker."

I nodded with another grunt, and her smile broadened in response. It lit up her entire face and made her blue eyes sparkle delightfully.

"It's a pleasure to meet you, Bayron."

"Likewise," I said, feeling a little stiff. I extended a hand towards her. "I will carry your bag. Is that all you possess?"

She shook her head, concern flitting through her eyes while she handed her bag over to me. "No, they said they would transfer my belongings to your ship."

"Yes," Kayog confirmed. "By the time we complete your marriage ceremony, her belongings should be sitting right next to your vessel, ready to be loaded onboard.

"Very well. Then let us proceed," I replied.

My stiffness bothered me. I should show more enthusiasm and warmth towards the female. The entire situation seemed to rob me of any rational thought or behavior. I could only hope she wouldn't perceive this as disrespect or lack of interest.

Appearing oblivious to my inner turmoil—although I knew him to be keenly aware of it—Kayog waved cheeringly at us to follow him.

"This way. The priestess is waiting for us in the small chapel right outside the docking bay," the Temern said, taking the lead.

We followed in his wake, Belle's bag clutched in my main right hand while she hurried by my side. The way she kept looking at me with awe truly unnerved me. I wanted to tell her to look ahead to avoid tripping instead of ogling me. But I couldn't figure out a way of saying it that wouldn't give away the fact that her insistent stare had shaken my otherwise unbreakable confidence—not to say overconfidence.

She would glance in front of her for a split second to see where she was going before her gaze zeroed right back in on me. Every time we made eye contact, she would beam at me. What in Khivolt's blood was wrong with that female?

"I hope you had a comfortable journey here," I said, trying to fill the heavy silence between us.

She nodded vigorously. "It was exceptional. The food was great, the accommodations were super comfy, and they had all kinds of activities to keep the guests entertained."

Instead of expanding further, she stopped talking and resumed staring at me with that intense expression. Two steps ahead of us, Kayog was walking quietly, his shoulders shaking from silent laughter I knew beyond any doubt was at my expense.

The wretch…

Thankfully, it was a short stroll to the chapel that catered to every religious denomination under the sun. With a simple vocal command, the barren walls would take on a holographic appearance matching the chapel-style of the chosen faith. A large aisle separated a series of benches on each side of the room. They could be lowered into the ground, their cushiony surface remaining at floor level to serve as comfortable mats instead, if needed.

A human female waited for us by the altar at the front of the room. She eyed me with the proper level of wariness, restoring my faith in my intimidating appearance, which my soon-to-be-mate had managed to shake with her awed stares.

"Bayron, Belle, please meet Isobel Biondi, the priestess who will preside over your wedding," Kayog said enthusiastically, while waving a feathered hand at the female.

She smiled politely, to which I responded with a nod. Belle waved back with a broad grin. I was starting to think my female showed excessive enthusiasm in all things.

"If you are both ready to proceed, please approach the altar," the priestess said. We complied, stopping a meter from her. "Great! Now please stand face to face and hold each other's hands."

I placed Belle's bag on the altar. Then once more we complied, only to realize my bride was missing a pair of hands to hold all of mine. Annabelle gave me an apologetic look accompanied by a nervous laugh—the first sign of uncertainty from her since her arrival. I didn't quite know how to interpret it. I cast a sideways glance at the priestess, who seemed amused by the situation.

"You can place your second pair of hands either on top of hers or hold her waist," the priestess said in a kind voice.

As hands on top of hands felt strange, I took a step closer and placed my hands on Annabelle's waist. It was soft under my touch and nicely curved inward. My female's lips parted, and her body slightly tensed, but not in a negative fashion.

"We are gathered here to celebrate the union of this woman, Annabelle Parker, and this Zamorian male, Bayrohnziyiek Skortheatis, in the sacred bond of marriage. Such union must be entered into freely, with honest intentions, a genuine commitment, and not for financial gains or deceptive purposes," the priestess said. "Annabelle Parker, do you freely and willingly take this Zamorian male, Bayrohnziyiek Skortheatis, to be your lawfully wedded husband, for better or for worse, through good times and hardships, in sickness and in health, until death do you part?"

"I do," Belle said with this same overeager excitement she'd been displaying since her arrival.

"Bayrohnziyiek Skortheatis, do you freely take this woman, Annabelle Parker, to be your lawfully wedded wife, for better or for worse, through good times and hardships, in sickness and in health, until death do you part?"

"I do," I replied, still a little baffled as to why I'd let the Temern talk me into a union I had not actually been seeking.

"Kayog Voln, do you confirm that you bore witness to this human female, Annabelle Parker, and this Zamorian male, Bayrohnziyiek Skortheatis, freely committing to be legally married to each other in accordance with human and galactic laws?"

"I do," Kayog said.

"By the power vested in me by the Clerical College of Earth and the United Planets Organization, I declare you husband and wife. Bayrohnziyiek Skortheatis, you may kiss the bride," Priestess Biondi said.

My mate drew in a breath, which she seemed to hold. Her blue eyes grew wide, her hands slightly shook in my hold, and I could almost feel her entire being buzzing with anticipation. As bizarre as her behavior felt to me, I couldn't deny that her apparent happiness to be mine and to be kissed by me rather flattered my considerable ego.

As soon as I bent my head down, Belle lifted her face towards mine and rose to her tiptoes. By human standard, she was of an average height. But before a pureblood Zamorian like me, she was tiny. Our lips met softly. It shocked me how disappointed I felt at her restraint behavior. Considering the restless eagerness she'd displayed since disembarking the shuttle, I'd expected her to all but devour my face. This rather chaste kiss left me feeling cheated... misled even.

I broke the kiss to stare at her with a slight frown. She licked her lips nervously, looking uncertain for the first time. Her eyes flicked between mine. Under different circumstances, I would have been amused by the fact that she didn't seem to know which of my four eyes to look at—a common occurrence with foreigners.

I couldn't say what she saw in my gaze or read on my face, but she took on a determined expression. Pulling her hands out of mine, she gently cupped my cheeks and drew my face once more towards hers. While my dominant side screamed for me to rebel at such boldness, I didn't resist and let her claim my mouth. This time, she kissed me with conviction, pressing her pliant body against mine. My main right hand found its way to her nape and gently fisted her hair there while the left wrapped around her back. Simultaneously, my secondary set of hands picked her up.

My tongue invading her mouth silenced her surprised gasp. She didn't fight or balk, instead slipping her arms around my neck and tilting her head to the side as I deepened the kiss.

Kromor's teeth! She tasted divine and felt so soft in my embrace! An unexpected flame stirred deep in my loins, forcing me to put an end to this kiss before I frightened my new mate with a dual bulge in my pants. While Kayog had assured me she knew what Zamorians packed, I suspected our wedding night would prove slightly traumatic for her once she saw me in the nude. I would spare her that shock for a short while longer.

I held her a few more seconds, studying her features while she looked at me with wonder laced with desire. That pleased me tremendously. I placed her back on her feet under the congratulatory applause of Kayog and the priestess.

Naturally, the wretched Temern gave me a smug smile when we turned to face them. The priestess made us press our thumbs into the signing boxes of the wedding contract before bidding us goodbye. Kayog lingered a moment longer.

"Before I leave you to get better acquainted, I will briefly remind you of the rules you have both committed to. As with all weddings contracted through the Prime Mating Agency, your union is to be consummated tonight. Normally, you would also be expected to hold the Zamorian wedding today, but I understand your culture requires it to happen on your homeworld."

"Indeed," I confirmed. "We will be heading straight there as soon as we part from you. It should take us two days to reach Xoccoris so she can be introduced to my clan."

"Excellent," Kayog said with approval. "As always, you must give this union a fair try for the next six months. Should that truly fail, then you only have to reach out to me, Belle, and I will find a new mate for you and cover the expenses of your relocation. For this reason, Bayron, you are not required to go through a full claiming during your Zamorian wedding. A binding will suffice until you are both convinced you truly are soulmates."

"That will not be necessary," I ground between my teeth, slipping a possessive arm around Annabelle's waist and drawing her against my side. "I do not fail. Therefore, this union will not either."

The look on the Temern's feathery face pissed me off to no end. At least, he spared me any smartass comment. I didn't love my mate. I knew next to nothing about her, aside from the fact that she seemed to have some creepy obsession with staring at me. But she was mine now. And I'd tear to shreds any male who dared covet or attempt to steal what was mine.

"I'm sure we won't fail," Belle echoed, her voice almost timid as she pressed herself against me.

Her reaction instantly doused my flaring temper. Not only had she not balked at my possessive claim, it seemed to please her.

This female was growing on me.

"Well, considering *I* never fail in my pairings, I have no

doubt your marriage will be a resounding success," Kayog said, his silver eyes taking on a taunting edge when he glanced my way, before winking at my mate, who giggled. "You will find a little something I've slipped into your luggage as your wedding present. I hope it will serve you well, my dear Belle. If either of you ever need anything, do not hesitate to reach out to me."

"We will," Belle said, her voice suddenly shaky, as if overwhelmed by emotion. "Thank you so much, Kayog. I knew the day I came to you, you'd make my impossible dream come true. You're the best!"

Her dream come true? Was 'I' her dream?

Kayog's face melted into a very tender expression as he gazed upon my mate. He extended a hand and gently caressed her cheek. Had he been any other male, I'd likely have broken his arm for daring to touch what was mine. But this gesture was far too paternal to stir my instinctive jealous possessiveness.

"It is I who thank you, dear child, for reminding me why I have the best career in the world. Never lose your bold enthusiasm and hunger for life. Never let anyone dim your light with their darkness. You are a bright beacon of joy, hope, and love, the likes of which we encounter far too rarely. I wish you all the happiness in the world."

"Thank you, Kayog," she whispered, her eyes shining with repressed tears.

The Temern bowed his head in goodbye before taking his leave.

CHAPTER 3
BAYRON

I slightly frowned as I watched him walk away, wondering what could have prompted such words from him, flattering though they were. My mate didn't strike me as the type who suffered from confidence issues that would require such encouragement. Did he fear *I* would dim her light? Or was he referring to someone or something else specific?

Confused, I turned to my female, who continued looking at the Temern until he exited the chapel. She then refocused on me, with an expectant look, this time laced with a hint of timidity.

"Let me take you to my ship. It is a long journey to my homeworld," I said, my voice once again taking that grumpy tone.

I wasn't upset or annoyed. I merely talked that way. Soon enough, she'd understand that. At least, it didn't seem to bother or concern her. She smiled and nodded. I let go of her waist, picked up her bag on the altar, and gestured with a hand for her to proceed. To my shock, she grabbed my hand instead and held it. By the way she looked at me and smiled, I realized she intended for us to walk hand in hand through the station to my ship.

Zamorian Hunters don't walk hand in hand with their mate!

I opened my mouth to say as much, but I couldn't bring myself to speak the words. It would undoubtedly wipe that awed expression she continued to stare at me with off of her face. I didn't understand why I fascinated her so much. But as unnerving as it sometimes felt, I also liked it. No one had ever looked at me as if I was the greatest wonder they'd ever beheld. Crushing her spirit over such a trivial thing wasn't worth it.

I grunted, closed my much bigger hand over her delicate one, and started walking. I had to control my strides so as to keep a comfortable pace for her. Otherwise, she'd have to half-run to keep up with me.

We only had a short stroll from this section of the space station to the ship hangar, where my vessel awaited us. But observing my mate as we walked was quite revealing. Belle possessed an inquisitive mind. Her eyes kept flicking in every direction as she took in our colorful surroundings. It was a pleasure barge filled with nightclubs, casinos, battle arenas, and naturally plenty of brothels and kink clubs. We couldn't see the latter from here, but plenty of holographic signs competed for the patrons' attention.

While some venues here qualified as respectable, this wasn't the type of place I wanted my mate hanging out in. To my relief, despite her blatant curiosity, Belle didn't seem to want to delay our departure so that she could explore the station.

"You come here often?" she suddenly asked as we approached the large, reinforced doors of the ship hangar.

I shook my head. "No. It was just a convenient rendezvous point, halfway from where you were and my last hunt. These places only tend to get you in trouble and make you part with your credits in dumb fashions."

She chuckled and nodded. "Agreed. But they can occasionally be quite entertaining."

"They can be," I conceded, pleased that she didn't appear to be a nightclub addict.

I had many talents, but dancing certainly didn't feature high on that list. While I enjoyed listening to certain types of music, shaking my massive body to its rhythm always felt awkward. Zamorians didn't partake in traditional dances. The closest thing I had seen in the human culture that resembled our versions of a dance was what they called Haka. But ours was, obviously, far more impressive.

The ship hangar's doors parted before us. As always, it bustled with activity from the space station's patrons arriving, departing, loading cargo or unloading the goods they wished to peddle or trade. Many visitors also simply slept in their vessel to save on the often prohibitive costs of lodging within the station.

Once again, my mate didn't seem to have enough eyes to take in our surroundings as she gaped with a marveled expression at the various ships in the hangar. A good third of them appeared to be on their last leg. Likely the vessels of gamblers, put together in a scrapyard after they'd lost their life's savings to games of chance, or mercenaries traveling incognito. Most of the other ships looked decent, with the handful of high-end, state-of-the-art vessels of VIP patrons. Those had their reserved parking spots in the most protected area of the hangar.

But the patrons themselves also held my mate's attention. She observed them discreetly, with a delighted expression. While I would have preferred her focus remained on me, I didn't feel any jealousy. The way she gazed upon them lacked any covetous edge… nothing like the possessive way she'd looked at me. In this instant, Belle reminded me of our younglings when they attended their first hunt.

It suddenly dawned on me that my female had likely not traveled much off her planet. While plenty of off-worlders visited Earth, interstellar travel remained very costly unless you owned a vessel. And the price for acquiring a good one could easily reach between three and ten times the cost of a standard home. Based on the information Kayog gave me about Belle, she had no real wealth to speak of.

I will make you visit more worlds than you can imagine or count.

That thought—not to say that silent pledge—pleased me. As strange as my female struck me to be, I liked that look of wonder on her face. I would give her many occasions to feel that way again, as was my duty as her mate.

"This is my vessel," I said, pointing at it while leading her in that direction.

Belle's eyes widened, and her lips parted with a marveled expression that had me puffing out my chest with pride.

"Oh, my God! It's totally badass!" she exclaimed, walking a bit faster in her haste to reach it. "It reminds me of a Cylon Predator."

"Cylon? I've never heard of that species," I said with a frown.

She giggled. "Not surprising. They don't exist. They were a fictional cyborg race in a classic sci-fi show on Earth. This looks almost like a phoenix rising. I love it!"

"I named it Ostros, after one of my homeworld's most dangerous birds of prey," I explained, now eager to show her my vessel. Considering it would be our home for much of the year, her reaction was encouraging.

As Kayog had informed us, three dock workers were standing next to my ship with an impressive number of crates.

Belle gave me a sheepish grin. "I hope you have enough room for my stuff," she said in an apologetic tone. "It's mostly my art supplies and equipment."

"There will be room," I grunted. "I already freed a room for you to use as your studio."

Belle stopped dead in her tracks and stared at me with a stunned expression.

I stopped walking as well to give her an inquisitive look. "What's wrong? You didn't want one?"

"Of course, I did! But… You really did that for me?"

I blinked, baffled by such a question. "Of course," I said, echoing her. "Why wouldn't I? You're an artist and my mate. It is my duty to anticipate your needs and fulfill them."

Of all the reactions she could have had, I never would have expected her to suddenly look so emotional.

"What is wrong, my mate?" I asked, unsure about what I had said to upset her.

She shook her head and gave me a shaky smile. "Nothing's wrong. Quite the opposite. You're just so perfect. I keep thinking I'm going to wake up any minute and realize none of this is real. That it is too good to be true."

For the first time in my life, I found myself speechless. I always had a snide or irreverent remark ready on the tip of my tongue for any situation. People usually addressed me with fear, resentment, or submission. The abrasive ways of the Zamorians —and even more so mine—didn't tend to endear us to others. But this? What did you respond to your brand-new mate, who was elevating you on a pedestal from whence you were bound to fall once she truly got to know you?

Why was she so awed anyway? By human standards, my appearance was freaky and my ways rude and barbaric. Why would my seeing to her needs move Bella so? Had she been so neglected in her life that the most basic of attention would touch her this much?

"Mr. Skortheatis?" one of the dock workers called out, saving me from this awkward situation.

"Yes," I replied, gesturing for Bella to resume walking as I headed towards the male. "I will open the hold for you to load my mate's belongings aboard."

"Thank you, sir," the human male said with gratitude.

They made quick work of bringing everything into my otherwise empty hold, while my mate bubbled with curiosity to explore the rest of the vessel.

"I will give you the tour first, then you can tell me where you wish me to put your various containers," I said to Belle as soon as the workers left.

"Sounds like a plan," she said with a beaming smile.

I couldn't help a smile of my own. I'd never met someone who was always so happy and enthusiastic. It was surprisingly contagious.

"It's a Xurgen vessel," I said smugly.

"Aren't they one of the most advanced species in the galaxy?" Belle exclaimed.

"They are. Ostros is one of five exclusive vessels of this model," I explained, puffing out my chest.

"It must have cost a fortune!"

I shook my head as the hold's doors opened onto the ship's main hallway. Its impressive width and high ceilings, with sleek asterium metal plates screamed high-end and luxury.

"On the market, it would indeed cost an outrageous price. But I didn't actually pay for it. They gave it to me."

"Oh?" Belle asked, tilting her head back to look up at me.

"It was the grand prize for the first-place winner of the Xurgens' second Grunux Hunt," I replied.

"Wow. You truly are a badass!"

"Thank you, my mate," I said with a grin before waving at a door to our left. "This is the holodeck. While the ship possesses an actual training room, I usually use the holodeck instead because of the advanced beast simulator programs. I have added a series of entertainment programs for you. But if they are not to your liking, let me know what you would prefer, and I will upload them."

"You're so sweet! I love holodecks. Sadly, I didn't get to use them as often as I wished on Earth. If you can't find me in the future, chances are I'll be in there."

Sweet?

While I appreciated the sentiment behind the epithet, the word itself stung. I was many things, but certainly not sweet. Considerate, thoughtful, and dutiful would have been acceptable adjectives to qualify my actions. But sweet?

However, Belle was already moving forward towards the next door.

"This is the armory," I said, taking her inside this time.

I simply couldn't resist showing off my equipment. At long last, my little human displayed the intimidated expression I'd begun to believe she didn't possess. She circled around the large room, looking at everything with the appropriate level of fear and admiration. My female paused in front of the display cases along the right wall with countless blades, daggers, and throw-weapons. She then gaped at my impressive collection of swords hanging on the wall above the daggers.

The central wall had every possible type of gun and blaster. On the left wall, behind a protective glass, my various battle suits hung neatly next to shelves on which rested my attachments and accessories. In the center of the room, four large racks held my battle staves, lances, and spears.

I picked up a couple of scythed blades and a pair of bladed staves—one in each of my four hands—making a series of acrobatic swipes; the staves flowing effortlessly around me without ever knocking into each other.

Belle's mesmerized expression stroked my overwhelming ego in all the right places. I could get addicted to this.

"I can't wait to see you hunt," Belle said.

"Soon, my mate. Soon," I replied while putting the weapons back in their place.

"Do you hunt often?" she asked, as I let her out to show her the mess hall.

"All the time. I only pause while waiting for the next worthy one to take place. I usually seize that opportunity to return to my homeworld."

"So what does that translate to? I mean, how many hunts do you do in a year?"

"It depends. Some hunts only last a couple of days, so I can fly to the next one right away and do five or six hunts in a single month. But then you have much larger-scale hunts that can last up to a month or more."

I led her through the imposing mess hall, which contained three large rectangular tables able to seat ten people each. I circled around the island at the back of the room with an encased cooking plate and stopped at the long counter behind it. With a wave of the hand, I showed her the food replicator as well as the fresh and frozen food storages.

"You will find everything you need here to sate your hunger. The replicator has premium recipes. I have added a variety of human delicacies to it. Let me know if there is anything else you would like added. However, I rarely make use of it. I rather eat handmade meals with meat I caught myself."

For the second time, Belle appeared intimidated. While it had pleased me the first time, this one threw me.

"I can make a mean steak and mashed potatoes," she said with a nervous laugh. "But I'm not exactly a gourmet cook, especially with alien meat that I've never worked with."

I recoiled, unsure whether to be shocked or offended. "Females do not cook," I said in outrage.

To my shock, it was Belle's turn to appear offended. "Women can cook just fine. *I* just happen not to be the best one at it."

I waved two dismissive hands. "Of course, a female can learn how to cook. But it's not because you *can* do something that you *should.* The kitchen is not a female's place. It is a male's duty to provide and feed his woman and offspring. You will not shame me by attempting to take over my role! Anyway, you don't have enough hands to be efficient in the kitchen."

Even as I finished speaking these words, I braced for what would undoubtedly be our first argument. She would fist her hands on her sides, take on a mulish expression, and start telling me all the ways in which 'I wasn't the boss of her' and 'I didn't get to tell her what to do' and especially that 'She could take care of herself just fine and didn't need a male to do that for her.'

Belle stared at me with round eyes, her lips parted in disbelief. The silence stretched for a handful of seconds—that nonetheless felt endless—then she shrugged.

"Hey, when you put it that way, who am I to argue? I wouldn't dare appropriate your duties. The kitchen is *all* yours. I gladly submit to being fed by my husband," my mate said with a smile and a strange glimmer in her eyes.

I couldn't decide if relief over her concession or suspicion about her potentially mocking me dominated inside me. In the end, relief won.

I grunted in approval. "Good. You will find I am an excellent cook. But come, let me show you the rest of the vessel."

"Okay," she replied, grabbing one of my hands again as I walked next to her.

Belle's need for physical contact was throwing me off. Zamorians didn't display affection or their relationship status in public like that. Our females showed their ownership and pride either vocally, or by adorning our braid with a token.

Is she even aware of this?

As an artist, my woman could make me the envy of my clan.

I gave her an assessing sideways glance as we exited the mess hall. I had looked at her online portfolio. Although I knew nothing of art, I thought she possessed an undeniable talent. And yet, something was lacking. The anatomy of the characters or creatures looked sound, her perspectives flawless, but they missed a spark of emotion, like she had drawn them out of duty rather than out of passion.

Hopefully, our travels would provide her with the subjects

that would ignite that spark. Nothing made me more alive than the anticipatory thrill before a hunt and facing danger as I battled against the most vicious predators of the galaxy. I wanted my mate to experience the same type of excitement with her work... but in a much safer environment than mine.

We quickly went through the guest quarters, and even faster through the machine room. My mate had not a single engineering bone in her body. She fawned over the massive bridge, even though she got cross-eyed looking at all the controls on the navigation board.

"You pilot this vessel by yourself?" she asked, stunned.

"Of course. However, it also possesses an extremely advanced artificial intelligence, which allows me to sleep, train, cook, and relax while it autopilots," I explained. "In case trouble arises, the self-defense and evasive maneuver modules will kick into action while raising the alarm so that I can come take over or assist."

Belle shuddered.

"Trouble? Does it happen often?" she asked warily.

I chuckled. "Occasionally, but it's rare. The hunts I attend are usually along safer sectors of the galaxy, ones heavily patrolled by the United Planets Organization's Enforcers. While Ostros is equipped with lethal weapons and defense systems, on the very rare occasions I got attacked, I toyed with the enemy long enough for the Enforcers to come handle them. Within minutes of me sending a distress signal, they would warp over and send the pirates running."

A strange expression flitted over Belle's face.

"What?" I asked, curious. "What thought just crossed your mind?"

"I... hmm... Honestly, I hadn't expected that response from you. I thought you would tell me all the ways in which you spanked them, wrecked their ships with yours, and sent them running while begging for mercy," she said, looking sheepish.

"I'm not saying that I disagree with your course of action, though," she added quickly, as if worried she'd offended me. "I think your approach is wise. I just…"

I chuckled as her voice trailed off. "I am an excellent pilot and a competent star fighter, but I'm not an ace. In a battle arena or on a hunting trail, there is no fight I will not see through. But out here in space, I have no problem deferring to the professionals. A good warrior knows how to choose his battles. I gain nothing by fighting pirates, but risk much instead. I may be ruthless and barbaric, but I am not a fool."

Belle beamed at me. "I'm really happy to hear that."

I caught myself returning her smile. Her cheerful demeanor was contagious.

"Come. Let's go see your studio," I grumbled.

To my shock, I found myself instinctively extending a hand towards her. My mate immediately took it, her smile broadening as she let me lead her to the crew quarters, which I had emptied for her. I couldn't understand what had prompted me to take her hand. It wasn't exactly the type of behavior I wanted to encourage. And yet, the way she smiled would likely incentivize me to do it again.

She's going to make me soft.

An unacceptable notion that I swiftly cast aside as I waved my hand in front of the motion detector of the door's digital lock.

"This is your studio," I said as the door slid open with a discreet swish. "You can set the panel so the door will lock, automatically open on approach, or require either a gesture or a vocal command to open. Most of the doors of the vessel currently open on approach if you are facing them."

"I have nothing to hide. Open on approach is fine," Belle said, her voice bubbling with excitement as we walked inside.

Barely two steps in, my mate froze, her eyes widening and her lips parting in shock as she took in the wide space. The diamond-shaped room had a large central area surrounded by an elevated dais lining the walls, with immense windows giving a view out into space. I'd left it empty but for three tall cabinets for her to store things in as well as a couple of tables.

Suddenly feeling self-conscious, I scratched the back of my nape while grumbling a justification as to its current barren state. "I emptied the room and repainted the walls off-white, since I read it is an excellent color for art studios. They were also talking about mid-value, low-chroma colors, but that encompassed too many colors. If you would prefer a different hue, you just have to ask, and I will change it for you. As far as furniture goes, I only put in the strict minimum so that you would have some storage space to put your things in until you've decided how you want to set everything up."

For a second, I thought Belle hadn't heard me as she continued to stare at the place. I hated how nervous this whole thing made me. I hadn't felt like this since the earlier days of my hunter training, when I desperately sought my father's approval.

Belle took a few hesitant steps inside the room, looking at it as if in shock. I wanted to believe it was pleasant shock, but I couldn't read her expression.

"This is for me?" Annabelle whispered, her back to me.

"Yes, my mate. It is for you to do with as you please."

She turned around and looked at me with eyes filled with tears. My hearts sank while my mind raced. What had I possibly gotten so wrong as to make her want to cry?

"What is it, Belle?" I asked, worry filling my voice. "Is this unsuitable? Please, do not cry. I will fix it. Just tell me what you need."

To my shock, she shook her head, smiling even as a tear rolled down her cheek. "It's more than suitable. It's perfect. *You* are perfect. I can't believe you did all of this for me. No one has ever gone out of their way for me like this. And you don't even know me yet."

Relief flooded through me, and the tension that had been

stiffening my spine evaporated. Tears of joy… a completely irrational human response I had forgotten about. The humans I usually interacted with—males and females alike—weren't the crying type, except at a funeral. And even then…

"I do not need to know you to do right by you, Belle," I said, slightly baffled by this argument, and yet flattered she deemed me perfect. "You are my mate. The day I consented to this union, it became my duty to always see to your needs. I do not intend to fail on that front."

She giggled while wiping her cheek with the back of her hand. "As I seem to recall, my husband never fails."

I puffed out my chest and struck it with both of my primary hands closed into fists. "That I do not," I growled proudly, amused to hear her echo my words to Master Voln.

She giggled again, the melodic sound rather pleasing to my ears.

"But when did you even have time to do this?" she asked, amazed. "You met Kayog barely two weeks ago, and I understand you were in the middle of a hunt."

"I am efficient," I said smugly.

Belle snorted and shook her head. "Clearly, you are. Thank you, nonetheless. I can't believe you would give me such a huge room and with such an amazing view into space. I love it!"

"I am pleased. Now come, let me show you our quarters. Then you can tell me which crates to bring, so that you can start settling in while I set a course for Xoccoris. It is a long journey home."

"Okay," Belle said, taking my hand again.

During our short stroll to our room, I could see my female's wheels spinning. A million questions fired off in my mind as I wondered what thoughts were crossing hers. With a bone-deep conviction, I believed they were thoughts about my vessel. She'd seemed impressed by it, and yet I could tell something bothered her.

"Holy cow!" Belle exclaimed when the doors to our private quarters opened before us. "This is bigger than my entire studio apartment back on Earth! You're only missing a kitchen!"

I snorted. "A bedroom is no place to cook. But there is a replicator and a small cooling unit by the mini bar in the living area," I said, pointing at the latter.

But Belle barely spared it a glance, too busy staring at my… *our* imposing bed. It exceeded the standard human sizes. Their King-sized beds were far too short and barely wide enough for the proper comfort of an adult Zamorian, especially one who liked to spread while resting.

"Sheesh, you need a car to travel across that," she muttered to herself.

I chuckled. "Wait until you see a proper Zamorian bed back home."

"They're even bigger?!"

I nodded with a teasing expression. "Mm hmm."

"Wow…"

Belle said that word with her hand gently caressing the dark brown fabric of the bedsheets as she walked towards the living area to the left. It had a large three-cushion couch with its back to the bed, a massive footrest in front, and a giant screen hanging on the wall across from it. To its right, the replicator was embedded in the wall above the mini bar. While the built-in cooling unit always contained a few cold beverages, I rarely consumed them. I usually indulged in a glass of my high-end alcohol collection. Opposite the living area, the breakfast table served more as a working desk than a place to eat.

"I've added a large amount of human entertainment programs and movies to the vidscreen library, as well as the most popular galactic content. Our com system is also able to connect to long range relays to stream additional programs that may not be available in the library," I explained.

"You really think of everything," Belle said with a smile.

"I do," I replied matter-of-factly, which made her chuckle. I walked back to the opposite side of the bed and pointed at one of the two large doors that occupied that wall. "This door on the left is the hygiene room. The one on the right is the walk-in closet," I said, opening it. "The left side is mine. The central cases and drawers, as well as the entire back and right walls are yours."

"Wow! Hangers, shoe racks, drawers, display cases!" Belle exclaimed as she walked through the large rectangular space. "I don't have enough clothes and shoes to fill all of this."

I frowned. "I thought human females always complained there's never enough room in their closets for all of their attire?"

The most adorable redness crept up her cheeks, and she took on an embarrassed expression. "It is true for many women. But, aside from the fact that I've never been a shopping freak, my finances didn't really allow me to splurge on clothes. I usually save for my art material," she confessed.

My frown deepened as I grunted in understanding. "Well, that shall be rectified. I will not have my mate lacking in clothes and shoes. I will acquire all that you need."

"Ooh! I don't really need anything. I'm not too big on…" Belle's voice trailed off as I glared at her. She scrunched her face, my expression having undoubtedly made it clear this wasn't open for debate. "Fine. I guess we can go shopping."

"We *will*," I corrected, my voice softening ever-so-slightly with contentment that she hadn't argued further. "Credits are not an issue. I am, after all, a top-ranking hunter."

As if I would allow my mate to have less than the elite of her species!

After quickly showing her the hygiene room—which once more seemed to impress her—I had her show me which crates to bring to our quarters and which ones to take to the studio. As we headed back to our room, the hover cart laden with her containers following us, I couldn't resist prying about what thoughts were still percolating in the back of her mind, and that she seemed reluctant to express.

The way her pale skin heated again confirmed my intuitions had been right.

"Speak your mind, my mate. Does my vessel displease you?" I asked, forcing my naturally growly voice to sound a little softer.

"Oh no! Not at all! I think it's an absolutely fantastic vessel. So high-tech and well-designed. It's pure luxury!" she replied, her sincerity undeniable.

"And yet, something about it displeases you," I insisted.

She hesitated and chewed her bottom lip, as if debating how to answer.

"You can speak freely to me. I will not be upset," I said in what I hoped came across as a reassuring tone.

"It's not that it displeases me," she said cautiously. "But… hmm… the entire vessel is kind of really brown."

I recoiled, stopping so suddenly that the hover cart nearly collided with me. I cast a glance around the large hallways, wondering how she could possibly fault their rather delightful brown color.

"What's wrong with brown?" I asked in a defensive tone. "It is a warm, strong, natural, and beautiful color."

Yes, I loved brown. Everything in this ship was in a shade of brown, from light beige to dark expresso. What was wrong with that? Many vessels were in lame metallic colors across the board, and a greater number still were all in dark grays.

"There's nothing wrong with brown," Belle replied in a soothing voice. "But you could make it livelier with some touches of reds, oranges, greens, blues, and even some bright yellows."

The horror I felt inside undoubtedly showed on my face as my mate burst out laughing before patting my arm reassuringly.

"It's not as scary as you're probably imagining," Belle said in an amused tone. "I could sketch what I have in mind to show you. And if you like it, maybe you'll let me make a few adjustments?"

I grimaced, hating the thought of all the ways in which she could deface my very virile vessel and turn it into a dainty, overly colorful ship. Unfortunately, if it was her wish, I couldn't challenge her on it. Females ruled over the dwelling and, in all the ways that mattered, my vessel would constitute our main dwelling.

"Very well," I conceded, making no effort to hide my reluctance.

She giggled and rubbed my upper arm in a soothing fashion. "Do not fret, dear husband. I promise you will love it."

I grunted in a non-committal fashion and resumed walking towards our quarters to deliver her crates.

CHAPTER 4
ANNABELLE

After Bayron's departure, I stared at the door without seeing it, unsure how I currently felt. My husband was a deliciously sexy beast. Hot and bangable didn't begin to do him justice. And how delightfully grumpy was he?

For all that, I didn't really feel the instant chemistry between us that I had hoped for. Sure, my toes had curled during our second kiss, after we'd exchanged our vows. However, as much as I wanted off-the-chart sexual tension between us, a genuine bond of affection held even more importance for me. I wanted the full fairy tale, with my beast head over heels in love with me. But was I being too over-the-top again?

Heaving a sigh, I began unpacking my clothes, while my mind continued to run wild with speculations and thoughts of my husband.

I had loved his possessive, neanderthal display when that guy had ogled me in the docking bay. Since then, though, Bayron had seemed more distraught than enthralled by me. My damn bluntness, excessive enthusiasm, and willfulness often grated on some people's nerves. Was he feeling the same about me?

I couldn't help staring at him. He was so freaking gorgeous.

Those muscles, those bulging veins, his fearsomely handsome face… I wanted to lick him all over. But it was clearly making him uncomfortable. He probably thought I was some psycho. Should I make some conscious effort to rein myself in to avoid freaking him out further?

Then I won't be myself.

Faking being someone tamer than I was would only work for so long. For this union to stand a chance, Bayron needed to fall in love with me just the way I was, in all my excessive ways. I just needed to remind myself that Kayog was never wrong. He'd deemed Bayron and I to be soulmates. That didn't equate with instant love. Like every couple, we'd face some challenges as we grew to know each other.

Patience, Belle. You've got your whole life to tame your Beast.

If only I could read emotions like a Temern. I'd kill to know what Bayron thought of me. Did he feel any attraction towards me? He hadn't looked disappointed by my appearance when I came down the shuttle. He'd also sounded pretty adamant that our union would succeed and that Kayog wouldn't need to find me a replacement husband. That was a positive sign, right?

I sighed again, annoyed with myself for overthinking things and allowing my usual insecurities to give me more stress than necessary. We'd been married less than an hour, and Bayron seemed determined to be the perfect husband for me. I needed to take a chill pill and spend the next six months showing him that I was also the perfect wife for him.

I quickly finished unpacking my clothes and my few pairs of shoes, using less than a quarter of the space Bayron had allocated me in the massive walk-in. However, the drawers in the central island were overflowing with the frilly and sexy lingerie and nightgowns I'd bought as soon as Kayog confirmed Bayron had agreed to marry me.

The thought of our wedding night had me hot and cold all at

once. I didn't want to think about it right now, or I might start panicking. Instead, I exited our room and made my way to my fabulous studio.

I couldn't believe he had freed up such a huge space for me and painted it the perfect color. After reading up on him, especially about the incident on Trangor during the first Great Hunt of the Ordosians, I hadn't expected him to be this attentive. I wasn't high maintenance, but having someone who actually cared about me and wanted to make me happy was a dream come true.

I set up a couple of easels and canvases, laid out my drawing and painting material on one of the tables, then placed my drawing tablet and holographic pose projector on the other. I mostly did digital illustrations lately as it was cheaper than traditional painting on a canvas. However, I already knew that I would not only do an oil painting of Bayron, but I'd likely also make a full height sculpture of him. I'd have plenty of room here to do all of this. I couldn't remember the last time I'd ever felt so excited at the thought of painting a subject.

As I reached for the last crate—a fancy one that clearly didn't belong to me, and that I assumed to be the gift Kayog had referred to—I bubbled with curiosity. Being a bit of a masochist, I had deliberately kept it for last. In a way, it was my reward for having completed my other tasks first.

My jaw dropped as soon as the silver container opened with a soft hiss. The squeal that escaped me, when I recognized the logo on the top box within, almost deafened me. A Zafell! Kayog had gifted me a freaking Zafell camera! That company produced high-tech, luxury art equipment.

The price of this camera alone easily exceeded a full year's rent of my former way-overpriced studio apartment. It not only took high-precision images, even from a great distance, but it also digitized them in 3D. The best part was that a section of the camera could be removed and act as a drone that you could either set to follow or control remotely. This was perfect for close-up shots of locations hard to reach, or of dangerous creatures. On top of being super silent, it even possessed a stealth shield so that the target wouldn't be alerted to its presence.

This would enable me to get badass shots of my husband during his hunts. I could already picture the type of epic drawings I could make from that. Buzzing with excitement, I checked what else my Temern hero had included in the gift box.

I felt weak in the knees at the sight of the complete Zafell suite. It included the fanciest drawing tablet with so many functions I'd probably need more than a lifetime to be able to explore them all, and the mother of all 3D sculptor projector mesh. It allowed you to manually sculpt a holographic mesh physically. You could assign the texture you wanted to the mesh, be it wood, clay, stone, or whatever other material you liked, and it would provide you with a similar resistance as the real thing. The difference? With it being all digital, if you screwed up, you could undo it and continue tweaking it until it was exactly what you wanted. You could experiment with colors, and only once done, commit it and have a laser cut the material you chose to perfectly match your design.

It even included a full set of sculpting tools, from carving, shaving, modeling, texturing, and polishing. I usually only worked with wood and clay, as I'd always found stone too hard on the hands. But this was opening me to a whole new world of possibilities. If Kayog had been near me, I'd give his feathery self a bone-crushing hug.

Once I'd sorted and carefully put away my gifts, I went searching for my husband and found him on the deck. Although he'd warned me that he wanted to get us quickly on the way to his homeworld, it still surprised me to see us already deep in space. Take off had been so smooth and silent, I hadn't felt it at all.

Bayron looked at me over his shoulder as soon as the doors

parted open to let me in. It was uncanny to have him staring at me with four eyes. I never knew which one to look at, although I tended to focus on the bigger, lower pair. I gave him a timid smile, which he didn't return. Instead, he watched me approach with an unreadable expression that made me feel super self-conscious. Once again, I wished I could read his mind or—at the very least—his emotions to get a sense of what thoughts my arrival had triggered within him.

"My mate? Do you require assistance?" he asked.

I shook my head, wondering if this was his subtle way of telling me I had no business on deck, unless I needed his help with something.

"No. I… hmmm… I finished putting away my stuff and setting up my studio. I thought I would join you here and maybe spend some time in your company," I added with a nervous laugh.

A strange emotion flitted over his alien features, so briefly I couldn't even begin to interpret it. I braced for him to tell me now wasn't a good time and to leave him be. Instead, he gestured at the copilot's chair near him.

"Of course. Have a seat," he replied.

Despite the relief that flooded me, I hastened to the chair, feeling even more nervous. I settled down under his intense stare, tucked a strand of hair behind my ear, and clasped my hands on my knees to keep them from shaking.

When nervous, I tended to suffer from an acute case of verbal diarrhea. In this instance, my brain decided to break with tradition and take an impromptu leave of absence. I stared at Bayron, my mind completely blank and my tongue having turned to lead.

A slight frown creased Bayron's brow as he observed my stiff demeanor. God, he had to think he'd married a major freak.

"Every time we're together, you stare at me," Bayron grumbled. "Why? Does something about my appearance bother you?"

My eyes nearly popped out of my head, my cheeks felt on the verge of bursting into flames, and then the floodgates opened.

"Oh God, no! Not at all. I'm sorry. I don't mean to stare. It's just… I can't help it. I think you're stunning. I thought you were handsome in the hologram Kayog showed me, but you're even more perfect in person. You look so fearsome and strong. You exceed everything I ever wanted, and I just can't believe you're really mine. I'm just so in awe. I fear if I look away for even a second, you're just going to vanish. Every time I'm near you, I have to fight the urge to touch you to reassure myself that you're really there. And I… Oh man, I'm babbling."

I pressed my hands to my cheeks, which were burning with the embarrassment I felt. I'd only meant to reassure him of my positive perception of him, but now sounded like a crazed fangirl all but throwing herself at him.

Bayron shifted in his seat. For a split second, he almost appeared shy, as if he didn't know how to handle such compliments. But it had been too brief for me to be certain.

"I am your mate, and I'm not going anywhere. That said, I am… pleased you feel that way about my appearance. Your kind usually finds mine ugly and fearsome," he said in that growly tone I loved, but which also betrayed the shyness I had accurately perceived moments ago.

"I'm not like the rest of my kind," I said with a dismissive gesture, my own shyness also seeping through. "I really think you're gorgeous. I would love to draw you, if you'd let me."

I hated how I'd fallen back to that uncertain, pleading voice I always took as a child, whenever I asked my father for permission to do something I was pretty sure he'd deny me. I was a grown woman who had been steadily working on building her self-confidence. I no longer fell apart when rejected or denied.

He seemed taken aback by that request, his face broadcasting he didn't understand why I would want to draw him. Clearly, he had no idea how I saw him. But my drawings would rectify that.

Bayron grunted, then shrugged. "Sure. You may draw me, if it pleases you. After all, I am yours."

A wave of warmth washed over me upon hearing those words. It wasn't so much the fact that he gave me his permission, but his confirmation that he was indeed mine. All mine… It would take some time for me to stop pinching myself over this.

"Hmm… Are you hungry? Tired? Do you need anything?" Bayron asked, apparently eager to move the topic away from his appearance and my itch to draw him.

I shook my head. "No, thank you. We had a huge meal shortly before our arrival on the space station. Anyway, I'm much too excited right now to think about food. I can't wait to see your planet. I've never been off-world before. This is the greatest adventure of my life."

Bayron's expression softened in the most fascinating way. His blue eyes appeared to grow an even paler shade as he cast a gentle gaze upon me. "Xoccoris is but one of the countless worlds I will show you during our travels."

"I can't wait," I said with an excited grin. "Are we going to spend our honeymoon on your planet?"

Bayron frowned. "Honeymoon? What is that?"

"On Earth, it's the bonding time between newlyweds, right after their marriage," I explained. "It can last anywhere between a few days up to a couple of weeks. Wealthier couples can go for a month or more."

His frown deepened, giving the impression that his upper set of eyes were narrowing while taking on an evil edge.

"Bonding time doing what?" he asked.

"Just doing a lot of things together. Talking, visiting nice places, doing romantic activities like candlelight dinners, walks on the beach, guided tours, lots of cuddling and…" I caught myself just in time before saying 'having lots of sex' and shrugged instead. "You know, newlyweds stuff to cement the new bond."

Bayron grimaced as if he'd just bitten into something bitter or taken a whiff of something foul. Under different circumstances, I might have burst out laughing. He appeared so horrified.

"That sounds like a massive waste of time," he grumbled. "How are any of those useless activities strengthening the bond between mates?"

"Ah… I see that you are a true romantic!" I said teasingly.

"That, I'm certainly not," he said, almost sounding offended. "Is that something you require?"

I couldn't help but chuckle at the hint of panic I perceived in what would otherwise be deemed a grumpy tone. For a split second, I considered saying yes, if only to see how he would respond. While I would have enjoyed such activities with him, I didn't actually need them.

"Require? No," I answered honestly, laughing again at his obvious relief. "But be warned that I'm a cuddler. So mentally prepare for the fact that I will want to sit in your lap and snuggle with you often."

I couldn't believe the boldness with which I was saying this, when just moments earlier I'd been drowning in shyness and embarrassment. Bayron stared at me as if I was some bizarre insect that defied any logic, and as if he was wondering why the heck he'd consented to this union. Despite that, I didn't feel the usual sense of rejection that kind of stare usually gave me. For a reason I couldn't explain, I felt strongly that this was merely him expressing how much I baffled him, and not a display of regret he'd married me.

Bayron grunted and gave me a stiff nod in concession. God, how I loved a grump! It took all of my willpower for me not to get up from my chair, kiss him, and then plop myself into his lap to snuggle with him.

Apparently, my brain had finally gotten the memo that it should cooperate in me establishing some kind of pleasant conversation with my new husband. Words finally flowed naturally.

"So, since we're not going to your homeworld for our honeymoon, what should I expect once we get there? What are we going to do?" I asked.

"We are going to get you clanned and familiarize you with your new home before we head out for the next hunt," Bayron said, matter-of-factly.

"Get me clanned?" I asked, my curiosity piqued.

"Anyone who isn't born within a clan must earn the right to join and be accepted to become one of us," he replied calmly.

My stomach dropped. "Earn the right and be accepted?" I echoed, worry rearing its head again. "Does that mean I could be rejected?"

"Of course," Bayron said, as if that was self-evident. "Weaklings aren't welcome."

"But… But I'm not strong like you! From what I've read, your females are very tall and physically stronger than the average human male. There's no way I can match that!" I exclaimed, panic firmly taking root in the pit of my stomach.

Bayron snorted and waved a dismissive hand. "You're a female. Physical strength isn't required of you."

"So, it's a mental thing then?" I asked, refusing to yield to relief just yet.

"Yes."

"Like what?" I pressed when he didn't seem intent on explaining further.

He stared at me for a few seconds, then the oddest smile stretched his plush lips. "You'll find out soon enough."

I scrunched my face, not liking that answer one bit. "Or I could find out now, if you'd tell me. Why won't you? How bad is it? I probably need to prepare. What if I fail?"

"If you fail, that will mean Kayog was wrong," he deadpanned.

I huffed, feeling almost as offended as if he'd personally insulted me. "Kayog is *never* wrong. He said you and I are soulmates, then that means we are. Which also means I *will* pass your test," I said, lifting my chin defiantly, my growing panic giving way to a sense of certainty. "I may not match what you *think* you wanted in a mate, but I *am* what you need. How? I don't know. But time will prove it."

Bayron snorted, his gaze roaming over me with an amused expression in light of my little diatribe. "All I *need* is a good challenge and vicious beasts to hunt," he countered.

I shrugged, not in the least deflated by his comment. "Then you're about to get served. Everyone always says I'm challenging. So there! You'll need all four of them big hands of yours to rein me in."

Bayron leaned back in his seat, chuckling and far from impressed by my bluster. He was giving me that annoying look bigger dogs gave tiny pups who were barking their little hearts out, as if they represented any kind of a threat. It should piss me off, but my mind was too focused on how hot he looked with a sarcastic expression on his handsome face.

"Well, you certainly are spirited… and optimistic. You just might pass after all." His tone remained taunting, yet I didn't miss the glimmer of approval in his blue eyes.

"You better believe it," I said smugly. "You're not getting rid of me that easily."

"I do not intend to."

That took me aback, but also had every shade of warm fuzzies wrapping all around me. It wasn't just the words that affected me, but also the way his voice had dipped deeper while its rumbling increased. Its possessive undertone did funny things to me.

I shifted in my seat, biting my tongue not to ask him what he actually thought of me and of our pairing. Instead, I moved on to another topic I'd been wondering about.

"Kayog mentioned you had not signed up for the PMA," I said.

"That's correct. I had considered it from time to time, but never felt a strong urge to proceed with it," he replied.

"Then why did you accept?" I asked, genuinely curious.

He shrugged. "Kayog contacted me and told me about you. As you say so well, he is never wrong—or at least, he's never been so far. Meeting a mate is challenging when you live a somewhat nomadic life like I do. I'm still young, and I'm not our clan's heir. Therefore, there was no rush for me to marry and have offspring."

My shoulders slouched. "Oh. Does that mean you only agreed because Kayog said you should, but you didn't really want a mate now?"

Bayron chuckled and shook his head. "No. I never do anything I do not wish to. Soulmate or not, I would not have consented to marry you if I didn't feel the time was right or if the thought displeased me. I am glad to be mated."

My heart leapt. "You... you are? I don't... disappoint you?"

He recoiled, stunned by my question. "Disappoint me? Why would you? You are not what I expected, but I enjoy a surprise. You are attractive and possess an interesting personality. And while your behavior is confusing to me at times, I find you intriguing. I look forward to discovering every single one of your nuances."

My cheeks heated with pleasure at finally hearing his thoughts about me and finding them to be this positive. I gave him a timid smile and squirmed some more in my seat, which seemed to amuse him.

"Yeah, I can be a little overenthusiastic and sometimes too forward," I confessed with a sheepish grin. "It's okay to tell me if I annoy you, or to shut up if I babble too much. It can be grating—if not overwhelming—for some people."

"I do not get overwhelmed," Bayron retorted, sounding slightly offended. "Only weaklings can't handle forwardness. I expect you to speak your mind. I will take an overly enthusiastic female any day over a mousy, fearful, and boring one."

"I'm glad to hear it," I said, beaming at him. "Just so you know, I'm going to make you like me, Bayrohnziyiek Skortheatis. I'll make you head over heels for me."

He snorted. "Challenge accepted, my mate."

I smiled, then tilted my head to the side, pondering. "If you didn't sign up for the PMA, how did you meet Kayog? As soon as he and I spoke, back on Earth, he realized you would be the perfect match for me. That means he must have known you quite well. Are you friends?"

Bayron huffed. "Friends is definitely not the term that comes to mind when I think of that Temern. He derives far too much pleasure from taunting me," he said with a growl in his voice.

His tone immediately set off my protective instincts towards Kayog. "You're not allowed to hate him! Kayog is fabulous!"

"I do not hate him. I have the utmost respect for the male. But I'd still love to pluck him."

"HEY!" I exclaimed, outraged.

He burst out laughing. "Calm yourself, little human. I will never touch a single feather on his head. After all, I owe him."

"How so?" I asked, leaning forward as overprotective outrage gave way to curiosity.

"After an unpleasant incident on Trangor, he had been called in to mediate the situation with the Federation and the local population," Bayron explained. "I had used a clever method to accumulate more kills than my competitors—one that didn't actually break the rules. But that still got some people calling for me to be expelled from the event. Kayog's evaluation proved there were no grounds for that. It was in large part thanks to him that I was able to complete the Hunt."

I chewed my bottom lip, pondering how I wanted to exploit this opening to dig deeper into the subject. "Isn't that the incident that led to Serena Bello getting arrested by the Ordosians?"

His face immediately closed off. "You've heard of her?"

"Everyone has. Her family is very influential. They stirred quite an uproar when there were talks of their daughter being executed for saving lives," I said cautiously.

"I didn't lure the beasts anywhere near the area where the Ordosian females and younglings were located," Bayron said in a defensive tone. "Assuming those creatures were even the ones I had been dealing with earlier, they would have traveled a very great distance from where I interacted with them. After Serena and I parted ways, I moved southwest. She traveled north for at least a couple of hours before she encountered the Flayers that threatened the locals."

From the tension in his voice and the way his muscles bulged, this was clearly still a sore topic for him. Could the Flayers that attacked the locals have really been different ones than those he had been luring to the border for the Ordosian hunters to kill, and then for him to reap the reward?

Does it actually matter?

I didn't doubt that he had never intended to harm the locals, and that it hadn't been deliberate negligence on his part that caused the incident. However, it troubled me that he didn't seem to find his tactics to get ahead in the competition unethical.

My tongue burned with the desire to challenge him on that, but now didn't feel like the right time. I didn't want us spending our wedding night arguing over an incident from his past.

"Well, however those monsters got there, I'm just glad that, in the end, it all worked out for the best. Word is that Serena is extremely happy with her husband, and his family adores her and their kids," I said in a soothing tone.

To my relief, Bayron instantly relaxed. I realized then that he had expected me to condemn him, as most humans—and likely others—also had.

"She is," he confirmed in a grumpy tone.

"You've seen her again?"

He nodded. "I've participated in a few more Great Hunts on Trangor over the three years since that incident. Serena usually comes to say hello to her hunter friends at the base camp. Last time, she brought her sons."

"Oh wow! That's awesome! I wonder if I'll get to see her the next time you have a hunt there," I said, wistfully.

"It might happen sooner than you think. After all, we'll be heading to Trangor right after we leave my homeworld."

I perked up and stared at him with bulging eyes. "For real?! Your next hunt is on Trangor?"

"Yes."

I didn't mean to let out the high-pitched squeal that escaped me. Bayron froze, his shocked expression almost making me burst with laughter, but embarrassment took over as I gave him an apologetic look.

"Sorry. Like I said, I can get a little overenthusiastic."

He snorted and shook his head. "You truly are a strange female. Thankfully, it doesn't bother me."

"Let's just hope your parents will feel the same," I mumbled, dreading how my colorful personality would be perceived over there. "I'm assuming I will meet them when we reach Xoccoris?"

"Yes. You will meet my mother, father, and older brother."

My stomach knotted with apprehension. "How much do they know about me and our wedding? Are they aware that we're in a six-month trial period."

All amusement faded from Bayron's face. A deep frown settled on his brow as he stared at me with a stern expression. "Why do you ask? Are you already planning on leaving me?"

"Heck no! I told you I intend to make you crazy about me. But…"

"But?" he echoed when my voice trailed off.

"What if your family finds me lacking and asks you to dump me?" I asked with a small voice.

The feral expression that settled on his face and the angry growl that rose from his throat should have terrified me. Instead, they resonated straight in my nether region and had my toes instantly curling. Damn, my Beast was magnificent!

"No one meddles in my marital affairs. You are *mine*."

Cue exploding ovaries. I closed my legs tighter to silence the dull throbbing caused by the possessive way in which he'd just claimed me triggered.

"Okay," I whispered in a submissive voice that seemed to please him. "So… Are your father and brother hunters like you?"

Bayron shook his head. "No. While every Zamorian male is a trained hunter, we are first and foremost warriors. My sire is our clan leader, and my brother is his heir. They lead our warrior army, enforce the peace, and handle all diplomatic matters with the other clans and off-worlders."

"But you followed a completely different path," I said, matter-of-factly.

He grinned. I loved the way it softened his features while also giving him a dangerous edge. Sure, it sounded contradictory, and yet there it was. Then again, my husband held a constant aura of lethal force and danger that was sexy as hell.

"I did," he said, sounding rather pleased about it. "The beauty of being the second son is full freedom. Varkuth's future was decided at the moment of his birth."

"That's your older brother?"

Bayron nodded. "Granted, Varkuth could have renounced his

inheritance, but it isn't really done among Zamorians. Thankfully, my brother is a natural leader and loves being the heir. I have no patience for leading people, especially not idiots. The minute they became a nuisance, I'd crack their skulls and move on. Truth be told, I'm a bit of a loner. I like being able to go wherever the wind takes me, with no shackles."

"Except now you're shackled with a mate," I said in an apologetic tone.

He smiled, his face taking on that softer expression again. "A mate is different. If we are indeed soulmates as Kayog claims, then you are exactly who I need by my side."

I returned his smile, feeling myself melting inside.

Just as I was opening my mouth to ask him another question, a beeping sound emanating from his navigation board interrupted me. Bayron returned his attention to the console and tapped a few things on the interface.

I didn't understand diddly squat about piloting a ship. Considering I had miserably failed to learn how to fly a hovercar, it wasn't surprising vessels with even more complex systems spanked me raw.

"Something wrong?" I asked.

Bayron shook his head. "Long-range scanners detected another vessel headed in our general direction, but it's not on a collision course. Its flight path indicates it's not in pursuit and is not a threat."

"You're worried about pirates?" I asked warily.

"Worried is too strong a word. But you should never let your guard down in this sector," he said in a reassuring tone.

"So, you're going to be piloting all night?" I asked, unsure if I felt bummed out or relieved, although the former sentiment dominated.

Once again, he shook his head. "No. I will let the ship's A.I. take over in a half-hour or so once we've entered a safer area. Then you and I can go cleanse together and then couple."

My stomach did a series of somersaults, while my jaw dropped at his bluntness. Granted, as per the PMA rules, we had to consummate our union tonight, but I hadn't expected him to express it so crudely. For all that, the throbbing between my thighs—that had faded since his last growl—reared its head with a vengeance. I looked forward to finding myself helpless beneath him as much as I apprehended it.

Judging by the feral smirk that stretched his lips, I believed Bayron had guessed what conflicting thoughts his words had stirred within me.

"Do you have a sigil, an emblem, or a sign that represents you?" he asked.

I recoiled, the complete switch of topic nearly giving me whiplash. "No. Why?"

"You need one for our Zamorian union. You must provide me with it sometime tomorrow. It can be anything you want, but it should fit on a medallion."

My eyes widened while excitement bubbled inside of me. "I can draw one. Are we talking family crest or just a symbol that sums up who I am?"

"A mix of both. It should be something that says who you are, what you aspire to, or how you would wish to be known. Something that people will automatically recognize as Belle whenever they see it."

"Okay. I can do that," I said with enthusiasm. "I'm guessing that's another thing you're not going to give me further details about?"

He snorted. "You guessed right, my mate."

"You're impossible," I mumbled with fake anger, making him chuckle.

We spent another twenty minutes making light conversation until we crossed into what Bayron deemed a safe region. It all looked the same to me. But then he activated the vessel's artificial intelligence, set it on autopilot, and turned on the stealth shield before turning his attention back to me.

Without a word, he rose to his feet and extended a hand towards me. I swallowed hard, took his hand, and let him lead me back to our quarters.

CHAPTER 5
BAYRON

As we entered the room, my mate looked as if she couldn't decide if she wanted to couple with me or run for dear life. This duality in my female, from moments of incredible boldness followed by a timid fragility, stirred me in all the right ways. I had no use for a weakling, but there was nothing more enticing than an attractive female that needed my protection and for me to handle her gently.

And gentle I would be.

"Are you afraid, my mate?" I asked in my softest voice.

Belle swallowed hard, eyes as round as saucers, and yet shook her head. "I'm not afraid. Just really nervous. I… I don't want to disappoint you, and—"

"You will not," I interrupted, forcefully. "Do not worry about trying to please me. Tonight, our bodies will make each other's acquaintance. This is about shedding whatever fears or misunderstandings there may be. And it is also about laying down the foundations of a bond of trust and of affection between us. We are very different anatomically. It is vital that we clearly communicate our expectations, likes, and boundaries."

Belle smiled, part of the tension stiffening her shoulders lessening. "Thank you. Yes, I would like us to be able to discuss things openly. You *are* huge," she added with a nervous laugh.

I smiled and began removing my clothes, starting with the skin-tight black t-shirt I wore to delay a little longer the moment she would face my cocks. My mate's lips parted with a mix of wariness and awe. Kromor's teeth, I loved the lustful way in which she looked at my body. Human females were often drawn to very muscular males. On that front, I certainly wasn't lacking. But the two sets of arms didn't appeal as much to many of them. My female couldn't seem to be happier that I possessed them.

Snapping out of her apparent trance, Belle reached for the hem of the skirt of her bohemian dress—as Kayog had called it —and lifted it over her head with shaky hands. I couldn't help a smile at the sight of the frilly, see-through, and barely-there white lingerie she wore. There was no question in my mind she'd put it on to seduce me.

The way my mate balled her dress in front of her stomach— covering the belly fat that I'd sometimes heard humans refer to as their paunch—expressed loudly how self-conscious she felt.

"You are well made, my Belle. Do not be shy or hide your beauty from me. Everything I see pleases me tremendously. And with four eyes, I do see you quite well."

Annabelle giggled nervously, a lovely blush settling on her cheeks as she lowered her arms. Then, as I had done with my shirt, she tossed her dress onto the dresser.

"Thank you. You're crazy hot yourself," she said in a small voice.

She reached behind her for the magnetic clasps of her bra at the same time I began undoing the ones from my pants. Eyes glued to my groin, Belle froze halfway through lowering the left shoulder strap of her bra when the waist of my pants cleared my cocks.

As I never wore underwear, they were both on full display. Even soft, their girth and length exceeded those of a fully erect, standard human male. I hated the fear that finally settled on my mate's face as I finished removing my pants.

"Do not be afraid, Belle," I said in a soothing voice.

"You… You're massive. They're *both* massive. I…"

She didn't finish her thought, words apparently failing her.

"According to Kayog, we are soulmates," I said softly, taking a careful step towards her. "Which means that, despite our obvious differences, we are meant for each other in all the ways that matter. I will never hurt you, and I will never demand anything from you that you are not ready for, or comfortable with. Finish removing your clothes and join me."

Still looking a little shaken, Belle complied. She looked confused when she saw me settle at the edge of the bed rather than lying down on it. We would shower together before moving on to coupling. But we had something else to do first.

She made to sit beside me, then emitted a soft gasp when I wrapped both of my left arms around her to draw her onto my lap instead. I'd expected my female to try and move her right leg as far left as possible to minimize contact with my cocks, but she paid them no mind. Instead, Belle stared at me like a panicked bird, her breathing labored as she tried to control her wariness.

I reached for my long braid with my main right hand and extended it to her. As expected, surprise and confusion replaced my mate's fear as she instinctively took the braid in her hands. She gaped at it for a second before giving me a questioning look.

I smiled and gently caressed her cheek. "Aside from my mother, you are the only female to have ever touched my braid, and who ever will until the day I draw my last breath."

"What?" Belle whispered, taken aback even as she glanced back at my braid with an air of confusion.

"Our females like to arrogantly refer to a Zamorian male's braid as his leash," I said in an amused voice. "In many ways, it is true. From the day we begin our warrior training, we no longer cut our hair, aside from a little trim to keep it healthy. Our braid is a sign of status and a source of pride."

I almost purred when Belle caressed my braid with a fascinated expression, while she hung on my every word, all worries temporarily forgotten, as I had hoped.

"There are only three reasons to cut a Zamorian male's hair. The first is the day he shames himself so greatly as a warrior that he must be stripped of all his ranks and titles, and for all to witness his dishonor. The second is if he commits a crime so great he gets banned from the clan. In that instance, it is not just the braid that is cut off, but the entire head is shaved, and a special oil is applied to the scalp to keep the hair from growing back for at least six months."

"Ouch! Brutal," Belle said with an air of sympathy.

"Save your compassion, my mate. For one to get cast out of a clan, their crime has to be so evil that even death would be a kindness they do not deserve. Xoccoris is as beautiful a world as it is harsh. One does not fare well there all alone."

"Right," she said, lowering her gaze back to my braid as she gently caressed it again.

"And the third is when a female repudiates her mate. It is essentially severing the bond that binds them," I explained.

"Woah! Considering the other two extreme reasons to cut a Zamorian's braid, this one seems overly harsh simply because a woman wants to end her union with her husband," Belle exclaimed.

"Marriage is a very serious matter on Xoccoris. Zamorians marry for life. If you recall, Kayog mentioned that you and I could settle for a bonding and not a claiming, since we have a trial period. A bonding can be severed with each member of the couple simply parting ways. It is a committed relationship, but not a lifetime engagement. You could call it a trial period as well. Only a grievous and unforgivable offense would drive a female to repudiate her mate."

"Could a male repudiate his wife?"

"He could, but I cannot think of any instance when that actually occurred," I said. I pointed at my braid between her hands. "This is our bond. Unbraid it."

Once again, Belle complied.

"It is yours to do with as you please. Per our traditions, our females do their husband's hair however they see fit, adorn it either with ornaments they create themselves or have our crafters make to their specifications."

"Really? What kind of hairdo?" she asked, her legendary enthusiasm seeping back into her voice.

"Anything you like, as long as it is braided. Once we get home, you will see the other clansmen, which should give you a better idea of what our females do."

"I can't wait to see it! You're going to have the best hair any Zamorian has ever had," she boasted as she finished unbraiding it.

I chuckled. "I'm counting on it, my mate. Now come, let's go cleanse ourselves."

To my delight, Belle no longer looked tense. Although it would return once we got into bed, I hoped that showering together would further help diminish how intimidating she found my body.

Despite that, her shyness crept back in as we entered the hygiene room, and I made her stand before me. I couldn't understand why she wanted to hide her belly and generous hips by clasping her hands in front of her. Silly woman. I *loved* her curves. Females weren't meant to be bags of bones or lean like a warrior. A male's hands needed some soft flesh to hold, to caress, and to worship.

I clamped down on these thoughts as I felt blood rushing to my groin. Now wasn't the time to have my cocks pointing at her like angry swords.

I reached for her hands and gently forced them apart.

Stretching her arms wide open, I slowly let my gaze roam over her nudity. Belle's face heated as she visibly struggled not to turn her body away.

"Do you have any idea how desirable you are to me, Belle? Your body is beautiful."

She blushed and gave me a timid but grateful smile. "You're too kind. Pudgy would probably be a more accurate adjective."

"Just the way I like it," I replied forcefully. "I want meat on my woman."

"That's more like fat," she said in self-derision.

"But all the flavor of the meat comes from the fat," I countered teasingly. "That just makes you even more delectable."

Belle burst out laughing, her shyness waning, and her pretty blue eyes sparkling as she gazed upon me. "You know, for an intimidating grump, you sure know how to make a lady feel good about herself."

"Only my mate," I grumbled, forcing myself to sound even grumpier, making her laugh again.

Its musical sound delighted my ears. I didn't have much of a sense of humor, and I certainly wasn't the entertainer type, but I would strive to make her laugh whenever I could… if only for selfish reasons.

I turned on the water, letting it rain down on us, a little hotter than lukewarm. After drawing my mate closer, I proceeded to wash her, keeping my touch clinical as I covered every inch of her body in soap. Belle's breath caught in her throat when my primary hands rubbed over her breasts while my secondary ones worked on her hips and down towards her pelvis. But I didn't linger there, moving further south. My goal wasn't to arouse her—even though she was showing every sign of it—but to make her comfortable with my touch, however intimate it became.

I had to pinch my lips to repress a triumphant smirk when a quickly repressed whimper escaped Belle as my hand flittingly settled on her sex, only long enough to apply the soap before moving on.

By the time I rinsed her, my female was vibrating with frustrated desire. In a short while, I would gladly sate her need. For now, I turned her away from me and proceeded to wash her hair, with my main hands giving her scalp a gentle massage, while my secondary pair loosened the knots in her shoulders and back muscles.

When I finished, Belle looked completely languid and relaxed, just as I had intended. With my height of 7' to her 5'6, I was towering over her. I therefore kneeled before her so that she could reciprocate. Although I had washed my woman's hair last, I indicated for her to start with mine instead and wash my body after. I would spare her for as long as possible the moment she would have to touch my cocks.

While small and delicate, Belle's hands gave me the best head scratching, which had me loudly purring. She giggled with delight, which only had me purring louder. When she moved on to wash my shoulders and chest, she touched me with an awe and reverence that did strange things to me. If my mate reacted to me this way, when we barely knew each other, how much more wondrous would it be once she had fallen in love with me?

I rose to my feet as her hands moved lower to wash my pelvic area. Although the girth of both my appendages still intimidated her, my female didn't let it deter her. A wave of pride swelled within me when Belle summoned that bold and undaunted side of her. She didn't shy away from my cocks, staring them head on mostly with a fascinated curiosity.

She worked up a lather, then reached for my main cock, which was slightly bigger and longer than the bottom one. Belle closed her right hand around its narrower base. Her fingers couldn't quite touch around it, but as her palm moved up my length, where the circumference widened, the gap significantly increased before narrowing again near my tip. I wiggled it, making her gasp in surprise.

"Did the head of your peen just move?" she exclaimed, bewildered.

I chuckled. "Yes. I can move it up and down, but only slightly left and right."

"Oh, my God! Whatever for?!"

Her shocked expression made me laugh. "So that I can aim at a Zamorian female's second cervix. Just like we have two cocks, they have two vaginas. But the cervix of the second one leads to their storage area."

"Storage?" Belle asked, her eyes all but popping out of her head.

"Sperm storage. When our females have already coupled, their main cervix will close to trap the sperm inside their uterus. If they have sex again before that attempt at conception has resolved, they can hold the seed of their lover within the reproductive tracts of their antechamber—which would be a smaller version of the uterus. If the couple failed to conceive, the female can transfer the stored semen to her uterus, even if her mate is gone hunting or off to war for extended periods."

"Oh wow! That's wicked! I think some snakes on Earth work like that, too. But... but why do you have to aim for it? Shouldn't your second penis shoot straight into that second cervix?"

I smiled. "In theory, yes. But we rarely use it for reproductive purposes. Our main cock releases our seed, unless it has gotten injured. We use the smaller one to urinate. However, both provide sexual pleasure to our mate—and to ourselves. The bulbus—the enlarged part in the middle—can also swell like a knot to lock our seed inside the female and increase the chances of conception."

"That is so cool! So I guess you never have the problem human males do when they need to pee but can't because their boner blocks their ability to do so," she said, both amused and awed.

I laughed. Although I wasn't familiar with the term 'boner', in the context, I could guess at her meaning.

"You are correct. It normally isn't a problem for us. However, should our main cock ever get injured or amputated, our lower cock would take over and serve both purposes. In that case, an erection would make it highly difficult for one to relieve the bladder."

"Damn. But what about the female? Does her antechamber become a uterus if hers becomes damaged?"

"Yes. Zamorians have back up organs for almost everything, except legs," I said smugly.

"That's truly amazing," Belle said wistfully.

Her fingers carefully traced the 'necklace' on the side of my cock. We referred to it that way because it resembled a string of pearls, which greatly enhanced our females' pleasure.

"No testicles," she whispered, as if to herself.

"Inside our bodies. Why expose such a vulnerable thing to be abused? I've seen human males doubled over in pain from a mere flick on their balls," I said disdainfully.

Belle laughed while nodding. She then lifted her head to give me the oddest look, filled with gratitude and something else I couldn't define.

"Thank you," she whispered, without explaining further.

I didn't need her to. My goal had been to give Belle a chance to grow comfortable with my body and quell her fears. Mission accomplished. I merely smiled. She reciprocated then proceeded to finish washing me.

Once properly rinsed, we stood beneath the dryer—or rather, I crouched while she stood—so that she could brush my hair. My mate was taking her role as 'owner' of my mane quite seriously. Although her fear had abated, Belle started displaying some healthy levels of nervousness.

That task done, we headed back to the bedroom. I stopped next to the bed and drew her into my embrace. My woman came willingly, slipping her arms around my neck. I loved the soft warmth of her naked body against mine. I lifted her up, my secondary hands holding the back of her thighs as she wrapped her legs around my waist. My main right hand gently caressed her back while my left held her nape. I felt her stomach quiver against mine when she felt my hardening cocks between us.

"Remember, my mate, tonight is about pleasure and making each other's acquaintance," I said in a soft and reassuring tone. "Do not worry about the PMA, or any perceived expectations. There is only you and me here. We will do as much or as little as you feel comfortable. And don't worry, if we go that far, I will only use one of my cocks."

I couldn't help but chuckle at the crimson shade her cheeks took upon hearing those last words, as well as at her nearly palpable relief. While some humans, both male and female, enjoyed penetration through their back opening, I highly suspected my mate had never done it before. While I wasn't opposed to the idea, Belle wasn't ready for it, and maybe never would be. Either way, I would be fine with her decision.

I captured her lips in a gentle kiss. She immediately responded, pressing her chest to mine. My tongue no sooner teased the seam of her mouth than my female parted her lips in a welcoming fashion. By Khivolt, I would never tire of her taste and of the soft texture of her tongue around mine. A searing flame ignited in the pit of my stomach as more blood rushed to my loins.

I had not expected that Belle would stir my fire so strongly, so soon. I had to clamp it down for fear I would unleash my passion on her. Tonight was about her pleasure, proving to her that I was a worthy mate, and a true protector.

Tilting her backward, my main left hand still holding her nape, I broke the kiss to caress her face and neck with my lips.

Simultaneously, my right hand roamed over her back before slipping to her front to cup one of her breasts. Belle moaned, her breath hitching when my secondary hands holding her thighs pressed her core even more tightly against my erect cocks.

Gently thrusting upwards, I rubbed my lengths against her to stimulate her clitoris and start getting her wet. To my delight, she pushed her pelvis forward to increase the friction while her hands explored my chest. The way I had her bent back, many females would have hung on to my shoulders or to my arms instead, for fear of falling over. But not my mate. That implicit display of trust moved me deeply.

After nibbling on her earlobe and sucking on the tender flesh in the crook of her neck, I pursued my journey downward. Belle sank her fingers into my hair when my lips reached her left breast. As my tongue teased her areola, the wondrous feel of her nipple hardening in response to my ministrations sent another wave of lust straight to my cocks. I licked and laved the little nub, reveling in the delicately salty taste of her skin and the musical sound of her moans in my ears.

For a second, I considered finally laying her down on the bed before joining her to continue pleasuring her. However, I decided against it, wanting to push further the level of trust she was already willing to grant me.

After rubbing my cocks a few more times against her core, I suddenly lifted my mate upward, settling her legs on my shoulders while I buried my face between her thighs. Belle cried out, her hands fisting my hair with enough force to give my scalp a nice sting. She bent her head backward, her breathing coming out louder and in shorter bursts interspersed with sighs of delight.

My female didn't panic or cling to me with the energy of despair. Instead, she loosened her grip, caressing my head with one hand and lifting the other one to fondle her own breast. My hearts swelled with a possessive pride to see how she gave herself over to the pleasure I was providing her, confident that I wouldn't let her come to harm.

But her divine taste on my tongue and the intoxicating scent of her musk soon had my brain too addled with lust to think straight. I devoured Belle with an almost crazed frenzy, the fingers of my primary right hand slipping into her opening. Kromor's teeth! She was warm, slick with desire, and exquisitely tight. Had I not been Zamorian, I would have worried about her ability to take me. Still, it would require care and patience to get her to adjust to my girth. However, my natural lubricant—which also acted as a muscle relaxer—would make it easier for her to stretch and receive me with minimum discomfort.

I'd been so drunk with desire, feasting on my female, that I never saw her climax coming. Belle shouted, her body seizing then all but collapsing while spasms of bliss coursed through her. Had I not firmly held her, she would have plummeted to the ground.

A deep growl rose from my throat as my abdominal muscles contracted painfully with the need to throw my female onto the bed, ram myself home, and give free rein to the burning desire clamoring for me to ravage her. Instead, my tongue still lapping at her palpitating sex, I closed the short distance to the bed, and carefully laid her down onto the mattress.

I reluctantly stopped devouring her, my lips moving upward to kiss the soft cushion of her belly and tease her belly button with my tongue. Even as Belle was starting to come down from her high, I slipped two fingers inside of her, scissoring them as they moved in and out. After my female had loosened a little, I inserted a third finger to further prepare her to receive me.

Moving up towards her chest, my mouth reclaimed one of my mate's stiffened nipples, while my main hands caressed her body and fondled her other breast. Belle arched her back, lifting her chest towards my face for greater contact. I chuckled when she spread her legs wider to facilitate access for my secondary hand making love to her.

She emitted a strangled gasp followed by a deep moan when I crooked my fingers inside her to rub the sensitive bundle of nerves I'd read human females possessed. Thrilled by her response, I accelerated my movements, reveling in the sounds of Belle's building pleasure as she once more began to crest.

My woman cried out again. Her hands—that had been caressing my hair, shoulders, and upper back—stiffened, her nails digging into my flesh in the most wondrous way as she soared. Even as it stroked my ego to find my mate so responsive to my touch, it also tortured me with a searing desire. My cocks throbbed and ached with the need to claim her.

Eyes locked on Belle's face, still dissolved in an air of pure bliss, I removed my hand from her. Licking my woman's delectable juice from my fingers, I settled between her thighs, opening them wide for me. Still half-dazed, she tried to refocus on me. I smiled and leaned down to capture her lips in a passionate kiss. Despite the fire raging in my loins, demanding I claim my female, I restrained myself. I willed my natural lubricants to exude from the pores of my cocks as I began to rub them against her slit.

She gasped, surprise settling on her features, no doubt in reaction to my lubricant's effects manifesting themselves. Zamorian females often reported a slightly cool sensation, followed by a little tingle, which quickly evolved into an aphrodisiac-like effect that made them ache to be possessed. Apparently, Belle felt the same. She lifted her pelvis to press it against mine, her response to my kiss becoming hungrier, and her hands on me more feverish.

I rubbed myself against her a couple more times before pressing the tip of my lower and smaller cock against her opening. Despite her arousal, how wet she was for me, and the extra slickness provided by my natural lubricant, Belle's body resisted my intrusion at first. Silencing the urge to force my way in, I gently rocked in and out, inserting myself centimeter by centimeter, while coating her with more of my lubricant.

To my relief, her inner walls surrendered relatively quickly, welcoming me at last in their tight embrace. A deep growl of pleasure rumbled through my chest at the burning heat of her sheath wrapped around my cock. Moving slowly at first, I gradually increased the speed and strength of my thrusts as Belle begged me for more. With my main cock rubbing against her clit with each stroke, my female rapidly neared the edge again.

An inferno raged in the pit of my stomach, each movement sending electric tendrils running up my spine and down my legs. My skin was on fire, the sensation exacerbated by the heat of my woman's silky skin against mine. Slipping a hand between us, I closed it around the tip of my main cock, squeezing it hard and roughly stroking it even as I continued to thrust in and out of my mate. Between two kisses, I whispered encouraging words to Belle until she fell apart again beneath me.

Her inner walls clamping down on my lower cock had me gritting my teeth with a loud snarl as it nearly forced my orgasm from me. But I would climax with my main cock inside of her, fill her with my seed, and mark her as mine over and over until she was properly claimed.

I released my cock and rubbed her clit instead to keep her flying high while I pulled out. Without slowing the movement of my hand, I flipped her around and put her on all-fours. Holding her up, I began inserting my main cock into her slit. Belle moaned, showing no signs of pain, despite its bigger size.

Leaning forward, I fondled her breasts with my main hands while continuing to massage her clit. I kissed her back and nape, flooding her with pleasurable sensations to drown out any discomfort from me taking her. But I soon found myself trying to rein her in instead. I couldn't tell if Belle was acting under the aphrodisiac properties of my lubricant, but she was rocking back and forth, trying to impale herself on my length. As much as I wanted to ram myself home, I forced her to follow my careful pace.

I'll be damned if I hurt my mate on our first night.

It took a few moments longer for her body to finally accept me. When it did, I thought I would die with pleasure. My main cock was so much more sensitive. In no time, my almost pained grunts of bliss were mixing with the sensuous sighs of my woman. I could feel myself losing control as I began taking her deeper and harder. Her plump, round behind felt divine in my hands as the slapping sound of our flesh meeting marked the increasingly unbridled tempo of our coupling.

From the way she trembled, Belle would soon be overtaken by another orgasm. As much as I dreaded that it would sweep me away as well, the need to give her pleasure exceeded any other thought. Even as I pounded into her, I began tilting the tip of my cock each time I pulled out in order to graze her sweet spot at the same time.

My wife went off like a rocket.

I shouted, the tightening of her inner walls around my cock tearing some semen out of me. I ground my teeth hard, refusing to yield to my climax yet, and continued to pump in and out of my female with wild abandon.

By Khivolt, she feels so insanely good!

The searing fires of a thousand dragons were consuming me from within. My skin felt on the verge of combusting as wave upon waves of nearly intolerable pleasure surged from my loins and crashed over me with each stroke. I arched Belle closer to me, needing the feel of her skin against mine. I pressed her back to my chest. My main arms wrapped possessively around her as I readied to finally surrender to bliss.

I scraped my tusks against the soft flesh of her neck, fighting the primal urge to bite, to brand her. My labored breathing mingled with hers and the throaty way in which she chanted my name as she prepared to fly again. Between the tip of my cock rubbing her sensitive spot and my fingers working her clit, Belle once more fell apart in my arms. This time, I followed her.

My spine seized, as if struck by lightning. My vision blurred, and my head swam as ecstasy swept me away. I emitted a savage roar as my seed shot out of me, filling my mate in blissful spurts.

I collapsed onto my back, my cock still buried deep inside my female. Holding her tightly in my arms, I covered the side of her face and neck with kisses, while waiting for the room to stop spinning around. I wished she'd been facing me instead. Reluctant to pull out of her just yet, I continued holding my mate a while longer, until I'd fully softened. When I finally removed myself, I turned Belle around, only to gather her even more closely in my embrace.

She lifted her face to look at me with an air of adoration that nearly destroyed me. In that instant, I knew I'd burn down entire civilizations if needed so that she would always gaze upon me like this. I reclaimed her mouth in a tender kiss nonetheless charged with the wave of possessiveness that surged through me.

"You are mine," I growled, almost angrily.

Belle smiled and gently caressed my cheek. "As you are mine…. *My* Beast."

That word should have been offensive, but the way she said it and the possessive pride in her voice somehow made it sound like a badge of honor. Before I could question it further, my female snuggled deeply against me, her face buried in my neck. Dismissing the thought, I closed my eyes with a content smile.

I'd been claimed.

CHAPTER 6
BAYRON

I couldn't stop staring at my female. She looked so delicate and fragile in her sleep. I pulled down the blanket to feast my eyes on the delicious curves that had procured me such intense pleasure. Belle didn't even stir when I closed a hand on the round mound of her right breast. I wanted to flick its nipple to see it harden, like it had done so many times for me last night.

Kromor's teeth! I wanted to wake my mate and claim her again. I'd taken Belle three times already, having selfishly interrupted her slumber to sate the irrational hunger she awakened in me. Although she'd been a more-than-willing participant, I didn't want to turn her off with my constant attentions. I also suspected she'd soon become raw—assuming she wasn't already—after the relentless assault I'd unleashed on her.

But the way her inner walls grip my cocks...

Swallowing back a frustrated growl, I leaned down and pressed a soft kiss on her forehead before carefully rolling out of bed. I pulled the cover back over her, my gaze lingering a second longer on her face before I went to get dressed.

Belle slept too deeply. She'd been all but wrapped around me when I first woke. That I managed to untangle myself, grope her breast, and get out of bed without her even so much as batting an eyelash screamed at her complete lack of proper survival instincts. It wouldn't surprise me if she had a dreadful situational awareness. Thankfully, I had not planned on taking her with me when I went hunting. Having her safely tucked away at our base camp would do wonders for my mental health.

I headed to the deck and reviewed the ship's trajectory and flight logs to make sure everything was in order. In the absence of any warnings or attack reports on the navigation channels for the sector, I left piloting to the A.I. and made my way to the holodeck.

Training constituted an intrinsic part of my life. One could almost say I needed it to live, just like water, sleep, and general sustenance. From the moment we were able to walk, Zamorian males learned how to fight and hunt. While many did it out of duty, true passion drove me.

Nothing—or rather very few things—compared to the thrill of the hunt. I craved the adrenaline rush from knowing a single miscalculated move, or the slightest moment of distraction, could result in grievous injury or death.

I began with a few warmup exercises, intending to then summon a grummoll. It was undoubtedly one of the most vicious beasts on Xoccoris. While I'd faced off against these massive beasts more times than I could count, brushing up on fighting them made sense. After all, an important challenge awaited me upon our return to my homeworld.

Despite my height of 7' those creatures easily towered over me by at least a couple of heads. Both my main arms could barely manage to fully wrap around a single one of its front legs. But then, it wasn't a good idea to get too close unless you wanted an unpleasant encounter with the spear of its extensible tongue.

After stretching, a twenty-minute run, and one hundred chin

ups—twenty-five per hand—I initiated the gauntlet program. That was the beauty of training on the holodeck.

The open layout with a series of inconspicuous poles scattered about the flat terrain was deceptive. Each of those poles would unexpectedly deploy various bladed weapons at random heights in an attempt to split me in half. Others would have spiked chains flailing around, guillotine-like mechanisms, or murder holes to shoot poisoned darts at me.

While training on the holodeck was completely safe, it wasn't pain-free. The neural stimulator at the base of my nape would register any contact the traps successfully made with me and inflict pain matching the type of injury received. It could quickly get debilitating for an unskilled fighter. Thanks to randomization, even though I'd trained a billion times with this program, I never knew what would be coming at me, which kept me on my toes.

And did it ever come at me with a vengeance.

I'd been steadily increasing the difficulty level, but this morning, the program proved particularly fiendish. Armed with a blade or spear for each hand, except for my main left one that held my shield, I dodged, parried, blocked, and attacked the various implements of pain trying to kill me.

Adrenaline pumped through my veins as two spiked chains came at me from different angles, while the murder holes of a third pole fired a barrage of poisoned darts. I jumped over the first chain, batted away the second one with one of my spears, and simultaneously blocked the darts with my shield. No sooner did I land from my jump than a fourth pole surged from the floor right in my path. I barely had time to drop to the ground before a large blade extruded from it at lightning speed, spinning like the deadliest of fans.

But this was no time to rest.

A split second after my back touched the floor, spears with serrated blades shot out of the two poles that had previously attacked me with chains. I rolled sideways out of the path of the first one, pushing myself up onto my knees half a blink before the second spear would have impaled me. The viciously sharp tip smashed into the floor less than two centimeters in front of me.

The soft swish of the holodeck's door opening distracted me long enough to almost get decapitated by another rotating blade coming furiously at my face. I ducked, feeling its flat side brush against the top of my head. Shooting to my feet, I ran away from that particularly savage section of the gauntlet. The words forming on my tongue to warn my mate not to advance died as soon as I got a glimpse of her face.

"Wicked!" Belle whispered with a marveled expression.

She whipped out a small device from the deep pocket of the wide blue dress she was wearing. Even as I avoided more deadly attacks from the simulation, my female threw a little sphere in the air, which almost instantly vanished.

Stealth cloak...

Belle then took pictures of me. I realized then that she was using the stealth camera Kayog had gifted her to record my performance at the same time.

I had intended to interrupt the scenario the minute I saw her walk in, but not so much anymore. A part of me wanted to stop —although I hated incomplete trainings. However, the way my female was barely repressing little whoops and gasps of wonder as she observed me was stroking my ego in the most delectable way. The need to show off and impress her took over, and I went all out.

My father always warned me against such things. Should I get wrecked in front of my brand-new wife, the humiliation would be hard to live down. At least three times, I came too close to meeting my demise. While years of experience allowed me to keep my cool, Belle held nothing back, shouting in fear for me then whooping some more when I prevailed.

By the time the simulation ended, I strutted towards my mate as the poles vanished. Chest puffed out, I bunched my biceps to appear more impressive.

"You're so freaking amazing!" Belle exclaimed, clapping her hands.

"Thank you, my mate," I replied in a growly voice, my hearts bursting with pride.

The way she always looked at me with such awe was quite intoxicating. It would become a dangerous addiction. I'd been a little reckless during my training in my irrational need to display my talent for her. At least, I'd done it in a safe environment.

As the youngest son, I'd always had to do more to get some attention. Being the firstborn and the heir to the leadership of the clan, Varkuth had both been blessed and cursed with having everyone focused on him. Between those making sure he excelled in all things to become the perfect clan leader, and those who spied for the slightest sign of weakness they could exploit, my brother always had to be on his toes.

At times, I had envied him. Today, I praised the gods for having been spared this constant scrutiny. But that didn't make me crave admiration and attention any less. And my mate was naturally filling that need... beyond my wildest hopes.

However, aside from enjoying how she stroked my ego, I rejoiced at Belle's reaction to seeing me in action. I wanted to believe it foreshadowed a positive response from her to the claiming ritual.

"I'm serious!" she exclaimed. "I don't understand how someone so big and muscular can move so fast and with such fluid movements. You seemed to be performing an acrobatic dance... although of the lethal kind. Every other second, I wished I could have frozen you in time to sketch you in action."

A wondrous warmth spread in my chest as she continued to shower me with praise.

I shrugged, trying to appear nonchalant to hide my slight embarrassment before such enthusiasm. "It's just training. And I believe your cameras will give you all the stills you require," I said in a grumbling tone.

"They will! Although it's not the same as drawing a live subject," she said. "By the way, your eyes were orange while you battled. How come?"

"It is a natural physiological reaction for Zamorian males," I explained. "Fierce combat or great anger will automatically trigger it. However, we can deliberately activate it to make ourselves look more fearsome when trying to intimidate an opponent."

"That's really awesome," she said pensively, her gaze roaming over me in an assessing fashion. "You're going to have to train for me fully naked."

I recoiled, my jaw dropping in shock. "Why in Khivolt's name would you want me to train naked?"

"So that I can see how your muscles move under the skin," Belle said matter-of-factly before gesturing at my groin with her chin. "You can wear some tight undies to hold the twins still. A jockstrap of some kind would work fine to keep them from dangling all over the place and getting in the way. What? Why are you looking at me like that?"

I didn't need a mirror to know what kind of horrified expression was plastered all over my face. "I do not wear *undies* and especially not *jockstraps*," I growled, my voice filled with outrage.

"I noticed," she deadpanned while calling the stealth camera back to her. "I simply suggested it to make things more comfortable for you. But hey, if you want the twins flapping in the wind and getting a close shave by all those crazy rotating blades, that's all you. Either way, I'll enjoy the show."

"They're not twins. In case you didn't notice, my lower cock is slightly smaller, but the necklace is bigger," I grumbled.

Belle didn't respond. I grunted in annoyance when she

merely stared at me with an obnoxious expression that seemed to imply "Yes, and your point is?"

That just made her smile.

"Anyway, you're assuming I will train naked, which I won't," I continued, wanting to get the last word.

"Really?" she replied, not fazed in the least. "I seem to recall that, just yesterday, while showing me the studio, you were saying how, as my husband, it is your duty to anticipate and fulfill my needs. Here, I'm actually stating what my needs are. Are you recanting on that pledge?"

I grimaced and glared at my female. Belle held my gaze unwaveringly, an irritatingly smug expression on her face.

"You'll see, a jockstrap isn't so bad. As you probably don't own any, I'll make you the perfect one," she said in a cheerful voice, sparing me the ignominy of having to concede defeat.

"I need to shower," I ground through my teeth, annoyed beyond words. "I'm drenched in sweat."

"Want me to wash your back?" Belle asked.

I froze, unsure whether she was mocking me or genuinely offering. Surely, she didn't think me incapable of washing my own back? But all teasing had melted from her face, replaced instead by what looked like a hopeful glimmer.

"If you wish," I mumbled.

The way she beamed at me and the heated once over she gave me—brief though it was—erased any thought of mockery. The fire that had been raging inside me while I watched her sleeping ignited again in the pit of my stomach. I didn't argue when she took my hand and pulled me after her out of the holodeck.

Not being one to be led, I took over with my longer strides, although not walking so fast as to make her scramble to keep up. With each step, my cocks stiffened as memories of how warm and tight she'd felt inside had me aching with need.

No sooner were we standing under the raining water than my

hands were all over my mate. Before long, I had Belle pinned against the wall while I thrust passionately in and out of her. To think I'd worried coupling between us might be a challenge for a few weeks. My female was quickly adapting to my girth—in no small part aided by the muscle relaxant of my natural lubricant. But more importantly, her libido appeared to match mine—a good thing, considering how hungry she had me for her.

The second time I made her climax, I joined my voice to hers and gave in to bliss. I could have gone at it a while longer but forced myself to restrain my ardor as we washed each other. Anyway, I needed to feed my female.

After we got dressed, I took her to the mess hall.

"What would you like to eat?" I asked as she settled at one of the benches by the island.

"Oh, you don't need to go out of your way for me. I'll be fine with a toast and some jam, or a bowl of cereal…"

Belle's voice trailed off when I deeply frowned at her, my scowling expression making it clear this wasn't an acceptable answer. As if the first meal I'd serve my mate would be bread and jam. Did she think me incapable of making something more elaborate?

"But if you insist, I'm quite open to whatever you're in the mood to prepare. I'm not difficult, and I like trying new things," Belle said in a submissive tone that turned me on.

"Good answer," I said in a rumbling voice. "I understand humans often have a steak with sauteed potatoes, eggs, and a side of fruits or vegetables for breakfast."

"Yes, that's when you want a copious breakfast," she responded carefully.

"And that is what you shall have," I said in a tone that brooked no argument. "You do like all of these things, right?"

"Well, yes, but—"

"Then it is settled," I said, interrupting her.

I was beginning to suspect that as much as she wanted to be

taken care of, my mate would show reluctance at openly requesting things that she considered non-essential. What a contrast with the bold way in which she pretty much imposed her will about having me fighting naked. But as Belle had accurately quoted, it was my duty to anticipate and fulfill her needs. If she thought she didn't deserve to get spoiled, I would have to set her straight.

I had stocked the kitchen with all the meats and produce my research had claimed constituted the humans' favorite diet, including spices. I brought out three steaks, a pile of potatoes, half a dozen chicken eggs, and a few fruits. The way Belle gaped at the amount of ingredients before me made me chuckle. She'd soon find out what impressive appetites Zamorian males possessed.

I made quick work of washing the potatoes before starting to prepare them, my main hands peeling while my secondary ones cut them into cubes.

"Holy shit! How do you do that?!" Belle exclaimed, her gaze locked on my hands. "I can barely peel an onion without cutting myself. How does your brain handle two completely different tasks simultaneously?"

Amusement and pride swelled within me. Other species often had similar reactions to seeing us easily perform things in parallel.

"It is an acquired talent," I conceded. "Our younglings fumble with this in their early years. As their brains further develop, so does the independence of the two pairs of hands. You can walk while searching a bag or untying something without having to think about it. Your brain manages two sets of limbs—your legs and your hands. The same way you learned how to do that, we learn how to handle a third set."

"Well, I don't really count on that front. I mean, it's a miracle that I can talk and walk at the same time without face planting!"

A rumbling laughter rolled out of my throat. "You manage just fine, my mate."

"Barely," she said, looking playfully dejected.

"And this is one of the reasons *I* am the one who cooks in this couple," I said smugly, further showing off my dexterity by spicing the meat while completing the dicing of the potatoes. "Once we reach Xoccoris, I will prepare fresh meats I will have hunted for you. You will *love* Zamorian cuisine."

"I look forward to it," Belle replied with enthusiasm. "You guys have any desserts?"

"We do not really have too many sweets. Our food is mostly savory. But I'll make you cakes and pastries, if you want them. You should also enjoy our version of chocolate," I said, reviewing in my head all the Zamorian recipes that could qualify as desserts. Worst case scenario, there were plenty of cookbooks available online, human or otherwise. "You say you're not much of a cook. Then who used to cook for you?"

"Restaurants…" she said with a sheepish expression. "When I wanted a proper meal, I'd order something. Otherwise, when I cooked for myself, I usually went with the path of least resis-tance. Frozen meals, sandwiches, salads, and canned soups were my go-to. I couldn't afford a replicator but would use the hell out of the one at my father's place whenever I would go stay with him for a while."

"That doesn't sound like very healthy eating habits. Your sire didn't cook for you?"

She chuckled, her face taking on a wistful expression. "Dad is a carnivore. For him, cooking comes down to sprinkling some steak spices onto a big slab of meat, slapping it into a pan for half a second on one side, a quarter of a blink on the other side, and he calls it good. That's his meal, no side dishes or anything."

"That's a recipe for suffering from serious nutritional defi-ciency," I grumbled, making no effort to hide my disapproval.

Belle smiled. "Oh, I agree. I told him as much many times,

but Dad always shrugs it off. It doesn't really matter because he's usually taken care of while in the military. When he's deployed, the cooks prepare most of his meals with the right nutrients. Ditto when he's stationed in some base between assignments. Supper, he has to handle."

She leaned forward, inhaling deeply the aroma of the potatoes with a greedy expression. Clearly, my mate liked good food. It therefore baffled me how little effort they invested in cooking.

"What of your mother?" I asked.

My mate shrugged, her face closing off despite her attempt at appearing nonchalant. "My mother left us when I was a baby. I've only seen her four times in my life and spoke on the phone to her just about as many times. So no, she never cooked for me."

"I see," I replied, feeling terrible for having brought up a sore topic for her. Ignoring the million questions firing off in my mind, I held my tongue. Belle would open up to me in her own time. "Well, your days of frozen meals and canned soups are over."

I 'slapped' the steaks onto the hot pan with a flurry, making her giggle. The sizzling sound quickly filled the room. While it cooked, I cracked all six eggs, then deftly cut the fruits, setting them in a bowl on the plates.

"Oh, my God! This smells so good," Belle said as I started putting a generous portion of potatoes on each plate, then the eggs and finally the steaks.

We settled at the table by the window looking out onto space. My mate didn't have to be told twice to dig in. The moan that escaped her after the first bite resonated straight in my cocks.

"The next time I say anything as stupid as toast and jam will be fine, feel free to tell me to shut the hell up and accept whatever meal you deem appropriate. This is divine!" Belle said before shoving another large piece of steak into her mouth.

I couldn't wipe the grin off my face. I always wondered what it would be like to be the official provider for my household. Never in a million years would I have imagined it would feel so wonderful.

Despite eating with a healthy appetite, Belle gave up halfway through, too full to continue. Her crushed expression as she looked at the large amount of food remaining had me laughing again, both with pride and amusement.

"Don't look so sad, my mate. I'll have other great dishes for you later," I said in a sympathetic tone.

And then I proceeded to gulp down my two steaks and mountain of sides before cleaning her leftovers. I had a healthy appetite… on all fronts.

Once we finished, Belle helped me clean up the mess hall. We made a small detour to the studio for her to pick up her drawing pad, and then she followed me to the deck.

I had some research to do in preparation for my next hunt. As I never liked leaving the ship on autopilot for excessive amounts of time, I often worked from the pilot's chair. My woman would keep herself busy browsing through the recording of my earlier training to select the stills she wanted to draw. As much of a loner as I was, the idea of having her working next to me held a certain charm.

I settled in my usual seat, expecting Belle to sit in the copilot's chair. To my surprise, she pushed back on my shoulder when I leaned towards the console to call up the holographic screen of my computer. My inquisitive look turned to shock when she plopped herself onto my lap.

"What are you doing?" I asked, baffled.

"Cuddling," she replied, as if it was self-evident.

"Cuddling?" I asked, horrified.

"Yeah. You know, that thing couples do when they want to share an intimate moment together."

"Oh! You wish to couple again?" I asked. Although I wanted

to get to work, I wouldn't object to another round with my mate, if she had need of me.

"No, silly, not sex! I just want to sit on you and feel you around me," she countered, looking at me as if she was starting to question my intelligence.

"But that's useless and makes it inconvenient to work," I argued, more baffled than ever.

"It's not useless, silly goose. It's pleasant and affectionate."

"I'm not a goose! Do I look like a bird to you?" I objected with a frown.

"Definitely no feathers on you. But you are acting silly like one," she said with a bratty grin.

"I'm not acting silly. And my people don't cuddle," I retorted, hoping to put an end to this nonsensical argument.

"Well, mine do. You said your body was mine. Which means I can use it to snuggle whenever I feel the need," she deadpanned.

I glared at her. "Female, you seriously need to stop using my words against me."

"Stop growling," she said in a sing-song voice. "I'm not using your words *against* you. I'm using them *for us* and merely reminding you of your own wisdom. Plus, happy wife, happy life. Your body is just too perfect not to cuddle with whenever possible. Give it time. Soon enough, you'll be the one asking for snuggles."

Without waiting for my response, Belle placed a resounding kiss on my cheek, and leaned back against my chest with a contented purr. She stuck the key from the stealth camera into her pad and started viewing the recording.

I glared at her for a while longer, annoyed by her lack of submission, flattered by her need for contact with me, and aggravated by how pleasant she actually felt on me. The wretched female was truly trying to soften me.

Swallowing back a growl, I loaded the information files

provided by the Galactic Hunters Federation regarding the vicious creature we would hunt on Trangor. As I began reading, my main right arm wrapped possessively around my mate with a will of its own. Belle caressed the back of my hand before giving me a sideways glance over her shoulder. She smiled with an air filled with such hope, affection, and happiness that it turned me upside down.

Kromor's teeth… unable to resist, I smiled back.

CHAPTER 7
ANNABELLE

The two days it took us to reach Xoccoris flew by much too fast. Bayron and I were just starting to find our footing around each other. A couple of weeks at least, just the two of us, would have permitted a closer bonding.

After a somewhat awkward start—thanks to my freakiness—something sweet was blossoming between us. Unsurprisingly, my husband didn't quite get me. Heck, I hardly understood myself. However, I loved that, as much as he grumbled at my grabby, touchy-feely ways, he still yielded to make me happy.

I couldn't say for certain if the reluctance towards displays of affection was a cultural thing, or just my grumpy beast's personality. But I strongly suspected it was a mix of both. Although I didn't mean to, I'd been pushing his boundaries. In a way, we needed that to get to know each other. He'd been a good sport about it so far. Now that we'd be throwing his family and clan into the mix, how would he react to me challenging his ways? And more importantly, how would *they* react to me and my quirkiness?

With nerves knotting my insides and thoughts of all the ways in which I could make a spectacle of myself filling my mind, I failed to even appreciate the alien landscape as we began our descent towards his clan's compound. My brain only registered that it looked like a gigantic, fortified city. However, instead of the network of streets lined with individual dwellings, it contained a few large buildings, which I presumed acted as apartment complexes.

Once more displaying his dexterity, Bayron flawlessly landed our ship inside the massive hangar. To my surprise, no welcoming party awaited us. In fact, you could all but hear crickets from the complete absence of any living soul, aside from the two of us. I cast a concerned glance at Bayron, who seemed totally unbothered by it. Catching my stare, he gave me a questioning look. I smiled and shook my head, implying there was nothing.

Could it be the way of his people?

As was his wont, Bayron picked up the little bag I'd packed for our stay here. According to him, we'd only spend a week. Therefore, it made little sense for us to unload everything from the ship.

As we exited the hangar, my hand itched with the need to reach out for one of his for comfort. The large, reinforced doors on the side wall opened into a short, but imposing hallway, with another set of reinforced doors at the end. The latter parted before us, revealing the city in all its splendor.

Bayron's obsession with brown finally made sense. While I wouldn't have described the city as having quite the industrial style, it boasted similar features. Between the exposed dark wood and dark metal beams, brown stones and bricks, huge windows, and the clean, sharp lines of the architecture, the entire place screamed order and discipline. The wide streets and greenery, seamlessly incorporated in strategic places, kept the place from looking sterile and gloomy.

Where the ship hangar had been a ghost town, the city streets teemed with activity. I was almost getting whiplash from my head turning in every direction to look at all the giants moving about. The females were just as imposing, although a slender version of their males. They all towered over me, with an average height of 6'4. Judging by their well-defined muscles, the females could break my jaw with a single slap. And yet, they remained quite feminine, like a fitness athlete rather than bulky like a female bodybuilder.

Their sexy attires—mainly cropped tank tops that exposed their navels, and skirts of varying lengths, from very short to below-ankle—made me feel frumpy. I'd put on one of my favorite boho dresses, slightly cinched around the waist to give me a more flattering figure, and with long puffy sleeves. Now, I almost felt like I had a potato sack on instead, when compared to the curve-hugging outfits the other females wore.

That every single local locked their four eyes on me as we walked past them only made me all the more self-conscious. I stole a nervous glance at Bayron, who once again appeared unfazed. To the contrary, he seemed to be prancing like a peacock.

I kicked myself for not questioning him further about his people. As I understood it, he'd been away for a few months. As his clanmates, and with him being the son of their clan leader, shouldn't they all be greeting him warmly, instead of these mostly indifferent stares at him, and curious ones at me? The absence of anger or annoyance from my husband some-what reassured me. Maybe his people really weren't into displays of affection of any kind—a hard concept for a hugger like me.

No one spoke to us. They just made zero effort to be discreet about ogling us. Bayron breaking the silence partially saved me from fully freaking out.

"It is normally a five-minute walk to my family's fort, but with your shorter strides, it should take about ten minutes," Bayron explained in a gentle voice. "It is not too late for us to use a ride instead, either a hover car or a mount. I just figured you'd like to get a glimpse of the compound first."

"Walking is fine," I said too quickly, no doubt giving away how I welcomed delaying as much as possible the moment I'd stand under the scrutiny of his family.

His knowing smile confirmed he wasn't duped. He pointed at some of the massive buildings I had noticed during our descent.

"These are the fortresses of the main bloodlines forming our clan. Each fortress contains countless individual dwellings for the various families within. The head of the family is a Clan Chieftain, and also one of my father's generals," he continued, before pointing at another massive structure. It vaguely reminded me of the carapace of a turtle, with spikes on top and huge windows all around. "This is the Great Hall. While each fortress possesses its own smaller version of it for bloodline gatherings, this one is where the clan as a whole convenes whether for social or political purposes."

"Is that where we're going to have our Zamorian wedding?" I asked, wondering what it looked like inside.

He chuckled and gave me the oddest look. "No. That's definitely *not* where it will happen."

I frowned, worry about what my acceptance into the clan involved resurfacing. We couldn't be married according to his custom until I'd been welcomed into the clan. Bayron hinted that my mental strength would be put to the test. But how? I enjoyed horror movies, so I could deal with a bit of stress. I had no problem eating gross things—my father had seen to it when he'd given me basic survival training. Could it be based on morals and values? I considered myself a pretty decent person, but what would this alien species consider as right and proper?

Before I could attempt to pry further, Bayron pointed at another impressive structure. The shape of that one brought to mind a crown of thorns sitting on top of a ring made of dark wood and brushed metal.

"This is the arena, and every Zamorian's favorite place to hang out," he said with a shit-eating grin. "You will visit it very soon."

My frown deepened, as did my worry. "Why do you say it like that?"

"Because it is exciting," he said with a far too innocent face.

My husband was up to something, but once again I didn't get the opportunity to give him the third degree about it—not that he would have answered. In the past couple of days, it had become quite clear that Bayron couldn't be coerced or sweet-talked into revealing anything he didn't want to.

"And this is the Skortheatis Fortress," he said, gesturing at it with both of his main hands, pride filling his voice. "My blood-line has led this clan for generations. My dwelling within... *our* dwelling... once belonged to my great-great-grand-father, Breiziksanyiek. Despite being the firstborn, he forfeited the honor of being Clan Leader in favor of his younger brother. He didn't want to rule, he wanted to fight. And he was probably the greatest warrior of our history."

"Wow!" I said, genuinely impressed, before another troubling thought crossed my mind. "So, when you say dwelling, are we talking about individual apartments, or you have a room in your parents' house?"

I flinched as soon as the words left my mouth. I hadn't meant to make it sound as if he was still squatting at his parents' home. To my relief, he didn't seem offended.

"No, I do not live in my parents' house, the way you're thinking," Bayron replied with an amused tone. "Each dwelling is independent and self-sufficient. You could compare it to a human townhouse, most of them with their own backyard. While there are common areas for families to mingle, you can do your own thing with your mate and offspring and ignore everyone else, if you so wish."

"Cool," I said, feeling relieved. While I liked the idea of a close-knit extended family, I didn't want third parties constantly in my business.

However, that relief was short-lived as we approached the massive doors of the fortress. It almost felt like entering the cyberpunk version of an industrial castle. A big hall greeted us, with off-white walls and exposed, thick wooden beams. Like the rest of the city, the large hallway beyond the vestibule had clean, crisp lines, and a minimalistic décor. Here, life-size statues of fearsome Zamorian warriors lined the walls at regular intervals. I could only presume they were former clan leaders or great warriors of Bayron's bloodline.

Instead of those statues, I had almost expected to find warriors in futuristic gladiator attire with their lightning spears guarding each side of the entrance. But once more, no one awaited us. I was starting to think we were being shunned.

Do they disapprove of Bayron marrying a human?

That fear had plagued me from the moment Kayog had mentioned no Zamorian had ever married a human before. And the continued indifference the return of the 'Prodigal Son' had elicited was seriously getting to me. I wasn't in love with my husband yet, but despite some awkward moments, I genuinely felt we were off to a good start. The possibility that his family could get in the way of the future we were building together terrified me. I wanted to keep my beast.

As if he'd read the thoughts running through my head, Bayron gave me a sideways glance and answered my unspoken question.

"My family awaits us in the gathering hall." He gestured with his chin at a massive set of doors about twenty meters ahead. "The side corridors on our left and right lead to the dwellings. You will see ours shortly."

"Okay," I said in a small voice, my pulse picking up.

Suddenly, the echo of our footsteps in the large space sounded deafening, competing with the roaring of my blood rushing in my ears. Summoning every ounce of my willpower, I tried to control my breathing and force a confident expression on my face.

That lasted only the time it took for the gathering hall doors to open.

I couldn't tell if someone inside had opened them for us or if a motion sensor had activated them. But my brain had more important things to deal with—namely the more than one hundred Zamorians gathered in what felt like a mix of a throne room, dining hall, amphitheater, and ballroom.

The vaguely octagonal room had dining tables lining the walls, all of them empty. A series of short stairs led down to the central part of the room, which reminded me of a dance floor. However, in-between the stairs, the majority of the clanmates present sat on a mini version of cushioned bleachers. And straight in front of us, on the opposite side of the room, elevated on a dais, a fearsome Zamorian sat next to his mate.

I didn't need Bayron to tell me they were his parents. His father was his spitting image, with the same long black hair and blue eyes, although with quite the impressive collection of scars. However, his mother couldn't have been more different, with silver white hair and golden eyes. To his father's left, another Zamorian male sat on a slightly smaller chair. His resemblance to my husband made it obvious he was his big brother. But the long scar on his left cheek made him all the more fearsome.

They sat on unpretentious 'thrones' made of carved wood, with metal edges and a burgundy cushion. Clearly, they didn't need all the glitter and fancy stuff other monarchs or heads of state surrounded themselves with. Their mere presence screamed their authority and power.

And everyone's intimidating gaze was leveled on me.

I realized I had reached out for Bayron's hand when every double set of eyes shifted to our joined hands. I swallowed hard and cast a nervous sideways glance at my husband, fearing he'd be aggravated with me. To my utter relief, he gazed at his clan-mates with a smug expression before turning his attention to his parents. Simultaneously, he gave my hand a gentle, encouraging squeeze. That, more than anything else, gave me the boost of courage I needed.

Bayron had freely agreed to marry me. He'd told me more than once that I was his and that no one would meddle in his marital affairs. I needed to tell my insecurities to piss the hell off. He was *my* husband, *my* beast, and according to Kayog, *my* soulmate. However intimidating his clanmates and family might be, I wouldn't be cowed by anyone.

We walked down the five steps to the floor, then made our way towards the throne. I couldn't believe I managed to get there with a somewhat graceful gait, and not stumble or faceplant. Fuck me sideways… I felt like an oddity in a freakshow.

"Mother. Father. Brother," Bayron said in Universal, as sole greeting as we came to a stop a couple of meters in front of the throne dais.

"Son, you have returned," his mother replied in a neutral voice, also in Universal.

"And accompanied, at that," his father added.

"Bye," his brother said.

It took me a second to realize he hadn't said 'bye' as in telling him to leave, but 'Bay' as an even shorter version of Bayrohnziyiek.

"I have," he said, nodding at his mother before turning to his father, "and I am, indeed. Please meet my mate, Annabelle Parker. Belle, meet our Matriarch, my mother, Feidinsaya. Feidin for short. Our Clan Leader, my father Ugrulsayiek, commonly called Ugrul. And my brother, Varkuthsenyiek, or Varkuth."

"I am honored to meet all of you," I said, annoyed that my voice didn't sound more confident, but at least relieved it didn't shake.

My heart sank when none of them responded. Ugrul gave me

a slow once over, as if attempting to figure out what his son could possibly find attractive in me. Feidin tilted her head to the side and pursed her lips like someone trying to decide how they truly felt about something presented to them. Varkuth seemed more interested in looking at his brother with a Mona Lisa smile.

"Annabelle Parker, are you standing before us to be bonded to my son?" Ugrul asked at last.

His voice was so deep, and the rumbling so powerful, I could have sworn the stone floor beneath my feet had trembled.

"Yes, Sir," I replied.

"Ugrul," he corrected with a slight frown.

I opened my mouth to apologize, but Bayron interrupted me.

"No, she's not," he said sternly.

I jerked my head towards him, shocked. What did he mean by that? Had he decided he didn't want to marry me according to his people's ways after all? We were supposed to give this a fair try for six months. Things had been going well between us—at least I thought so. Was he…?

"Oh?" his mother asked.

"We're not here for a bonding but for a claiming," Bayron replied, lifting his chin defiantly.

Feidin's face closed off. Varkuth's brow shot up in surprise, while Ugrul frowned.

"You are not *required* to do that this soon," his father cautioned.

"I *choose* to do that," Bayron retorted in a tone that brooked no argument.

Behind us, the clan whispered, apparently just as stunned. I remembered then that Kayog had mentioned Bayron didn't have to fully claim me until the six months were up. While I didn't know jack shit about how any of their rituals went down, I at least understood that the bonding was a non-permanent wedding that you could walk out of if things didn't work out. But a claiming was for life.

I didn't understand why my husband seemed so determined to make our union permanent from the get-go, but I was fully onboard with that. Beyond the fact that Kayog's blessing made it a guaranteed success for me, I loved Bayron's determination to make us work, to want to keep me forever, even though he wasn't yet in love with me.

I had never realized just how desperately I wanted to belong to someone who truly wanted me. To this day, I still struggled with abandonment issues, mostly caused by the actions of my mother, but also somewhat by my father.

"What of you, Annabelle Parker? Do you also choose a claiming over a bonding?" Feidin asked, an unreadable expression on her face.

"Bayron and I are soulmates," I said, stunned by the firmness and strength of my voice when my knees were all but wobbly. "We don't need a bonding. As per my vows, I married him for better or for worse, until death do us part. He's mine, and I'm his. I want a claiming. Oh, and you can call me Belle."

Under different circumstances, the way both of his parents and his brother simultaneously raised their left eyebrow in surprise would have been hilarious—if not a little creepy. But it was the glimmer of approval in Feidin's yellow eyes that made me feel warm inside. Ugrul's expression remained unreadable.

"Do you know what a claiming involves, Belle?" Varkuth asked with a semi-taunting, semi-amused expression.

I shifted nervously on my feet and cast an uncertain look at Bayron. But he was staring somewhat defiantly at his elder brother.

"No," I conceded sheepishly.

The explosion of laughter in the room startled the heck out of me, making me nearly jump out of my skin. I flicked my head this way and that, trying to figure out why they thought this so amusing. The shit-eating grins cast my way all seemed to infer I would hate whatever awaited me.

"Tell me, little human…" Ugrul said, placing the palms of his secondary hands on the armrests of his throne and the elbows of his primary arms on his knees as he leaned forward to look intently at me. "Do you enjoy danger?"

My stomach dropped upon hearing his words, which echoed the question Kayog had asked me during our first meeting.

I scrunched my face and shrugged. "Danger that I have some control over, yes. I like scary stuff, but not really to be in the middle of it."

Everyone laughed again, including Ugrul and Varkuth. I was feeling stupid, even though I didn't think they were mocking me. Their laughter was laced with disbelief and a sliver of pity, the way you feel sorry for someone clueless who just got in over their head. Still, my anger flared, especially when Bayron said nothing, content to cross his thick arms over his massive chest.

"I'm glad I'm provoking all of this hilarity. But how about you just tell me what this claiming is all about?" I snapped.

Far from being offended, Ugrul snorted—apparently amused by my temper flare—and echoed the words Bayron had previously spoken to me. "You will find out soon enough." He then refocused on his son. "Are you certain you want—?"

"Yes, we are," Bayron said, interrupting his father, his tone all but daring him to challenge his will again.

"Very well, then. If it's a claiming you want, a claiming you shall have…" Ugrul said, the way one gives up on a hopeless case, before casting a glance at his wife.

He didn't speak a word. Feidin simply rose to her feet. To my surprise, she reached for her husband's braid, elegantly adorned with bejeweled rings along its length, letting it slide through her fingers in a gentle caress. The way Ugrul's face melted as he looked at his mate while a purr rumbled from his broad chest totally threw me. There had been something incredibly possessive and sexy in the gesture. For some reason, it reminded me of a wild creature marking her territory… and that territory enjoying being claimed.

Varkuth also rose, heading towards Bayron while Feidin came to stand before me. Damn, she was tall! I felt scrawny before her. The neutral expression on her face made her seriously intimidating.

"Come then, Belle. We shall prepare you for your claiming," Feidin said.

Without waiting for my response, she started strutting towards the exit. The long black skirt, with a slit up to the middle of her left thigh, gave a glimpse of her endless, sexy leg with each step. Her silver mane, down to the small of her back, swayed in tandem.

I cast a semi-panicked look at Bayron. He nodded at me in an encouraging fashion. After a last squeeze of my hand, he released it. Swallowing hard, I hurried to catch up to his mother.

But after barely a few steps, a male sitting on the left 'bleachers' suddenly growled at me in a menacing fashion, making me yelp and almost lose my footing. I gaped at him, my palm pressed over my heart while I gave him a 'What the fuck?' look. Some of the females sitting near him chuckled, one of them rolling her eyes.

Just as I was regaining my bearings and resuming walking towards Feidin—who was looking at me with a less-than-impressed expression—a different male to my right started growling. He was louder and looked even more vicious, then slammed his main fists on his chest.

My steps faltering, I cast a worried look at Bayron over my shoulder. Teeth bared, he was glaring at the male who had just growled, looking like he wanted to come crack his skull. Standing next to him, Varkuth was pressing a hand to his brother's chest, clearly to keep him from intervening.

They have the right to do this, and Bayron isn't allowed to stop them!

Was that the test? Surely trying to scare the bejeezus out of me couldn't be the acceptance challenge into the clan? Whatever this was, they apparently expected me to just take it. I could do that, and then Bayron would have some explaining to do. Lifting my chin, I forced myself to put one step in front of the other. As I made my way to Feidin, four more males growled and emitted threatening sounds towards me, two of them standing up to bunch their muscles and make terrifying faces at me.

For a split second, I thought they were going to attack me, but they stood right in front of their seats. And then a freaking behemoth rose from his seat and came to stand near the doors. The roar that erupted from his throat nearly deafened me. But I was too petrified to even wince at that. With a height of at least eight feet and nearly twice the width of Bayron, he had to weigh a minimum of four hundred pounds—all of it pure muscle.

If I had not emptied my bladder before getting off the Ostros, I would have peed myself. I froze in place, mouth gaping, as I stared at the most terrifying person I'd ever met. His eyes had turned orange, a common trait with Zamorian when they were angry or were entering combat mode. Head bent all the way back to look at the giant, I almost forgot to breathe.

Him brutally slapping his chest with both his main fists, spreading his secondary hands as if to reach out and grab me while roaring savagely snapped me out of my petrified state. I yelped, taking a couple of involuntary steps back while shaking like a leaf. For a split second, I thought he would pick me up with one hand and smash me onto the ground like a ragged doll, shattering every bone in my body.

I couldn't think straight as he continued to emit feral sounds, stomping his feet, bunching his muscles and gesturing the way a wild beast would to chase off a would-be trespasser on his territory.

"Bayron!" Ugrul's voice exclaimed sternly behind us.

I looked at them over my shoulder. To my shock, this time

both my husband's brother and father were holding him back. Except, instead of looking furious at the behemoth who was threatening me, Bayron was glaring at *me*.

What the actual fuck?!

I realized then that he had also been growling. But another loud roar from the giant had me shouting, my entire body jerking with fright as I turned back to look at him.

"Enough, Krogal. You've made your point," Feidin said, looking both annoyed and unimpressed.

She grabbed my wrist and pulled me after her while the terrifying mountain of muscles straightened, all anger apparently faded as he watched me walk past him with a smug grin on his face.

Too traumatized to speak, I just let my mother-in-law lead me to the elevator in the right hallway leading to the dwellings.

"What the heck was that?" I asked, finally recovering my voice as she pressed the button to what seemed to be the penthouse. "Why were they threatening me? Is that the mental test Bayron hinted at?"

Feidin snorted and shook her head. "I can see why *you* would interpret their behavior that way. But no, Belle, they were not threatening you. They were presenting for you."

"Presenting?" I asked, baffled.

"Showing off their attributes, their strength, how intimidating they are," she replied, sounding amused.

I blinked, even more confused. "Whatever for? Why do it by trying to scare the living daylights out of me? And why did Bayron look mad at *me* instead of at those males bullying me."

The elevator coming to a halt spared Feidin from answering. She waved me out as soon as the doors parted. I complied, determined not to let her off the hook if she tried to dodge.

A large set of wooden doors closed off the small antechamber we were standing in. As I suspected that they would open onto the living space of the dwelling, I appreciated the privacy they provided, instead of having the family exposed as soon as someone came out of the elevator.

To my relief, Feidin walked out of the elevator and stopped to face me. "It is not bullying, it is courting. These males were expressing their interest in you and showing what great protectors they would be with their strength and ability to terrify enemies. And your response to Krogal was quite flattering to him."

"WHAT?! Hoooold on! Wait a freaking minute! First off, I'm already married. They have no business courting me!" I exclaimed, feeling offended by this blatant disrespect for my husband. "Second, I was scared shitless. This was *not* me responding positively to that giant, *at all*. I thought he was going to bash my head in!"

Feidin tilted her head to the side, studying my features for a few seconds as if she wanted to make sure I was speaking the truth.

"For my son's sake, I'm glad to hear it. But no, Belle, you are not married yet. Your human wedding has no legal value here," she added quickly when I opened my mouth to argue. "Until you have been claimed or bonded according to our customs, you are deemed fair game. Should Bayron fail in his attempt to claim you, or should you decide not to claim him after all, these males will vie for your attention, especially Krogal. And I can see why…"

The mysterious way in which she pronounced that last sentence struck me as odd. But too many questions were pressing themselves over my tongue.

Feidin turned to the large doors, pushing them open. My jaw all but dropped at the stunning room thus revealed. It felt like walking into a luxury penthouse loft, flooded with light from the humongous, floor-to-ceiling windows. Once again, the décor favored the industrial style but this time with rustic vibes as well. Looking past the excess of brown and beige, I could already picture the wonders I could achieve with such a magnificent canvas.

"Bayron is quite possessive of you," Feidin continued while leading me towards a large room at the back. "Your reaction to his cousin hurt him."

"But I wasn't turned on or flirting," I countered, feeling it was all unfair.

She opened the door to the most insane bedroom I'd ever seen. Bayron had not been kidding when he'd said a Zamorian bed was even more massive than the one we shared on his ship. It was large enough to put two Krogals side by side, spread-eagled. Although scarce, each piece of furniture was of exquisite craftsmanship, once again made of wood and metal. Next to a huge seating area, tall patio doors gave way to an imposing terrace with a breathtaking view over the city.

"No, but you were scared," Feidin said matter-of-factly while reaching for a white garment on the bed. "We Zamorian females do not scare easily. A male who manages to prompt such a reaction as the one you displayed is definitely a keeper for us. My Ugrul made me faint with terror."

She held the white dress in front of me to measure it, then burst out laughing upon noticing my horrified expression.

"Then I'm glad Bayron didn't come at me that way. I like getting scared watching movies, not in real life," I muttered, repressing a shudder at the thought of Krogal, then gestured at the garment with my chin. "Is that a Zamorian wedding dress?"

To my surprise, Feidin's face shed any sign of amusement. She frowned at me with a slight air of concern as she shook her head. "Not exactly. It's a sacrificial gown."

"WHAT?" I exclaimed, taking an involuntary step backward. "What the heck kind of claiming is this?"

She lowered her main hands holding up the dress, then folded the garment over her forearm. "During a claiming, a male has to prove that he is a worthy protector for the female he covets."

"Prove it how?" I insisted.

Fighting to silence my growing panic, I reminded myself that Kayog knew what a bonding and claiming involved. He never would have sent me to some freaky place to get slaughtered.

"Bayron must prove himself by saving you. And you must prove your trust in him by allowing him to," Feidin said, her intense gaze studying my features as if to read whether I had it in me.

"Specifically, what does that mean?" I asked, getting annoyed at the vague responses. "You want to put me in a 'sacrificial' gown. Am I to be sacrificed if he fails?"

Feidin snorted and shook her head. "If he fails, you will not be sacrificed. However, you are to be shackled in the arena as a sacrificial offering. A grummoll, one of Xoccoris's most vicious predators, will be unleashed in the arena. Bayron must keep it from coming close enough to harm you and defeat it."

"Seriously?" I asked, incredulous.

"Seriously," Feidin confirmed. "Although my mate and first-born son always standby to save the bride in case the aspiring groom gets overwhelmed, all the males who growled for you earlier will be on standby. They will protect you or jump into the battle if you ask for help because you believe Bayron will fail."

"So, what you're saying is that you guys want me to agree to be shackled in an arena where you're going to throw in the craziest beast there is on your planet, and then wait for Bayron to come and single handedly rescue me?"

"In essence, yes."

"This is so freaking cool! I loved the part where Belle gets rescued by the Beast when a bunch of rabid creatures tried to kill her. Now I truly get to be the damsel in distress saved by her prince!"

"Excuse me?" Feidin asked, looking utterly lost.

I giggled and waved a dismissive hand. "Never mind. It's just a human fairy tale I love. But yeah, I'm totally fine with this whole thing."

She stared at me, looking as if she couldn't decide if my response thrilled or baffled her. "You agree? I thought you said you didn't want to be in the middle of danger?"

"Right, but Bayron is going to keep me safe," I said with a shrug. "He's super hardcore, and he's hunted the most savage monsters out there. He's going to kick that grom-whatever-its-name creature of yours without breaking a sweat. It's going to be *epic*! I love watching him fight."

I grinned, already buzzing with excitement.

Feidin appeared speechless for a moment, then all tension bled out of her as she gave me a slow grin.

"You're a strange human," she said, pensively.

I snorted and gave her a teasing smile. "Everyone who knows me would agree with you."

She looked amused. "You know, I think I like you. There might be more fire inside you than that meek exterior lets on," she said in an approving tone. "Your fragile appearance is very appealing to our males. Frankly, you stir my own protective instincts."

"That's nice… I guess. But no offense to those other males, I'm not interested. I have Bayron," I said cautiously, examining her features to see how she would respond to my words.

"I'm glad to hear it. Had you refused to participate in the claiming, it would have implied you deemed Bayron unfit to protect you. He would be publicly shamed, and your union voided," Feidin explained.

"Whoa! Why would he take such a big risk without first making sure I was onboard with that?" I asked, baffled. "I mean, sure, Kayog says we're soulmates, but we still have to get to know each other."

"He did it to protect you. He likely had not wanted you

spending the duration of your voyage here panicking about what was about to happen," Feidin replied with a shrug. "Truth be told, without the Temern's assurance that you are indeed soulmates, I would have opposed this claiming."

I stiffened, giving her a shocked look. "Opposed it? Could you do that?"

"Of course," she replied, as if the answer was obvious. "I am the Matriarch of this clan. Our males may be loud and intimidating, and my mate may be the Clan Leader, Zamorians are first and foremost a matriarchy. I could not prevent a bonding, but I could stop a claiming, if I didn't believe the couple could truly last. Divorces are a horrible thing and a stain on both the Matriarch who allowed that marriage, and the clan as a whole."

I frowned, feeling uneasy by that comment. "I don't think anyone enters into a union with the intention of divorcing. But isn't it better that people who fall out of love divorce rather than remain trapped in a miserable and loveless marriage?"

"That's what bondings are for—a committed long-term trial period that allows the couples to determine whether or not they are truly meant for each other."

I bit my tongue not to argue with her. Butting heads with my mother-in-law right before my wedding didn't seem like a wise course of action. In principle, I agreed with her statement. Nowadays, it often felt like people gave up on their vows at the first hurdle. But I also didn't believe in condemning someone to a lifetime of misery if things really didn't work out after both parties had made every genuine effort they could to save their union.

"So, you want me to put on this dress?" I asked, shifting the subject to safer grounds.

"Yes," Feidin said with a firm nod. "If you want, you can change here. However, I understand humans tend to want privacy. In which case, you can go to the hygiene room," she added, waving at a large set of doors on the left side of the bed.

For a split second, I considered going to the bathroom. Aside from my slight body-image issues, stripping in front of a stranger, my new mother-in-law no less, who also happened to have a body to die for, made me quite self-conscious. Yet, the overly nonchalant way in which she had offered felt like both a challenge and a test.

Sucking it up, I yanked up the hem of my potato-sack dress to lift it over my head. As soon as I started removing it, Feidin's lips stretched in a discreet smile, a glimmer of approval flitting through her yellow eyes. She barely spared me a glance, turning away towards the dresser near the door.

A part of me suspected she had done so as much to go fetch something in the drawer as to grant me some privacy. The amount of time she fiddled with the contents of the drawer before retrieving a small box only seemed to confirm it. Even from where I stood, I could see that everything in that drawer was neatly organized. I appreciated this discreet thoughtfulness.

By the time she returned with the box, I had finished putting on the dress. It had a Grecian style to it and reminded me of ancient Rome's vestals attire. Although it hugged my curves a bit more than I was normally comfortable with, it actually felt great on me. Judging by the once over Feidin gave me, she also seemed to approve.

She opened the box and presented it to me. I gaped in awe at the stunning medallion inside. I didn't know the metal it had been made from—although it vaguely resembled some kind of pale gold—but it perfectly represented the stylized tree of life I had drawn as my symbol, per Bayron's request.

"Oh, my God! This is exquisite!" I said, taking it with reverence. I noticed then the chain attached to it, making it a necklace. "I can't believe you got my design turned into this so quickly. I love it!"

Feidin smiled smugly, pleased by my reaction. "Well, you cannot have a claiming without it."

"Really? Why? How does it work exactly?" I asked, my gaze locked on the medallion, which seemed to have little indents at the back, like for some locking mechanism.

"You'll find out soon enough."

My head jerked up, and I scrunched my face at my mother-in-law. "What's with you guys and that phrase? Why not just tell me?"

"Because seeing your annoyance is too amusing," she said in a teasing voice. "What does this symbol mean anyway?" Feidin asked before I could think of a clever comeback.

"It's my version of a stylized Tree of Life," I said, suddenly feeling nervous about exposing the very personal reasons behind that choice. "The Tree of Life represents our personal development, our uniqueness, and individual beauty. It starts as a weak sapling, and battles through adversity to expand its roots and spread its limbs towards the infinite. For the longest time, I devoted my energy spreading myself outwards, overcoming my challenges and embracing the world, because I didn't really have any roots. In truth, I didn't know where to plant them or where I even belonged. But now I finally do. Whatever I was growing towards can only become stronger thanks to the foundation Bayron and I are laying down together."

As I had braced for her to mock my romantic babbling, the gentle, almost maternal look she leveled on me instead wrecked me. My mother had essentially been a stranger to me.

"Family is everything," Feidin said in a soft voice. "If it is roots you want, then you couldn't have picked a better mate. No matter how violent the winds, no matter how powerful the floods, my Bayron will always keep you upright until the roots binding you are so strong and so deep that nothing will ever be a threat to you."

My throat tightened as I nodded at her words. "I want that very much."

"Then let's get you claimed," Feidin said enthusiastically,

while picking up a small flask from the same dresser drawer she had recovered the medallion from.

It looked like a bottle of perfume. She lifted it in front of me and sprayed some over me. It had a rather delicate scent, so subtle—at least to my human nose—that I didn't really understand its purpose.

"Hey! What is that?" I asked, instantly worried by the almost evil grin on her face as she did so.

"It's brumar sweat. A potent pheromone that attracts grummolls. Come on, it's time to put you up for sacrifice."

CHAPTER 8
BAYRON

Standing in the middle of the arena, with every unmated male of marrying age split in two groups on each side of me, I watched my Belle approach, led by my mother. Our single females had formed a path, standing on each side of the entrance of the arena. They chanted while throwing shabira petals at my mate, for luck and fertility.

Belle looked stunning in the sacrificial gown that hugged the delicious curves of her body. While I found the boho dresses she liked to wear rather pretty, I hated how they hid her shape. No matter how many times I had to repeat it, I would get my mate to realize she was perfect just the way she was, paunch and all.

It had been bold—not to say reckless—of me not to warn her about what the claiming entailed. But at a visceral level, I had known she would consent. Belle wanted me… wanted us. Her reaction to my training sessions had heavily hinted that she would be fine watching me in a real battle. Granted, this time she would also be in relative jeopardy. However, over the past couple of days, my female had demonstrated that she implicitly trusted me to keep her safe.

Up on the dais overlooking the arena, my father and brother

stood side by side in front of their respective chairs. My mother would join them after she had restrained my mate. My father emitted a powerful war cry that resonated throughout the space. The crowd of mated people and those either too young or too old to partake in a claiming, responded with loud shouts of encouragement and excitement.

I echoed my sire's cry, spreading my four arms, each holding a lethal bladed weapon. The single males around me grunted menacingly, semi-crouching as they began the mating dance. They turned their eyes orange, as did I, which made us even more fearsome. Off-worlders failed to understand how it was a seduction dance. Each male moved savagely through the dance, their movements synchronized as they followed the ancestral choreography. And yet, it was what allowed the more fearsome to stand out by performing the same gestures as everyone else but more threateningly.

From stomping their feet, slapping their chests, shouting, grimacing, and mimicking a flurry of powerful attack moves, they showed what formidable opponents they would be. And they were formidable.

As the groom, I got to yield my weapons as I performed the same choreography. There could be no greater shame than to be outperformed by weaponless males. Judging by the intensity with which Krogal danced, he was truly taken by my mate.

Remembering how Belle had reacted when he had presented for her still stung. I had to remind myself that, as a human, she probably hadn't found that attractive. However, she had made no mystery she loved a fearsome brute with a cuddly side. And Krogal undoubtedly qualified as both. No one could rival his strength and savagery in battle, not even my father. But off the battlefield, he was the gentlest veterinarian. Once she got to know him, I didn't doubt Belle would grow extremely fond of him. Everyone did…

So I danced like my life depended on it.

While her eyes sparkled with awe as she took in the five dozen males performing for her, my mate's gaze would only stray for a second before refocusing on me. Her smile radiated pride as my mother led her past us to sacrificial pillars.

Embedded in the stone platform in the center of the arena, they framed a rectangular altar that the bride could sit on if she so wished. As the battle sometimes stretched for a bit, she might as well be comfortable to enjoy the show. Mother attached the chains from the manacles on Belle's wrists to a pillar on either side from her. Their length allowed the female to get up and move by a couple of meters in any direction around the altar. At each corner of the platform, a blue flame burned in a large brasier.

We continued dancing until my female was properly shackled.

I emitted a final war cry, echoed by the other males as we simultaneously stopped dancing. As always, performing a Thasnak got the adrenalin flooding through my veins and my blood raging. Seeing my mate thus helpless and restrained also had the latter boiling with a different type of urge. But now wasn't the time to let my dominant side distract me from the task at hand.

A vicious roar off to the left seemed to chime in its agreement with that thought.

My mother exited the arena, followed by the females. The single males filed out after them, climbing into the safe area in front of my father's box. It was elevated enough to keep them out of reach of the beast, but close enough that they could quickly jump into the arena to intervene and protect Belle should things go awry.

As if I would allow that to happen.

While my protective side appreciated that extra layer of security for my mate, it offended my ego that my failure would even be deemed a remote possibility.

The single females split between two sets of balconies on each side of my father's box, while my mother went a level higher to sit next to him. The grummoll roared again as if in response to the ominous sound of our giant bumar drums resonating over the arena.

I cast a possessive look at Belle. Although she was sitting on the altar, her entire body vibrated with excitement. The thrilled expression on her face whipped my bloodlust into a frenzy.

With a loud grinding sound—intended to ensure the fighters in the arena wouldn't be taken unaware that the beasts had been unleashed—the metal barrier of the holding area slowly parted to release the grummoll.

"Oh, my God!" Belle whispered, a sliver of fear entering her voice when she at long last beheld the creature.

Just shy of three meters tall and two meters wide, the grummoll wouldn't win any beauty contests. To my mate, its body would look like a cross between a giant gorilla and a Pitbull with leathery skin and scales. The head had no visible nose, just a giant eye in the middle surrounded by a lot of smaller ones. Their whitish color devoid of pupil made them all the creepier. Below, a giant maw opened into a terrifying tunnel of death filled with needle teeth down to the back of its throat. Six vicious hooks protruded from its lips, ready to latch onto prey to keep it from escaping while it began chewing on its victim.

But its tongue, not its mouth, constituted the biggest threat. The wretched thing could stretch over nearly two meters, the pointy tip acting like a harpoon. Once it had penetrated a target, the tip would open inside, turning into a grappling hook that would inflict horrendous damage if the tongue was yanked out. Worse still, even out of range, the grummoll could open the tip of its tongue like a blooming flower to shoot acid darts over ten meters.

The sickly whitish-blue color of its underbelly indicated the vulnerable areas. Thick bone plates behind its smaller eyes protected the brain from fatal injury. The other ways of swiftly dispatching the creature were a perfect stab in its central eye, or the fragile spot right behind it. Except, a bunch of long spikes coated in the same paralytic acid as his darts covered its back.

I gave Belle a reassuring smile before charging the beast.

For a claiming, I couldn't use a blaster or any other types of long-range weapons. It didn't matter. I would do just fine with my bladed weapons. As I closed the distance with the grummoll, I activated the energy shield from the bracer of my main left hand.

The real challenge would be to keep the beast beyond shooting range from my mate. If the grummoll got close enough to her, he would spit a dart at her. Should that occur, an energy field would trigger around the edge of the platform she was shackled on. However, that would be deemed a failure on my part.

No wonder I loved hunting alone: no one else to worry about keeping safe. Right now, I had to avoid getting gutted by the beast while blocking any dart it might fire Belle's way. With the amount of pheromones my mother had sprayed on my female, the grummoll seemed determined to get to her as quickly as possible.

Its massive paws pounded the ground, the sound resonating above the drums, then its dagger claws dug into the packed dirt to help propel him further ahead. For such a huge creature, it moved at lightning speed. Even though I came straight at it, the grummoll ignored me and shifted slightly to the left to continue dashing towards the altar.

I rammed the side of its front right leg. My brain rattled in my skull from the force of the impact. Although the grummoll stumbled left, it recovered in a blink and whipped its head in my direction. I barely had time to take a step back and raise my shield to avoid getting harpooned by its tongue shooting straight for my face.

Simultaneously, it swiped its paw at me. I had expected that, knowing there would be no avoiding it. The blow didn't sting any less, sending me flying a few meters back. I went into a roll as soon as I landed—thus softening my fall—and flowing back onto my feet. Arms and legs pumping, I chased after my prey, which had resumed rushing towards Belle. I didn't spare her a glance, refusing to get distracted.

Despite its height, the slant of the grummoll's back made it easy to climb, further helped by its short tail acting almost like a step. Using my momentum, I ran up onto the middle of its shoulders, careful not to get pricked by the folded quill-like spikes on its back. It immediately reared to knock me off. I swiftly stabbed the spears in both my secondary hands downward.

Fighting to keep my balance, I missed the main eye but took out at least two smaller ones. The tips of my spears struck the protective bone plate behind them, and the creature reared while opening its gaping maw in a deafening roar. Had I not begun slipping off, I would have attempted to stab more at its face and throat. Furthermore, acid was beginning to ooze from the needles on its back and would wreck my boots if I remained there much longer.

Although the grummoll shot its tongue out again, it couldn't recurve it over its head to get at me. I collapsed my shield and jumped down to the left side of the creature seconds before it dropped back down onto its front paws from its attempt to buck me off. Had I landed behind the beast, it would have kicked me, likely shattering a few of my bones in the process.

As I had hoped, it tried to swipe at me with its front left paw. I dove beneath it, raking its underbelly with the daggers of both my main hands while rolling to the other side. The grummoll screeched, its front legs temporarily buckling from the pain as purplish blood gushed out from the wounds.

The crowd shouted its approval as the beast tried to back away, its torso lowered to protect its underbelly. But even as it temporarily retreated, it pursued its attack, repeatedly launching its harpoon tongue at me while I was still lying on the ground. I rolled right, just in time for the grappling tip to hit the dirt behind me with a thunderclap sound. I reactivated my shield while turning onto my back, raising it half a blink before the tongue stabbed at me again.

Belle shouted in panic when the grummoll charged me, clearly intent on trampling me underfoot. Pushing off my back, I jumped onto my feet, my shield still raised to deflect the darts it was firing at me. I didn't try to run away—there wouldn't have been enough time. Although it felt like the creature moved in slow motion, it was upon me in seconds.

Waiting until the last minute, I pivoted out of the way, spinning with my blades extended at a low angle to slash at the vulnerable flesh at the base of its flank. The beast roared in pain. To my shock, instead of moving away from me like it had previously done, it started falling to the side. On instinct, I latched onto the talon-like hooks that framed its mouth, using them to help me climb onto its head before it could fall on top of me.

I'd never witnessed such a behavior from a grummoll before and couldn't tell whether it had collapsed in reaction to the wound I'd just inflicted, or if it had deliberately attempted to crush me with its weight. But the speed at which it got back onto its feet made me believe it had been the latter.

The beast violently shook its head to get rid of me. I managed to slash a few more of its eyes before it brutally swiped the side of its face on the ground. That slammed my back on the packed dirt hard, almost knocking the wind out of me. I lost my grip on the two hooks around its mouth that I'd been hanging on to. The grummoll lifted its head just far enough to shoot its tongue at me again.

This time, I didn't try to avoid it. Moving at lightning speed, I caught the tongue right below the sharp tip and wrapped its length around my forearm. The beast's roar turned into a gurgling screech when I stabbed my right spear into its mouth. The grummoll reared then backed away, yanking me back on my feet in the process.

I flowed with the movement, holding tightly onto its tongue to prevent it from reeling it back in. Without missing a beat, I rammed my second spear even deeper into its gaping maw. Its body seized before being shaken by a violent spasm. I pushed both spears further in then ended it with a fatal blow of my dagger in its main eye.

The grummoll went limp, collapsing onto its stomach with a low grumbling sound.

The crowd erupted in a deafening roar as the drums went silent.

"Whoo-hoo!" Belle shouted, her voice the sweetest music to my ears.

After yanking my weapons free of the beast, I turned around to look at the crowd. I spread my arms wide, my bleeding weapons raised high in a victorious gesture. I slowly pivoted to look at the hundreds of clanmates gathered in the arena, reveling in their acclaim as they stood and shouted my name.

I then turned to face my mate. Belle also stood, her face radiant with joy, awe, and pride. She'd moved towards me as far as the chain allowed, her arms involuntarily tugging at the restraints. Feeling like a god, I marched towards my female, stopping a couple of meters in front of her.

Her confusion quickly faded when she saw my parents enter the arena, followed by the unmated females and the handful of males who had growled for Belle. Even though she had merely cast a curious glance at them, I hated the nervousness that settled in the pit of my stomach, especially seeing Krogal staring at her.

My female had exceeded my expectations. While she had feared for me when things got heated, she had been very vocal in cheering me on. Not once had I perceived any expression of fear for herself. Belle might not be a Zamorian female, but she certainly had the heart of one.

My parents came to a stop before Belle. As our Matriarch and Clan Leader, they always presided over any claiming or bonding. That I happened to be their son only made this time more special. And the pride in their eyes when they gazed upon me filled my hearts to bursting.

"Bayrohnziyiek Skortheatis, you have prevailed in your challenge," my father said in a booming voice. "You have therefore earned the right to free the Vaika."

Puffing up my chest, I took the key he handed over to me and strutted towards my Vaika—the sacrificial bride. Once more, Belle nearly vibrated with excitement. But it was the way she stared at me as if I were the greatest wonder in the galaxy that messed with me. For a moment, I feared she would throw herself into my arms the minute I freed her. I didn't know if my mother had warned her that it would be highly inappropriate. Thankfully, although her hands literally twitched with the apparent need to touch me, she kept her distance once I removed the shackles from her.

"Annabelle Parker," my mother said in a solemn voice, "my son Bayrohnziyiek has faced great danger to prove himself a worthy protector for the family he desires to build with you. Does he meet your approval? Will you have him as your mate?"

"Heck yes!! He's awesome! He's perfect! I mean, yes, I will have him as my mate," she said, her voice pitching in her excitement.

A few of the females surrounding us chuckled, while an amused smile stretched my parents' lips. Her eagerness had my chest further swelling with pride. I still didn't understand why she wanted me so fiercely, but I couldn't be more pleased by it.

"Then I shall give him to you," my mother said.

My father approached the large stone altar Belle had initially been sitting on and activated the hidden mechanism. My mate gasped as it rose from the ground by almost a meter to form a perfect altar, only for the top to slide open.

"Oh wow…" Belle whispered when it revealed a small basin filled with purifying water on the left and a case with a short staff and clean cloth on the right.

My mother retrieved a bowl and a few cloths, which she handed to my cousin Noca, who was also one of the unmated females. I removed my bloodied shirt and handed it to Krogal, along with my weapons. As my mother began to cleanse my face, chest, and arms, my father turned to Belle.

"May I?" he asked, gesturing at her necklace.

She stiffened, her hand protectively closing over the medallion. It had been an instinctive reaction, but an interesting one, nonetheless. Snapping out of it, she removed the necklace and warily handed it over to my father.

Belle's lips parted in surprise when he removed the medallion from the chain and affixed it at the end of the short staff.

"What is that for?" she asked my father, gesturing at the staff with her chin.

As was his wont, my father gave her a mysterious look and his favorite infuriating answer. "You'll find out soon enough."

Belle grimaced and glared at him with undisguised annoyance. "You're impossible."

"You have no idea," my mother retorted, her back still turned to them as she placed the soiled cloth in the bowl Noca was holding.

Using a second clean cloth, she wetted it in the purifying water then took my braid to rub the cloth over it. Belle gasped, an expression both outraged and baffled, settling on her features. My mother cast a glance at my mate over her shoulder and smirked.

"My Feidin should be the one outraged," my father said with a chuckle. "His braid is hers until he is mated."

Belle recoiled. "But he——"

"Is *not* mated yet," my father interrupted in a soft but firm voice. "At least not according to our laws. And only they count for us. Feidin gave you a pass because you first married according to your customs. Otherwise, she'd be entitled to challenge you to a duel for that trespass."

This time, Belle blanched. I glared at my father, who didn't notice. Technically, his words were accurate, but as we never had a marriage with an off-worlder before, it had never been an issue. Obviously, I had known my mother wouldn't challenge my mate for that perceived slight, but I hated that they were causing her distress over it.

And yet, as rulers of our clan, I could understand their need to define boundaries and remind her that she now lived under very different cultural rules. A stern reminder to me as well to make sure I provided Belle with all the necessary information and guidance to keep her from unknowingly offending someone, which would inevitably occur. You didn't learn and assimilate an entire new culture overnight.

"And I would have, had you been Zamorian," my mother said while giving Belle a taunting look. "But that would have been after I'd spanked my second born for allowing another to touch his braid without my blessing to begin with," she added, her stern expression making it clear she was no longer teasing.

I realized then she had felt disrespected by my actions. There was no question in my mind she had intended to give me an earful about it in private later.

"Apologies, Matriarch," I said in a subdued tone. "It had never been my intention to disrespect you. Sadly, there are no guidelines for off-world unions. I should have erred on the side of caution."

Mollified, my mother gave me a small smile. "All is forgiven." She placed the cloth she'd used to clean my braid in the same bowl Noca held, then started undoing the plating.

"I carried you for ten months. I gave you birth, raised you, and nurtured you into the great hunter you've become. Today, I release you."

My throat tightened as my mother finished unbraiding my hair then combed her fingers through its length. She turned to Belle and gestured for her to approach. My mate cast a nervous glance at my father then me before complying.

My mother extended my hair to her. Belle took it with great care.

"Annabelle Parker, I give you my son," Mother said, releasing my hair. "From this day forth, no female but you shall touch his braid or have any claim over him. Plait it while repeating after me."

Belle nodded, a nervous expression settling on her face as she carefully began braiding my hair.

"Bayrohnziyiek Skortheatis, I bind you to me, hearts, body, and soul," Mother said, Belle echoing her. "I bind you as my protector and as the protector of our home and of any offspring we may be blessed with."

Once more, my mate repeated my mother's words. But this time, she stopped looking at the hair she was still braiding to lock gazes with me instead. That did funny things to me.

"I bind you as my life mate, as my best friend, and as my lover," mother continued. "For as long as you draw breath, you are mine. And for as long as I draw breath, I pledge to love and honor you, to nurture our bond, and to be your safe haven."

Belle finished repeating that last sentence at the same time she completed my braid. When my mother nodded at my father, my mate cast a curious look at him. I grinned as the long-awaited moment of my final claiming was upon us.

My sire activated the short staff before handing it to Belle. Confused at first, my mate took on a horrified expression when the medallion turned red and started emitting intense heat.

She gaped at my father. "You cannot mean for me to—"

"Claim my son?" my father finished for her when her voice

trailed off. "You wanted a claiming. It is a permanent bond. You must seal it."

"By branding him?!" she exclaimed looking first in horror at my sire before turning to me, clearly hoping I would side with her.

"Yes," my father said in a tone that brooked no argument. "It is our way."

"But… But that's… I can't do that!"

My hearts seized, and my back stiffened as I stared at my female in shock. "You *must*, unless you no longer wish to claim me."

"Of course I want to claim you. But I don't want to maim you!" she exclaimed.

"You're not *maiming* me, you're *claiming* me," I countered.

For a second, she looked at a loss for words. "My people banned the practice of branding chattel to mark ownership as it was deemed cruel and a form of torture. And you want me to do it to you?"

"Chattel doesn't have a say in the matter. They didn't consent to be owned or to be marked," my father countered. "My son *chose* a claiming, with all that it entailed, when he could have settled for a bonding. All Zamorian males proudly bear the mark of their mate."

Belle's shoulders slumped in defeat. The way she looked at the short staff, you'd think it was a weapon she'd been asked to shoot me with.

"Don't your people use painful methods to mark their flesh with the name of their lover, of their offspring or merely as adornments on their bodies?" I asked in a soft voice. "There are countless new painless methods of tattooing. Yet many humans continue to prefer the painful method with a needle."

She frowned, slowly nodding. "Right," she conceded. "But burning seems much worse."

"It actually takes a lot less time—seconds instead of hours or even days with a tattoo—and it heals faster," I replied.

"I just don't want to hurt you," she finally said in a small voice.

"What will hurt me is to be rejected should you refuse or be unable to seal your claim," I said, refusing to accept the possibility she could actually not go through with it.

I'd worried about her being too scared to be a Vaika in the arena, but not this. How could she have loved being a sacrificial bride, and now be terrified at the thought of putting her brand on me?

To my relief—and that of my parents—my words appeared to get through to her. Belle swallowed hard and gave me a stiff nod.

"Okay. Where… Where should I do it?"

I hated the trembling in her voice. "Here," I said, pointing at my chest where my left heart was located. "Right in the center."

"Okay," Belle repeated.

"Steady your hands, human," my mother said in a semi-taunting voice. "You want a clean burn. Messing it up would require a skin graft to fix the damage, and then you'd have to brand him again."

Under different circumstances, I would have chuckled along with the other single clanmates surrounding us. Instead, I glared at my mother. While I agreed—and was even grateful—for the much-needed warning to my mate, she could have handled it in a more diplomatic fashion, considering how traumatized Belle already was.

Then again, we Zamorians weren't known for being the diplomatic type.

Belle cast a "I didn't need to hear that" look at my mother then returned her attention to my chest. She took in a deep, forti-fying breath, then raised the short staff. Pride swelled within me at not only the determination she displayed but also at the unexpectedly steady fashion in which she pressed the brand on my chest.

The sizzling sound of my flesh burning and the scent of charred meat accompanied the sharp pain inflicted by the brand. A congratulatory roar rose from the crowd and the unmated surrounding me. I raised all four of my arms in a victorious gesture, a broad grin on my face as Belle completed the seal.

"Hold!" my father said to Belle when she made to remove the staff. "You only remove it once the red light on the staff turns blue."

Even as he spoke, I felt the brand cooling and then the prickling sensation of the staff's four tiny needles jabbing me with an antibiotic that would both prevent infection and accelerate healing. Within a couple of hours, scarification would be almost complete.

The light turned blue, and my mate removed the staff, looking awed at the flawless brand of her Tree of Life on my chest.

"You have laid down your roots, Belle," my mother said in a soft voice.

My mate gave her a quivering smile, her eyes misting. I instantly guessed she had shared with my mother the meaning of her chosen symbol.

"And by claiming my son, you have also claimed his people," my father added. "Welcome to the Skortheatis Clan, Daughter."

CHAPTER 9
ANNABELLE

Just like that, the Zamorian wedding was over. My medallion cooled almost as quickly as it had heated, and Ugrul handed it back to me. I felt disappointed when Bayron didn't put the necklace around my neck, watching me putting it back on myself instead. He also didn't put a ring on me and didn't brand me—not that I would have wanted *that* part. Additionally, he didn't kiss the bride or make any real pledge to me. I was starting to understand what Feidin had meant by declaring their people a matriarchy. On Earth, the father of the bride gave her away to her husband. In many cultures, she entered his family and took on his name.

Not here.

A Zamorian mother had to release ownership of her child—be they male or female—before their partner could claim them. In the case of a male, he became the property of his wife. But the wife became the property of the Matriarch. Skortheatis wasn't Ugrul's last name, but Feidin's. By marrying Bayron, I became a Skortheatis through his mother.

We didn't leave the arena right away. Feidin and Ugrul had us join them and Varkuth in their fancy VIP box. Meanwhile, the single males who had danced for me carried off the carcass of the grummoll.

Moments later, the females spread out in the arena, resuming their singing while my clanmates of all ages and genders joined them. They then launched into a mesmerizing show worthy of the fanciest circus. They didn't dance, but there was plenty of music, singing, acrobatic demonstrations—both with and without trained animals—and what seemed like wild, choreographed battle sequences. Four-armed warriors were truly a wonder to behold.

I noticed then that the single males had not returned.

"They are preparing our wedding feast," Bayron informed me when I asked.

"Oh okay." Then my back stiffened as a suspicion suddenly struck me. "Preparing the feast with what?"

Bayron chuckled, the taunting glimmer in his blue eyes confirming what I suspected.

"Oh, my God! They're cooking the grummoll, aren't they?!" I exclaimed.

"Of course," Bayron said as if it was self-evident. "I told you on the Ostros that once we arrived here, I would feed you fresh meals and meat that I hunted myself."

"Right… But a grummoll?" I asked, uncertain.

Bayron snorted. "It may not be a pretty creature, but it's quite tasty."

By the time the show ended, and we made our way to the Great Hall, I was hungry enough to eat half of the grummoll by myself. This place was a much larger version of the gathering hall in his parents' fortress. They had not decorated the way humans did a wedding hall, but the feast that awaited us more than compensated. The massive room could accommodate the entire clan, including the clanmates from the other fortresses.

The males had placed a table of honor on the elevated dais where Bayron, his parents, sibling, and I settled. All around us, the rest of our guests sat at tables where males served the food. It was so odd as I would have expected those brutes to be the cavemen type, demanding to be waited on, hand and foot, by their submissive females. But all such thoughts vanished as I stuffed my face with every dish presented. The grummoll, offered in a variety of preparations, was to die for.

Considering how fugly that creature was, who would have imagined it? Then again warthogs, monkfish, and sea lampreys also would never win a beauty contest, and yet were delicious.

The evening flew by, almost like in a dream. I remembered laughing a lot at the antics of the males bragging and of their females knocking them down a notch or two. The deceptively sweet Zamorian wine that flowed freely throughout the feast surely also played a part in it. By the time Bayron took me back to our dwelling inside the fortress, I was both tipsy and battling a food coma.

As soon as we exited the elevator into the vestibule of the penthouse, I faced Bayron and started kissing and caressing his chest. Although my brand on his chest looked surprisingly healed for such a short time—likely thanks to some nanobots—I avoided touching it.

"I don't think you're in any state to couple, my mate," Bayron said with a chuckle. "You do not seem to handle alcohol very well."

"I'm not wasted, just tipsy," I grumbled between two kisses on his chest, my voice a little slurred. "This is our official wedding night. Newlyweds always bang on their wedding night."

Bayron snorted. "Bang?"

"Mm hmm. You know, the monster with two backs… Doing the horizontal dance… Playing hide the snake in the cave… Well, snakesss in your case."

Bayron shook his head at me, looking amused. "The only horizontal thing you are going to do is sleep. You are jetlagged and drunk. Once you have sobered and are fully rested, we will 'bang' all you like."

I tried to argue, my own words making little sense to me. But my husband wasn't having it. Even reminding him that he was officially mine to do with as I pleased didn't sway him. When he removed my undies after discarding my dress, I perked up, thinking he'd finally caved in. He lay me down on the bed, joining me after swiftly shedding his pants and boots.

I purred loudly when the burning feel of his muscular body wrapped around mine as he drew me into his embrace. A part of me just wanted to snuggle and fall asleep, but another really itched to get down and dirty.

When I tried to get frisky again, he grabbed my wrists, pinning them to his sides while his primary hands immobilized me against him.

"I said sleep. It is not a request," he reiterated in a commanding voice that had my toes curling. "We may be officially married now, but I will never couple with you unless you are able to give your consent without your mind being artificially impaired in any way. We have the rest of our lives to 'hide the snakes in the cave.' And I can assure you that I intend to do so… often. Sleep, my wife. You are safe."

Another loud purr escaped me. I rubbed my face on his chest, kissed it, then rested my cheek on it. Soothed by the steady beating of his two hearts, I let sleep claim me.

I woke up to the distant sound of rain. I opened my eyes, disoriented for a second by my surroundings before realizing we were no longer on the Ostros but in our dwelling on Xoccoris. I abruptly sat up in bed, remembering my Zamorian wedding and uneventful wedding night.

My disappointment at finding Bayron gone from our

humongous bed vanished the minute I glanced out the huge windows to our private terrace. It wasn't raining outside. Therefore, the muffled running water sound had to be the shower.

I jumped out of bed to go join him there. However irrational some people might find me, it bothered me beyond words that we hadn't consummated our wedding last night. Granted, this was our second time getting married, but his people only acknowledged the Zamorian version. For my own sanity, it needed to be done right.

Sure, I also wanted my mate, but our failure to couple last night felt like a bad omen. If we couldn't get it going on during the most important day of our lives, what did that foreshadow for our future?

Yeah, I was superstitious.

I didn't walk under ladders. I didn't open umbrellas while indoors. And I didn't point at rainbows or at the full moon. However, as I was born on a Friday the 13th, I had mixed feelings about that specific superstition. Such a combination of weekday and date couldn't bring such terrible bad luck when it hailed the arrival of the wonderful little ray of sunshine that I was, right?

When I barged into the room, Bayron was already staring in the direction of the door. His sensitive hearing had no doubt given away my approach. He once again had that unreadable expression that made me nervous. What thoughts were crossing his mind right now? Was I disturbing his moment of privacy? Had he hoped to sneak out of the house before I woke up? Was he—?

"I can almost hear you thinking from here, woman. And by the look on your face, all of it is unfounded nonsense. Come to me," he said, extending a hand towards me.

He snorted at the eagerness with which I complied. God, I was pathetic.

"Did you sleep well, my wife?" he asked, drawing me against his half-rinsed body.

"Yes, thank you. Although I rather zonked out," I added sheepishly.

He chuckled. "Our Strovia wine certainly did a number on you."

I scrunched my face and nodded. "It did and ruined our wedding night," I concurred, feeling bummed out.

I raised a hand and carefully traced the outline of my symbol on his chest. I couldn't believe how quickly it had healed, all redness gone.

"It wasn't ruined," Bayron countered in a soft tone. "It was merely delayed. I've seen vids of some extravagant human weddings. I bet you that, by the time their reception was over, many of those couples were too wiped out to do anything that night other than to pass out in bed."

He had a point. I'd even attended weddings where the bride or the groom—sometimes both—got so wasted they were hungover for over two days.

"Okay, fair enough," I conceded, still caressing his brand. "I hated the idea of using a brand on you," I said pensively. "It seemed so cruel and violent. Am I a hypocrite for finding it beautiful now and loving seeing it on you?"

He covered the back of my hand with his and pressed it over the brand. "You should find it beautiful, my mate, because it is. Branding is only cruel when done against someone's will and for the purpose of causing pain and shame. I *wanted* this. I *want* the whole world to know I am yours."

"You're so fucking awesome," I said in a quivering voice while wrapping my free arm around him.

His chest vibrated with a rumbling laugh, filled with pride. "That I am, in more ways than one. And I'm about to show you just how much. I made you a promise last night about snakes and a certain cave."

My stomach flip-flopped, not only at his words, but also at the way his voice dipped at least an octave as he spoke them. Bayron drew me under the water that had been pummeling his back while we talked. He leaned down to capture my lips in a dominant way. My husband kissed like a champ. I had initially worried that his tusks would make it awkward, but he knew how to angle his lips just the right way to make it barely noticeable.

Even as his tongue invaded my mouth, its slightly rougher texture enhancing every sensation, he quite literally had his hands all over me. One held my nape to control the kiss, another fondled my breast, a third grabbed my left butt cheek, pressing my pelvis against his, and the last had slipped between my legs to fiddle with my clit.

To think my fellow human women thought males with multiple arms were freakish. If they only knew what wonderful sensation overload they could give.

"Already wet for me, my mate," Bayron growled approvingly against my lips, his tongue diving back in for seconds keeping me from responding.

I didn't need to. My moans, the shivers coursing through my body, and my hardening nipples did all the talking for me.

Bayron was a generous lover. Too generous in fact, as he hardly gave me an opportunity to reciprocate in his eagerness to pleasure me. As soon as he broke the kiss, I tried to go back to kissing his chest on the way down to the twins. I still hadn't given him a blow job. Every time I tried, he pulled a fast one on me and had me screaming with bliss instead.

As he did again just now.

I never even got to start crouching. He kneeled before me, immediately burying his face between my thighs, his wicked tongue going to work on me. In seconds, my hips gyrated in tandem with my increasingly labored breathing.

In the few days since our human marriage, Bayron had carefully studied my responses to his touch. He no longer went straight for my clit, working around it instead until it was painfully engorged and throbbing, aching for attention. His thick and long fingers would also move in and out of me, systematically avoiding my G-spot, until he had me mad with need. And then, he would latch on to them in a frenzy.

Bayron finally sucked on my clit at the same time he crooked his fingers inside of me. I went off like a rocket. A blinding light exploded before my eyes, and my knees buckled. By rights, I should have collapsed to the floor and probably busted my head open on the stone tiles of the shower. But as always, my husband caught me effortlessly, keeping me up while he continued to feast on me.

I'd never felt so safe with anyone, so cared for.

Still flying high, I drunkenly wrapped my arms around his neck when he lifted me up. Bayron's secondary arm behind my knees kept me wide open for him as he began rubbing his cocks against my core. I immediately started tingling in reaction to the aphrodisiac and muscle relaxing effects of his self-lubrication. My inner walls palpitated, and my stomach constricted with a burning need.

After a moment, he reclaimed my mouth as he began inserting his secondary cock inside of me. I wanted to believe we would eventually get to the point where he could go in directly with his main one without needing that first preparatory step—not that I minded.

The secondary cock had a thicker necklace—a string of bumps resembling pearls the length of the side edges. They swelled inside me in the most wondrous way, giving me extra sensations. As did the insane tip of his cock, each time it tilted inside me to graze my sweet spot.

In no time, my husband had me speaking in tongues as wave after wave of pleasure swelled within me. As soon as he felt me begin to crest, Bayron tightened his hold on me and accelerated his movements, thrusting deeper and harder, but still with restraint. A part of me wanted him to go wild on me. And he would.

However, I'd come to realize he only unleashed his passion once he was taking me with his main cock. Then, pleasure and pain would mix in the most mind-blowing fashion. I'd never imagine a bit of pain could be so exquisite. And yet, so far, everything with my husband had been sublime.

My climax crashed through me violently. I cried out Bayron's name as ecstasy had my entire body shaking in his arms. He emitted the sexiest of growls as his hand fisted my hair at the back of my head. He yanked it backward, so that he could stare at my face as I continued to ride my orgasm. That was another thing I'd realized with my husband. He loved my expression of bliss—his reward as he called it. The victorious snarling on his own face felt almost threatening. And yet, it only made me crazier for him.

As soon as I began to come back down, he pulled out only to slam his main cock home in one powerful thrust. I cried out, more in slight fear than any real pain. But I should have known he would have properly assessed my ability to take him comfortably.

He immediately set a punishing pace. His hand tightened around my throat. It didn't choke me, but gave me another sense of thrill, of the type of controlled danger I craved. Even though Bayron was now pounding into me, wrecking me inside, I couldn't seem to get enough. I couldn't say what I needed, but I wanted more. The aphrodisiac properties of his lubricant had to be the cause.

His lower cock rubbing against the seam of my behind had my rosette tingling. My breath caught in my throat when one of his fingers began to tease my forbidden opening. We hadn't discussed it, although that possibility had been hanging between us from the start. I didn't know yet if I'd be willing to go all the way on that front, but I trusted Bayron not to push me beyond what would be comfortable for me and not to rush anything.

Even now, I could see him studying my reactions while fighting his own urge to abandon all restraint and let passion take him over. Once more feeling safe, I gave myself over to my husband, letting him do with me whatever he pleased.

An inferno raged inside of me as his thrusts became more and more unbridled. Between his cock destroying me, and one of his hands massaging my clit, I was drowning in too much pleasure to really notice the initial discomfort of his probing finger. I had expected pain, but the muscle relaxer of his lubricants had worked its magic.

By the time I realized he had two fingers moving in and out of my rear in counterpoint to his cock, I was already cresting again. The odd sensation, far from unpleasant, was making me fuller than ever. Sensing me nearing the edge, Bayron started whispering encouraging words, laced with some dirty talk that further fueled my excitement.

My orgasm slammed into me with the violence of a tsunami. My spine seized, and my mouth formed a silent O, my body too shocked to form any sound. Eyes rolling at the back of my head, I collapsed in Bayron's arms. He roared as my inner walls clamped down on his cock. His seed shot out into me, bathing my battered insides while he continued to pound into me with almost feral grunts.

When his seed was spent, he gradually slowed down his thrusts until he came to a full stop. As was his wont after sex, my mate didn't immediately pull away, holding me close for a few minutes in a moment of tenderness that always made me feel cherished.

I could have remained like that forever and felt somewhat bereft when he finally pulled back to look at me. The tenderness in his blue gaze turned me upside down. We weren't in love with each other, but an undeniable bond was growing between us. He leaned forward and gave me the sweetest kiss, devoid of the wildfire that had consumed us mere moments ago.

"Wedding night banging handled," Bayron whispered against my lips in a teasing tone.

I burst out laughing before kissing him again. God help me, I was beginning to fall for my beast.

CHAPTER 10
ANNABELLE

After we got dressed, Bayron prepared a copious breakfast for us and let me braid his hair. Before I got too drunk last night, I'd spent a lot of time ogling the other males' braids to get a sense of how their wives styled it.

I didn't have anything to make Bayron's hair stand out from the masses just yet. Thankfully, Feidin had offered to take me around the shops in the city and introduce me to some of the crafters who could make special adornments based on my specifications. While my husband cooked, I'd sketched a few things I hoped could get made quickly enough that we'd get them before our departure in six days.

As we came down the elevator to the main entrance of the fortress, the few clanmates we ran into gave us knowing smiles that had my cheeks burning. Considering it was well past noon, they had no problem speculating as to what had kept us up there for so long. At least, my thoughtful husband had messaged his mother while I still slept to inform her that I would be late.

It embarrassed me that this should happen on my first girls' outing with Feidin. Bayron reassured me that she hadn't been upset, especially considering we had loosely said we'd go out in the morning with no specific time spelled out.

"Mother will join you in the gathering hall," Bayron said as we stood in the main hallway at the junction leading to the two corridors of the dwelling elevators. "She said it should take you no more than two hours to do your shopping. I have a few things to handle. I'll return at the same time you do and take you on a brief tour of the surroundings."

"Sounds like a plan," I said with excitement.

Last night, I'd kicked myself for not using my camera to record Bayron fighting to claim me. At least, Feidin had reassured me that they had a recording of their own. It wouldn't rival the awesomeness that could be achieved with the camera Kayog had gifted me, but it would be better than nothing.

My mind bubbled with ideas for at least two entire collections, with one devoted to my husband and another with the Zamorians as a whole as the central theme. I couldn't recall the last time I'd been this excited to paint. I planned on taking as many pictures and recording as many videos as possible before our departure. As we'd be spending a lot of time traveling from one hunt to the next, I wanted to have a maximum number of references to keep me busy.

To my dismay, Bayron didn't kiss me goodbye. He merely nodded, turned around, then left. That stark reminder of the fact that Zamorians didn't publicly display their affection didn't make it sting any less. As I watched him head out of the fortress, I debated whether I should bring that up with him or just suck it up. I didn't want to annoy him by being too clingy and needy. In truth, beyond my natural hugger inclinations, a lack of self-confidence largely fueled this need for contact. In many ways, it gave me confirmation that the person cared.

Heaving a sigh, I decided to leave it alone for now. Aside from the fact that I could live without it, I had pushed the boundaries of his comfort zone enough already. Turning on my heels, I made my way to the gathering hall. The motion detectors opened the doors seconds before I reached them.

An empty room greeted me, except for Ugrul sitting on his throne while conversing with another clanmate whose name I couldn't remember. Frankly, aside from Bayron's parents and his brother, the only other name I had memorized belonged to the behemoth that had scared the bejeezus out of me. I sucked with names, but never forgot a face.

When I hesitated at the entrance, not wanting to intrude in what could be private matters, Ugrul gestured for me to approach. Before I could reach them, they concluded their discussion and the male headed for the exit. He politely nodded at me on his way out. I responded with a smile and a timid nod.

Typical of every Zamorian male, muscles bulged on every inch of his body. Just like their women wore sexy, form-fitting clothes, the males also wore t-shirts that might as well have been a second skin, and tight pants that left nothing to the imagination. However, I had also spotted several males wearing short skirts, not quite kilts, not quite Roman, but every bit masculine. This made me wonder if it held any significance or merely indicated a different fashion taste. I had not glimpsed a single skirt in Bayron's wardrobe. I'd have to inquire about that.

Ugrul leaned back in his seat, watching me approach with the disturbingly unreadable expression Bayron sometimes had. Although he had called me 'Daughter' last night at the end of the wedding ceremony, I didn't feel like he had fully accepted me, unlike Feidin.

"Sit with me, Belle," Ugrul said, waving at his mate's throne.

I hesitated, wondering if it might offend her to have someone else—another female at that—sitting in her place.

As if he'd read my mind, Ugrul chuckled. "It's okay. I wouldn't have offered if it would disrespect my mate. She wouldn't hesitate to chop my braid off if I did."

Laughing nervously, I complied with his request. I sat down, slightly sideways to face him, and tucked a strand of hair behind my ear. It took every ounce of my willpower not to squirm under the intensity of his stare.

"So, what prompted a human to marry a Zamorian?" he asked in a conversational tone.

"A Temern," I replied matter-of-factly. "Kayog told me Bayron was my soulmate."

He pursed his lips and continued to stare at me as if he couldn't decide whether my answer satisfied him.

I frowned and lifted my chin defiantly at what struck me as further proof of his rejection of me. "You have a problem with that? You think he's wrong?"

He didn't recoil or appear angered by the challenging way in which I asked the questions. Ugrul merely continued to study my features while he seemed to think on how to word his response.

"I have no reason to doubt the word of a Temern," my father-in-law conceded at last.

"But?" I insisted.

"But I struggle with the fact that he would deem such a small creature as my son's perfect mate."

That cut deep. Although I'd just met him, it hurt with the familiar sense of rejection I always got from my mother. Once again, I realized how desperately I wanted to belong and be accepted. Bayron's family had held the potential for me to finally achieve a dream I'd held on to since childhood.

Refusing to let him see how badly his words had affected me, I lifted my chin defiantly. "Is it my height and size that bother you, or the fact that I'm an off-worlder?"

Ugrul snorted and crossed his ankle over his knee, a mocking expression settling over his handsome face. "In truth, both… But not for the reasons you think," he answered in a surprisingly soothing voice. "I've looked into human anatomy. Knowing how my son is hung, I frankly didn't think you could ever take him.

Clearly, I was wrong. However, will you be able to satisfy him in the long-term if you can only ever give him half the full mating experience Zamorians normally enjoy?"

I bristled at such an intimate and invasive line of questioning. It chafed all the more that it echoed some of the concerns that had been gnawing at me.

"This is a highly inappropriate question or conversation. What happens in the privacy of our bedroom is none of your business!"

"Calm, Belle. You asked my thoughts on your union to my son, I'm merely answering truthfully," Ugrul replied with a slight frown, his stern tone reminding me of a father scolding a difficult child. "I do not dislike you, Annabelle Parker. And I have no problem with the fact that you are not Zamorian. I can see why you appeal to Bayron. However, I am concerned about the viability of your union because of your specific human anatomy. I wouldn't worry so much had you both consented to a bonding first. But I fear the devastation that might ensue if your claiming fails."

Reining in my blossoming anger, I took a deep breath and tried to rationally respond to what I could see were genuine paternal concerns.

"Well, Bayron and I had a human wedding four days ago. As per the Prime Mating Agency's rules, we had to consummate our union on the first night," I said in a slightly clipped tone. "Had it been such a disaster between us, do you really think he would have asked for a claiming instead of a bonding?"

However, even as I said that, I remembered how my husband had fingered my rear end this morning when we made love. Was he already tiring of being only able to use one cock at a time instead of both? Was our sex life already growing stale for him?

"No, he wouldn't have," Ugrul conceded with a bow of the head. "And I genuinely hope that it will be sufficient for him in the long run. But what of offspring? Will you be able to bear him sons?"

I blinked, baffled by that question. "I am fertile, so I don't see why not."

"Compared to a Zamorian female, you are petite. Our offspring are massive, nearly twice the size of a human baby. Can your body handle that without getting damaged?" he asked, the paternal worry etched on his face this time doing quite a number on me.

I squirmed in my seat, not having thought of that. "Okay, that is a fair point. However, a human woman's belly stretches a great deal. Some women have carried octuplets and delivered them just fine."

"But with those multiple pregnancies, each newborn was usually very small. Has any human female pushed out such a huge baby as ours?" he countered.

"Doubtful, but that's what C-sections are for," I replied with a shrug. "They'll cut me open, yank the baby out, and patch me back up. No biggie."

Ugrul snorted and leveled his blue eyes on me, sparkling with an odd glimmer. "You have more spine than your small size would suggest, little human. For all our sakes, I hope you are correct. I genuinely want your union to be successful. You have no idea how much you have stirred our collective protective instincts. As much as I want you to give my son a couple of male heirs to help protect your home, I hope you will have many daughters. The thought of such a tiny, delicate little thing clinging to me for safety awakens a most potent yearning."

My throat tightened at the picture of Bayron holding our tiny baby girl while his father doted on our other one.

"A Temern is never wrong, Ugrul. If Kayog deemed me your son's perfect mate, then I am. And fate willing, we'll have plenty of rugrats to sate your protective instincts."

"Rugrats?" he asked, baffled.

I gave him a sheepish look. "Sorry. It's a cute earthling term to refer to babies."

"As in rats that dwell on rugs?" he challenged.

"You'd be shocked by the number of human expressions that would break your mind," I said with a mischievous glimmer in my eyes. "But I do hope we'll give you many grandchildren."

He smiled with a softness that messed me up. In that instant I knew I had indeed found my home. My roots were spreading.

The doors opening ended our conversation. Feidin entered with a brisk walk, stopping a few steps in. Although Ugrul had said that my sitting in her chair was fine, my spine stiffened with worry.

"Stop pestering Belle, husband. Off we go, Daughter," Feidin shouted over the distance, gesturing for me to come.

Ugrul snorted with amusement while casting an affectionate glance at his mate. I gave him an apologetic smile and hurried to join my mother-in-law.

For the next couple of hours, we toured the local stores and artisan shops. I placed countless orders, blossoming under the crafters' compliments when I showed them my sketches. Feidin's pride and approval in terms of the choices I made, from materials, colors, and design did wonders to boost my too-often shaky confidence. Although it would take at least two days for my orders to be ready, I nonetheless rejoiced in the fact that I'd get them before our departure.

By the time we returned home, a million new designs—some of which I could probably craft myself—filled my head.

~

Sitting next to Bayron in his personal shuttle, I didn't have enough eyes to take in the savage beauty of his world. The small vessel, shaped like a horizontal comma, had only two seats in the front and a small space for cargo or storage in the back. Bayron had placed a huge picnic basket there and some gear he claimed to be motorized surfboards. Once he'd heard of all the extreme sports I was into, he'd been adamant I give this a try.

It sounded like a freaking riot.

I'd been stunned to find out that Zamorians parked these small personal shuttles—commonly referred to as stingers— directly on the landing pads of their dwelling's terrace. I loved how truly independent we felt, despite living in the fortress with all the other families of his bloodline.

Xoccoris took my breath away. Vast forests, majestic mountains, large bodies of pristine water, and untamed wilderness separated the immense compounds that served as a city for the different clans. We flew over the closest neighboring clans, Bayron playing the perfect tour guide with backstories, juicy anecdotes, and thoughtful insights about each of them. He made a few detours to give me a glimpse of some of his planets' landmarks.

I would have loved to explore, but with the quickly waning afternoon, we'd never have time to surf if we didn't head there now.

"The beach is a twenty-minute walk from here," Bayron explained as he landed the shuttle near the tree line of a forest. "We could have landed closer, but I want to pick a few fruits and mushrooms for our meal after we're done surfing. It will also give you a chance to admire some of our flora and fauna."

"Lead the way, husband!" I said with my usual enthusiasm.

He snorted and shook his head with an indulgent smile. I loved when he gave me that kind of sweet expression. After activating the door at the back of the stinger—which opened up like a bird's beak, Bayron picked up the bag containing the motorized surfboards in one hand, the picnic basket in another, a large bag containing who knew what in a third, and then grabbed my hand with his fourth.

The stupid grin that settled on my face made him laugh. I didn't have to say anything for him to know how happy these simple displays of affection made me feel.

As we walked through the forest, Bayron recounted some of his childhood adventures with Varkuth. When he showed me the ruins of what had once been their version of a treehouse, I released my camera on roaming mode so that it would record our surroundings, but also Bayron and me. I was definitely making a few drawings of the two of us having a romantic walk in the woods.

My steps faltered as a thought suddenly struck me. Bayron stopped talking mid-sentence to give me a questioning look.

"Is there something wrong?" he asked.

I shook my head. "No, absolutely not wrong. But I just realized that you've taken me on a guided tour to visit the beautiful places of Xoccoris. We're now walking through the woods, hand-in-hand, on our way to indulge in one of your favorite local sports, and then we're going to have a picnic by the beach."

"Yes, and?" Bayron asked, confused.

"And that matches the type of things I listed newlyweds did during their honeymoons," I deadpanned.

Bayron bristled, the outraged expression on his face making me burst out laughing.

"This is not a honeymoon," he retorted, saying the word as if it was dirty and offensive. "I am merely familiarizing you with your new home."

"By making us do honeymoon stuff," I replied in a sing-song voice. "I knew there was a big softie behind that intimidating appearance of yours."

"I am not a softie," he growled, glaring at me.

My grin broadened. "Yes, you are. And I love that about you. You make me feel special."

Bayron opened and closed his mouth a few times, before scrunching his face at me, robbed of words. Despite his considerable ego and tendency to show off, my man often became quite shy in the face of gratitude or admiration not stirred by his hunting or combat feats.

Failing to find an appropriate response, he grunted and drew me after him.

"It's still not a honeymoon," he muttered under his breath.

I chuckled and gave his hand a squeeze. Honeymoon or not, this was the best date ever. I was about to ask him a question when he suddenly jerked his head to the left, tension stiffening his muscles. His pointy ears flicked, and he seemed to strain to listen to a distant sound. Worry settled heavily on my chest, constricting it.

The urge to ask him what he'd heard burned my tongue. I bit it to keep silent. Whatever it was could have as acute a hearing as he did. I wouldn't risk giving away our position. A strange air of worry and confusion settled on Bayron's face as he sniffed the air. He shook his head as if what he'd perceived made little sense.

As he began tapping some instruction on the interface of his bracer, I fought the urge to panic. Had he not been by my side, I'd be in full freak out mode right now, my fertile imagination picturing a horde of grummolls stampeding in our general direction.

Obviously, that wasn't the case. I would have heard the stomping of their paws, and the forest would have gone quiet had such a danger lurked around.

"It shouldn't be here," Bayron whispered disbelievingly. "Come quietly and stay behind me."

"Okay," I whispered back. "What… What is it?"

"A stone wolf," he replied in a tone that made it clear we shouldn't speak any further.

That he didn't pull out the dagger from his belt went a long way in reassuring me that he didn't expect a fight with a savage creature. We started walking, making as little noise as possible. Ten meters in, I finally perceived the sound that had caught Bayron's attention. It seemed to be the death rattle of a mammal, followed by a high-pitched whine.

A few meters later, the scent of blood and of meat in the early stages of rotting slapped me in the face. I braced for what would follow, but nothing could have prepared me for the heartbreaking spectacle that awaited us past a large tree on the left.

The alien version of a small-sized brown bear lay on its side. Its guts spilled out and congealed blood matted on the fur around its slashed throat, it served as feast for a swarm of maggots. A short distance away, a strange-looking wolf pup barely hung on to life. My heart seized for it at the sight of the deep puncture wounds around its right hind leg and the broken bone protruding through its leathery gray skin.

Bayron shook his head with a commiserating frown as he stared at the pup. "How did the ocaih get to you?" he asked, not actually expecting an answer from the pup.

"That's the ocaih?" I asked, pointing at the writhing remains while carefully approaching the baby.

"Yes. They often come to this area to hunt and are not a threat to people. They usually eat rodents and small creatures like the equivalent of your rabbits. That pup matched the size," he added, pointing at the little wolf with his chin. "But stone wolves don't come here at this time of the year. Once adult, they are vicious creatures. He must have gotten separated from his mother, and the ocaih snagged him. A shame. He clearly has a warrior's heart that he managed to kill his abductor and survive at least two days."

I gaped in disbelief at the ocaih's wounds before looking back at the little wolf. Only then did I finally notice the dagger claws at the tips of his small paws, to which the ocaih's blood and fur still clung.

"What are you doing?!" I shouted when Bayron pulled his dagger from its scabbard.

He looked at me as if the answer was obvious. "Giving him peace."

"What? No!" I exclaimed, rushing to the pup. "You said yourself that he has the heart of a warrior. He didn't survive this long just to be killed like that. We have to help him."

"He is too damaged, Belle. Look at his leg. It is broken in at least three places, and the bite wounds are infected," he countered in a soft but firm voice. "This can't be fixed. He will always have a painful limp and won't be able to properly hunt. Without a pack, his chances of survival are slim to none. And they will kill him if he tries to rejoin them. This planet is all about survival of the fittest."

"Following your logic, should I have been put down as well as a child?" I snapped in a harsh tone.

Bayron recoiled, shock and confusion settling over his features. I didn't wait for his response and opened the picnic basket he had placed on the floor next to him. It was unfair of me to throw this at his face. He didn't know the details of my difficult childhood. To my relief, he didn't press me, his gaze intense as he waited for me to expand further on that statement. I needed a moment to calm the maelstrom of emotion raging through me.

I retrieved a bottle of water and a plate from the basket and carefully approached the wolf. After pouring as much water in the plate as it could take, I placed it next to the pup's mouth. He emitted a pathetic growl and tried to raise his claws in what had to be his attempt at appearing menacing. However, despite the terrible damage he'd inflicted on the ocaih, I wasn't afraid. The poor baby visibly didn't have enough strength left to attack or injure me.

"My mother was always a selfish and self-absorbed woman. She liked to party and have fun, consequences be damned. She was impulsive and driven by whatever stirred her passion at that moment," I said, surprised by the bitterness in my voice.

After all these years, I thought I'd gotten over my mother's abandonment. Apparently not…

Bayron said nothing, his attentive expression encouraging me to continue. Simultaneously, he kept an eye on the pup, ready to intervene at the first sign of trouble.

The little wolf whined in a heart-breaking fashion when I first dripped some water over his snout. He weakly stuck out his tongue, catching a bit of the moisture. As I continued drizzling water, he began lapping with a bit more conviction, extending his tongue to the bounty on the plate.

"From what I've been told, my mother got pregnant with me because all her acquaintances had been settling down and having babies. She thought it would be cool to have one as well. But pregnancy didn't turn out to be as fun as she expected. My mother resented me because of the morning sickness, swollen limbs, back pain, and the fact that she couldn't drink or do drugs for months. The only reason she didn't consume any of that stuff regardless was my father."

"As was his duty as a protector," Bayron said approvingly.

I snorted in self-derision. I'd never really thought of it that way.

"Yeah, I guess you could say he was my protector. Mom, sure wasn't," I said, adding a bit more water on the plate before gently caressing the fluffy fur on top of the pup's head.

He flinched at first, as if he feared my touch but soon no longer shied away from it.

"When I was a little over six months old, my mother decided she'd had enough of being cooped up inside the house looking after a baby," I continued. "My father is a career military offi-cer, a Navy Seal. He had left on a mission only two days prior. Since she couldn't find a babysitter for me, Mom took me with her off the base to some big outdoor festival in the middle of nowhere. On the second day, the bulldog of a partygoer attacked me."

"No!" Bayron whispered.

"Oh yeah," I replied with a sad smile. "By the time they took him off me, he had shattered my right leg and shaken me so violently that it had damaged my spinal cord, broken a few of my bones, and given me some serious brain swelling and bleeding. They rushed me to the hospital, and I spent the following week fighting for my life."

Bayron frowned, his gaze roaming over me with a mix of anger—which I knew to be aimed at both the dog and my mother—and of wonder at how I had been mended.

I reached back inside the basket, my shoulders slumping when I failed to find something to feed the pup.

"There's no meat?" I asked.

Bayron shook his head. "I was going to fish for us."

"Then we need to take him back home right away. He needs food, and he needs help. We must clean that wound and fix his leg."

"Belle—" Bayron said in a reasonable voice.

"Don't, Bayron!" I interrupted in a harsh tone. "You're going to say that he's beyond help. That trying to fix him is only going to prolong his agony. That's what my mother said as well about me."

"I am *not* your mother," he ground through his teeth, outraged.

"No, you're not. But you're also not a veterinarian, just like she wasn't a doctor. They believed I stood a chance, a slim one, but a chance, nonetheless. My father—who's not even my biological father—is the one who told them to go ahead and do everything they could for me."

Bayron recoiled. "Not your sire? Did he know?"

I shrugged. "I think he suspected from the start. He knew my mother wasn't faithful, but he didn't really care. He was always off on missions. I suppose he just liked having someone home when he returned. However, I needed a spinal graft, and he was excluded as a relative or potential donor. My mother wasn't ready to deal with the years of recovery that awaited me, so she left."

"And he kept you?"

"Yes, Dad kept me. He hadn't signed my birth certificate when I was born, but he officially adopted me so that I could be entitled to all of his benefits. The Special Ops division enjoyed the best medical services available on Earth. It took three years and the most advanced medical treatments, but they fixed me. Had I not told you, you would have never known what a mangled mess I had been," I said defiantly.

"You are right. I never would have known. And I am forever in the debt of your father for protecting you the way he did," Bayron said cautiously.

"He didn't owe me anything, and yet he stepped up because I deserved a chance. And today, I am paying it forward to someone who owes me nothing. This pup fought this hard, he deserves a chance, too," I said, this time with a pleading tone.

"Very well," Bayron conceded with obvious reluctance. "Just do not get your hopes up too high, my mate."

I nodded. "Fate will decide. But we can still give her a nudge in the right direction."

Sighing in defeat, he retrieved the picnic blanket from the basket and carefully wrapped the pup in it. The poor baby's pained cry broke my heart, as did his feeble attempt to bite my husband. He looked so tiny in Bayron's primary arms.

I called back my camera then picked up the picnic basket while my mate grabbed the motorized surfboards and harvest bag with his secondary hands. A part of me felt guilty for derailing Bayron's plans for us. However, this was important and the right thing to do.

We quickly returned to the shuttle. To my relief, my husband used the emergency kit inside to sedate the pup. I held him in my arms throughout the trip back to the city. We didn't land at home but on top of a building I didn't know, which turned out to be the compound's medical center. An elevator took us down to the first basement where the veterinary department was located.

To my shock, the doors of the clinic opened on Krogal, wearing a white medical jacket.

CHAPTER 11
BAYRON

I couldn't believe I had allowed my female to talk me into trying to save the pup. All I could see was the life of pain that awaited it. But doing what I believed best for the creature would have undoubtedly created a permanent rift between my mate and me. After the compelling story of the trials she faced as a child, refusing to grant the pup the same mercy her father granted her would make me a monster in her eyes. Anyway, I couldn't bear the thought of breaking her heart by refusing. For once, I hoped Fate would prove my expectations wrong.

However, my concerns over the pup's welfare and my mate's reaction to it gave way to irrational jealousy as soon as we entered the clinic. Even in his medical jacket, Krogal continued to be a scary beast. I hated how skittish my Belle instantly looked in his presence. I hated even more that I had never stirred this level of wariness in her. The most intimidating male to her should be me.

My cousin interrupted his conversation with Dhalgal, the receptionist. Dhalgal smiled at us before casting a stunned glance at the still-sedated bundle in Belle's arms.

"Belle, Bayron, what have you brought me?" Krogal asked.

My mate blinked, as if his words had snapped her out of a fearful daze, then swallowed hard.

"We found a stone pup, grievously wounded by an ocaih," I said in a clipped voice when Belle took what I felt was much too long to respond.

It had barely been a split second, but her reaction to Krogal —involuntary though it was, and especially because of that— irked me to no end. He raised an eyebrow at my tone. The smug, knowing smile stretching his lips pissed me off even more. At least, he spared me the ignominy of calling me out on this display of insecurity.

My cousin reached for the picnic blanket wrapping the pup, and carefully opened it. His frown upon seeing the extensive damage to the leg only confirmed what I feared. By the way Belle's eyes misted, she likely read the same thing I did on his features.

"Please don't say he's beyond help. Help him, please. Please!" Belle pleaded.

My stomach knotted, and my chest tightened. I hated seeing my mate so distraught. Judging by how Krogal grimaced, her despair affected him just as badly. Zamorian males had no problem dealing with a female's ire, but her sorrow wrecked us.

"His injuries are very severe, Belle. I will examine him and see what—if anything—can be done."

"Thank you! Thank you so much," she said, with far too much hope.

His non-committal grunt once more echoed my misgivings. Still, he led the way to one of the smaller examination rooms in the hallway left of the reception desk.

After placing the pup on a table that made him look even tinier and more delicate, Krogal performed a quick manual examination. He asked a few questions as to the condition we'd found him in and what we had fed or administered to him before our arrival. I answered his questions, then Krogal went quiet as he pursued his examination. Despite his silence, his efforts to hide how hopeless he believed the pup's chances to be failed miserably… at least for me, who knew him well.

He then moved the wolf to a medical pod, which ran a full battery of tests. As data started populating the giant screen above the pod, Belle slipped a hand inside my primary one. I wrapped my secondary right arm around her and drew her to my side. It troubled me more than I wanted to admit that she would need comfort over a creature that was nothing to her. I didn't even want to imagine how devastated she would be had this been our child instead.

When Krogal turned to us at last, Belle all but stopped breathing while awaiting his verdict.

"It is very bad," my cousin said in a soft but serious tone. "I can stitch the bones back, but not fully fix them. He will have a limp. How severe? I can't say. It could be mild enough to merely be a bit of a nuisance. But it could also make it impossible for him to hunt. Only time will tell. A nanite treatment should have him able to stand and walk again in a couple of days or so."

"That's great news!" Belle said, excitement filling her voice.

"On *that one* front, it is semi-positive," Krogal said in a careful voice that hinted the bad news was still to follow.

"The infected wounds?" I asked.

Krogal shook his head. "The infection hasn't spread far enough to be problematic. I can clean the wounds and give him an antibiotics regimen over the next ten days that should eradicate all traces of infection. The problem is the ocaih's venom."

"Venom?" Belle echoed, worry descending over her features.

My cousin nodded. "You see how he's covered in a gray, leathery skin beneath that fur? Had he been older, his adrenal glands would have been able to produce a special hormone that thickens the skin. And when in combat, it hardens to something impenetrable, akin to stone."

"Hence why they're named stone wolves," Belle reflected

out loud, earning a nod from my cousin and me. "But what does that have to do with the venom?"

"The reason stone skin is so important for these wolves is because they have a very weak immune system," Krogal explained. "Any bacteria, toxin, or virus that enters their bloodstream can wreak terrible havoc. In his case, the ocaih's venom went straight for his endocrine system and attacked his adrenal glands. I don't think I can save them. At least, for the moment, I don't see how. Without that, the slightest scratch could result in terrible infections. He would basically be forced to remain locked up in a sterile and padded environment."

My chest constricted again at the sight of Belle's crestfallen expression.

"There have to be some endocrine experts out there who know of a potential solution," my mate argued in a pleading tone. "Technology is so advanced these days, there has to be a way!"

"I do not know, Belle," Krogal said in an apologetic voice. "Stone wolves are wild beasts that we usually leave alone. No one has performed extensive studies on them. I cannot promise any miracle, but I will do some research and consult with others to see if we can fix him."

"Thank you, Krogal. I really appreciate you doing this. It means a lot to me," Belle said, gratitude filling her eyes.

My cousin gave her a gentle smile, laced with timidity. Embarrassed, he quickly turned away to hide it, but not so fast I missed the glimmer of longing. So many of our females had hoped to claim the most imposing warrior in our midst, but none had found grace in his eyes. My mate had involuntarily succeeded where all others had failed. Had I not claimed her, I believe he would have.

Would she have accepted him?

She no longer seemed frightened by him. The careful way he had handled the pup had revealed just how gentle he could be with those under his protection. Another wave of jealousy rose within me. I forced it out of my mind. Belle had given me no reason to doubt her commitment to me and to our union. We had claimed each other, freely and willingly. She wasn't responsible for the desires she passively stirred within other males.

"The medical pod will work on him for at least a couple of days," Krogal explained while typing a few instructions on the device's interface to initiate the treatment. "I will give you regular updates on his progress."

"Thank you, cousin," I said with sincere gratitude.

"Yes, thank you," Belle echoed, beaming at him.

We exited the examination room and waved goodbye to Dhalgal on our way out. Both lost in our respective thoughts, we remained quiet on the elevator ride up to the roof of the medical center to get back in our personal shuttle, and during our short flight to our dwelling.

By now, it was well past suppertime.

"I'm afraid I cannot prepare you a meal with freshly hunted protein, as I had intended," I said apologetically.

"Don't apologize. I'm the one who derailed your plans," she said with a sheepish expression. "Thank you for sparing him and for taking us to your cousin. Krogal was so gentle with him. Do you think he can save the pup?"

I turned my back to her while unpacking the picnic basket to hide the jealousy rearing its head again.

"Krogal is an excellent veterinarian. From war beasts to tiny house pets, if it can be saved, he will find a way," I said, proud I managed to keep my voice neutral.

"That's wonderful. To think I'd been so terrified of him," Belle said with a chuckle. "He's like a big teddy bear behind that fearsome appearance."

I jerked my head around to look at her over my shoulder. Her wistful smile cut me deep.

"You like him, don't you?" I asked in a growly tone, immediately kicking myself for letting my jealousy show.

Belle's smile immediately faded, her eyes widening in surprise. Then shock and worry settled on her features.

"I don't *like* him the way you seem to imply," Belle said cautiously.

I turned around to face her. My mate sustained my gaze unwaveringly.

"You find him magnificent, don't you? You think him more intimidating than I am," I said, forcing myself to sound factual rather than accusatory.

My heart sank when Belle didn't respond right away. She chewed her bottom lip, looking like she was carefully choosing her words.

"Krogal is at least a good head taller than you are and almost twice your size," she said in a reasonable tone. "Anyone with eyes would be impressed. Yes, I think he's magnificent and incredibly terrifying. But that takes nothing away from *you*, and it especially doesn't make me attracted to *him*. I don't find you terrifying, and that's a good thing."

"How in Khivolt's name is that a good thing?!" I exclaimed, offended.

"Because I would never marry someone who scared me," she said, as if it was self-evident. "I'm human, not Zamorian. Had you come at me the way he did that first day we met, I would have been off that space station so fast, you'd have wondered if I'd been a mirage. Terrifying isn't appealing to me. You're intimidating in a sexy way… in the *perfect* way. I love how you make me feel fragile but safe. Krogal is just too big."

"Bigger and stronger… Shouldn't that make you feel even safer?" I argued, wondering why I was persisting, as if trying to convince her she should have picked him.

"Bayron, bigger isn't always better. There *is* such a thing as too big. I feared our first night together because I dreaded how big your twins would be. If whatever your cousin is packing is even remotely proportional to the rest of his size, there isn't a hill or mountain high enough for me to run to," Belle said with a shudder.

I couldn't help but snort, unreasonably pleased with her response. It wasn't my place to reveal what my cousin was 'packing' as she so eloquently put it. But saying he was well-endowed would be the understatement of the century.

Belle approached me and wrapped her arms around my waist. I drew her in, closing my own arms possessively around her.

"I already found my soulmate. And that's you," she said.

My chest vibrated with a rumbling purr of approval as I leaned down to claim her mouth. She responded with a fervor that immediately ignited a now familiar flame in my loins. I deepened it, enjoying the sweet taste of her lips and the softness of her body in my embrace. Then, with much reluctance, I broke the kiss. I needed to feed my female instead of sating my selfish desires.

Relieved to have that issue out of the way, I prepared our meal, and we ate in a relaxed atmosphere.

As soon as I entered the gathering hall, all eyes turned to me. My clanmates—the vast majority males—sat on the benches surrounding the floor, some having settled directly on it. A circular area in the central part of the floor had parted to expose the brasier, which burned with a delightful fire—a custom held from the old days when our ancestors would gather by the fire to talk.

"Has your mate already cast you out?" my brother teased, eliciting the collective chuckles of the people present.

"Hardly. I am too great a husband for that," I replied in the same taunting tone, earning me a few snorts. I pulled my braid in front of my chest, showing off the blue metal string—matching my eye color—which Belle had weaved into my braid with matching small beads in strategic locations. "And does this look like a braid of a male who's been cast out," I gloated.

A few appreciative nods greeted my words as they all admired my mate's handy work.

"It is indeed very nice, especially for a first attempt," my father conceded with a glimmer of approval.

I puffed out my chest, my legendary ego, laced with pride for my female, manifesting itself again. "It's even more admirable that Belle is still awaiting the delivery of the ornaments she ordered. She improvised with what was available in store so that I wouldn't walk around bare until she could execute her true vision for me."

Idriks, one of our most talented crafters, nodded. "Your mate has placed quite a few orders with me. I have completed a third of them and should finish everything in the next couple of days. I am quite curious how she will use them on you. They were quite beautiful and innovative."

My chest further swelled with pride. "My mate is an artist. Of course, she will make uniquely enticing things. Speaking of which, Belle is having a vidcom call with her father and will join us after. She asked if it would be okay to sketch your ugly faces during this assembly."

"No way she used that term," Kraslo countered mockingly. "After all, she claimed *you*."

I joined my laughter to theirs, acknowledging the nice jab. As I had suspected, they gave their consent. Many actually felt flattered to be the subject of an artist.

"I understand you brought back a wounded stone wolf," my father suddenly said, bringing the room back to a more serious mood.

I'd expected that would come up and heaved a sigh. "Yes. Belle was adamant we try to save it."

"Does she understand it is not a pet and likely cannot be tamed?" my father asked. "Assuming it survives and becomes an adult, that wolf roaming our streets could be a threat, especially for our younglings."

"I know, Father. Yes, she is aware. But I doubt she's worrying about anything past healing the pup. Once Krogal has done all that he can, we will assess the next steps."

Satisfied, my father grunted in approval. However, I remembered too well the maternal way Belle had held the pup. She would want to adopt him, like her father had adopted her. I didn't look forward to the conversation about releasing him to the wild, where he belonged.

As was usual during assemblies, my clanmates took turns bragging about their latest feat, epic battle, or duel. The handful of females present affectionately shook their heads at our need to constantly try to one up the other.

Kraslo was just about to start a tale of his own when the doors of the gathering hall parted on my mate. All conversation ended, every eye locked on her. My Belle scrunched her face in that adorable way she always did whenever she felt self-conscious. Her gaze flicking over every face, likely to assess what thoughts traipsed in my clanmates' minds, my female held her drawing tablet against her chest like a shield as she made her way to me.

I smiled encouragingly, possessive pride filling my hearts as she approached. Belle didn't understand how attractive she looked to me and to many Zamorian males. She was stuck with that human definition of beauty that held no appeal to us.

Although I'd left plenty of space on the bench next to me for Belle, I shifted a bit to the left to make even more room. To my dismay, instead of settling next to me, my mate climbed in my lap and rested her back against my chest, her head leaning against the left side of my neck.

Between the snorts, disbelieving gasps, and blatant gaping, I felt beyond mortified. I should have expected Belle would do that; she always did at home. By the way she stiffened in light of our clanmates' reaction, I suspected she hadn't planned this, and merely sat on me as a reflex the way she usually did.

I could almost hear her thinking as she likely debated whether to get off my lap and sit next to me instead. The Zamorian in me wanted her to do just that, but the husband in me didn't. These public displays weren't our way, but they were hers. Belle had made a lot of concessions to adapt to our customs, it was only fair I did the same for some of hers.

I wrapped both of my secondary arms around her, making it clear I didn't want her to move. My mate looked at me over her shoulder, and I gave her a reassuring smile. All tension bled out of her, and she beamed at me, grateful. For a split second, I thought she would kiss my jaw, but she reined herself in. I believed she would have done it had we not been in public.

"Are you afraid we will harm you that you seek such comfort from your mate?" Kraslo asked Belle, ever the taunting fiend.

I bared my teeth at him, instantly ready to demand a duel. My clanmates could taunt me all they wanted, but my mate was off limits.

"I'm not afraid," Belle replied, as if he'd asked a dumb question. "I just like to cuddle with my man. Why should I settle for a bench when I have my husband right here? I love the feel of his body around me and of his strong arms holding me safe. Why would I deprive myself of this comfort?"

The stunned silence that greeted her words reflected the shock I also felt, although pride superseded it. My Belle had previously told me how much she enjoyed snuggling with me. However, judging by the timidity she usually displayed around my clanmates, it once more took me aback—and flattered me—

to see how assertive she became whenever anyone questioned or challenged her relationship with me.

The slightly envious gazes the males cast my way further stroked my ego. But it was the somewhat disgruntled sideways glances a few married males gave their mates present in the room that almost made me burst out laughing. The unimpressed look on the females' faces only confirmed their husbands had their work cut out for them if they wanted public snuggles.

"Fair enough," Kraslo said, nodding in concession. He then resumed his tale. "The Azamphir Clan is livid that I have once more defeated their Gathering Champion in their own competition," he said smugly. "This time, the challenge was to mark as many shihi root locations as possible in twenty-four hours."

Belle frowned, visibly confused as to what he was referring to. He turned to my mate.

"The shihi is a bitter root that only grows in the wild under specific conditions. It cannot be cultivated. The Azamphir Clan uses it to make shinzan, a very expensive and wondrous liquor that they hold the secret recipe to."

Belle smiled gratefully at him for this clarification.

"How soundly did you defeat him?" my father asked.

Kraslo lifted his chin with arrogant glee. "I marked three times as many as he did."

An approving roar rose from all of us while he puffed out his chest.

"Marqen must be livid," I said with a chuckle. "How did you achieve such a feat?"

"By outwitting him, of course," Kraslo retorted. "Shihi is arduous to find. While their roots run deep, they only have small, vine-like branches with short leaves that could pass for grass blades. As they hide in the underbrush, especially the dense ones, you can spend a lot of time lifting ferns and bush limbs before you find a root," he once more explained to my mate.

"Sounds like a major pain!" Belle said, turning on her

drawing pad to sketch Kraslo as he spoke.

"That it is, unless you are clever about it," he replied with a mischievous glimmer in his eyes. "I dabbed some cressok musk on random trees in the area I was to hunt in. It attracts small rodents who feed on these roots. I only had to wait for them to gravitate towards the roots to stick in my marker."

"Oh, that *is* smart," Belle said, while the rest of us loudly expressed our approval. "But why didn't your rival use it as well?"

"Because he doesn't know about it," Kraslo replied, frowning as if the answer should have been obvious, a look shared by everyone else in the room. "I'm a chemist and mixologist. I spent weeks figuring out how to prepare that musk specifically to give me that edge."

It was Belle's turn to frown, all admiration fading from her face. "Isn't that cheating?" she asked.

My spine stiffened while shocked gasps resonated throughout the room. Kraslo straightened in his seat, his biceps bunching with anger as he stared at my female in outrage. Had she been a male, he'd already be on his feet, challenging her to a duel.

"Belle!" I whispered sternly.

My female turned her head this way and that, stunned by all the angry stares cast her way before she looked at me over her shoulder. But I turned my gaze to Kraslo.

"Peace, Kraslo. My mate meant no offense. She is unaware of our customs," I said in an appeasing tone.

"I didn't mean to insult you," Belle echoed in a small voice.

Mollified, Kraslo grunted in acceptance of her apology, although his expression remained disgruntled.

"I do not cheat," Kraslo said forcefully, the sting of the offense lingering in his voice.

From the look on Belle's face, she was clearly struggling to bite back her thoughts on the matter. As one of the few of my people who extensively lived off-world for the hunts, I knew well what foreigners thought of our ways. While I'd learned to shrug it off, it deeply stung that Belle would share their views.

"Accusing someone of cheating is one of the greatest insults you can give a Zamorian," my father explained to my mate in a gentle tone. "It is serious enough to be considered as sufficient grounds to ban someone from their clan." Belle recoiled, looking more baffled than ever. "My words confuse you. Why, Belle? What makes you perceive what he did as cheating?"

My female licked her lips nervously and gave me an uncertain look over her shoulder. I smiled and nodded encouragingly for her to proceed.

"I do not wish for my words to be deemed disrespectful," she said carefully.

Our clanmates nodded, all aggression gone.

My father smiled. "We will not take offense. You are the first human to come live in our midst. We would like to understand your perspective on the matter—whether or not we agree with it. Speak freely."

Belle shifted on my lap, squared her shoulders, and took in a deep breath before complying. "For us, any time you break the rules agreed upon or use workarounds to give yourself an unfair advantage, it is deemed cheating."

"Except he didn't break the rules," my father argued. "Nowhere did it state that he couldn't leverage the behavior of the local fauna to facilitate him finding the roots. So long as he only used whatever tools were permitted for him to prepare that musk on the field, then it's fair. His opponent could have attempted the same, had he thought of it or had the skills to do so."

"And I did," Kraslo chimed in. "I spent the first hour hunting for a cressok then preparing the musk. After that, I spent another hour dabbing the scent in strategic places. During that time, Marqen had taken a substantial lead. Had my plan failed, he would have utterly crushed me."

"I see," Belle said, her brow creasing as she still struggled with his explanation.

"You are still troubled, my mate. Why?" I asked.

She shifted once more on my lap, carefully choosing her words. "Well, I understand what he is saying. But for me, for humans in general, and I suspect many members of the galactic alliance, this would still be deemed… unethical."

Her use of that alternate word provoked a few snorts and amused glances.

"Why?" Kraslo asked, this time genuinely confused rather than offended.

"Because rules are meant to put everyone on a level playing field," Belle explained. "Sure, he could have tried to come up with his own version of your musk or an original method to give him an edge. The problem is that once everyone skirts their way around the rules, how do you truly determine who is the best at a given task?"

"The one who wins," I replied in an obvious tone.

"But that doesn't make him the best," Belle challenged. "No offense," she added sheepishly for Kraslo. "It makes him the cleverest for this specific round, but next time, Marqen will likely use that method as well, so it will once more be about who can come up with a new ingenious method."

"Exactly!" I exclaimed, my clanmates also expressing their agreement. "And the cleverest person will best the others again. I do not understand why this is a problem for you."

Belle sighed with frustration, her wheels spinning as she looked for a way to make us understand.

"On Earth, we have a major planetary athletic competition called the Olympics. Athletes from around the world compete against each other in a variety of disciplines," Belle explained. "We can only know who the fastest runner in the world is by making sure every single person is racing under the exact same conditions. That includes the same type of outfit and shoes, running at the same time, on the same type of surface and weather, and over the same distance. If someone took performance-enhancing drugs or propulsion shoes—"

"That would be cheating," I interrupted. "The rules are about evaluating each participant's natural personal performance and ability. Using any kind of enhancement would break the rule. In Kraslo's case, the winning condition only required the winner to mark the most roots by any means possible, while using only the authorized tools to help them achieve their goal."

"But he created a new tool with that tool. That breaks the rule, no?" Belle argued.

"Just like a survivalist who goes into the forest with nothing but a knife will build himself a tent with branches and leaves, a spear by sharpening the tip of a stick of wood, or a fishing net with vines. Those are all new tools created from the initial one. Is that cheating?" I asked.

"Hmmm. No, it's not."

"And yet, you are not convinced," my father said, tilting his head to the side with an almost fascinated expression.

"I'm sorry, Ugrul, but you're right, I'm not," Belle said in an apologetic tone. "I understand that this is the Zamorian way, and that for all of you it was fair, which is all that matters in the end on Xoccoris. However, off-worlders will not share that view, and it's why your people have… might have a poor reputation."

My father laughed. "You didn't need to correct your sentence. We are well aware of the negative way off-worlders perceive us, not that we care. But it makes me curious to understand the reason. There's nothing wrong with what we do."

"I wish I could explain better, but I'm not very eloquent," my mate said sheepishly. "I'm good at drawing, not with words."

"Then tell me this, Belle," I said in a soft tone. "You are aware of the incident involving me during that first Great Hunt on Trangor, three years ago. Do you think I cheated?"

My hearts constricted when my mate blanched, worry

settling on her face as she hesitated to answer.

"The Federation ruled that I had not, as did your hero, Kayog. And yet, I can see that you still feel I did," I continued in the same soft tone. "Why? Speak freely. I will not be upset."

She squirmed in my lap, her fingers nervously twirling her drawing pen. "The rules of the hunt were for you to claim the most kills while making them as clean and painless as possible for the creatures you were hunting. I've seen you battle, so I know what a formidable hunter you are. But instead of getting your own kills, you got the Ordosians to do it for you. That's... not fair. They were not *your* kills."

"Nowhere in the rules did it state that you could *only* claim your own kills," I replied calmly, while getting a horrible flashback of how I had been forced to defend myself before the Federation for fear of getting banned. "The rules clearly stated that we could claim any abandoned dead Flayer that had not been marked by another contestant. And that's exactly what I did."

"Yes, but you lured the Flayers to the Ordosians for *them* to do the work," Belle countered. "It would have been fine if the Flayers had just wandered there."

"How is *that* fine but not giving the odds of that happening a boost?" Varkuth asked, looking as baffled as I and everyone else felt.

"Because you effectively changed the rules," Belle said forcefully. "Here, among yourselves, everyone expects the competition to try and skirt around the rules to get an advantage. Out there, other galactic members do not. For everyone at that hunt, it was a contest of personal hunting skill, not a battle of wits on how to stretch the rules. They all wanted to prove that they could get the highest number of clean kills over everyone else. So you coming in and outpacing everyone by collecting kills others performed on your behalf was a major slap in the face."

"I see the point you're making," my father said pensively. "However, once they realized how my son had outsmarted them, why didn't they do the same?"

"Because that's not what they were there for! Just like the Olympic runners, they came there to compete with the finest hunters, and prove that they are the best at what they do. The prize and the title are only the icing on the cake."

"The prize and the title are everything! They are both the icing and the cake," Varkuth exclaimed, the rest of us agreeing with him.

"And *that* is where we all differ. For us, competition is about pushing your own limits, giving the best of yourself, and beating your own record. And that hopefully also results in you beating all of the others," Belle explained softly. "It's about honor, but also earning the respect of others."

She turned to look at me over her shoulder.

"Had they not stripped you of the kills the Ordosians made and that you claimed, you would have won by a landslide, but everyone would have hated you for it. To them, you would have stolen that victory because they were not *your* kills, as per the rules everyone else was following. Do you know who the true winner was?"

"Of course," I said, feeling annoyed. "It was a human named Donovan Craigh—an efficient and seasoned hunter."

To my shock, Belle shook her head. "Donovan won the title and the cash prize, but Serena was the real winner."

"What?!" I exclaimed, all of my clanmates also expressing their disbelief. "She forfeited the victory, even after the Ordosian kills I had claimed were given to her. It made no sense."

"No, sweetie, it made perfect sense. Like the other hunters, she only wanted credit for kills she had personally accomplished. To her, claiming the title and prize would have been unfair to those who hunted more efficiently than she did."

"Then how does that make her the winner?" my father asked,

his tone hinting that he was starting to question my mate's logic.

"Because she won the respect and admiration of everyone within the galactic alliance," Belle said with a passionate tone. "She put her life on the line to protect the weak and the innocent. She forfeited wealth and honors out of respect for the rules of the hunt, even though everyone would have gladly yielded to her. And through her marriage to an Ordosian, she has helped mend the rift with the Hunting Federation after the massacre of the innocent fauna by poachers among the hunters. Everyone in the galactic alliance knows and idolizes her. But ask anyone who was actually crowned the winner, and very few outside the hunters' circle will know the name Donovan Craigh."

Silence met her words while we reflected on them.

"Is that what you want of me? You expect me not to try to win at all costs?" I asked, my back stiff with tension.

"I would want you to kick ass like you always do and do your damnedest to win… but by following the rules, not skirting around them. You say you are the best hunter. Prove it. How do you know the real extent of your awesomeness if you use side methods to win?"

"Who cares?" Kraslo asked. "Winning is winning. Losers can boast about how they improved their personal performance as consolation."

My clanmates cheered Kraslo's words. Belle didn't comment, her face taking on a resigned expression. It would take more than this to change a mentality so deeply ingrained in our culture. Although I understood her reasoning, I didn't know that I could merely discard my own. If I didn't, would she grow disappointed in me? Ashamed of me? Resent me?

Our imminent journey to Trangor might put our union through its first real test.

The gathering hall's doors opening instantly chased away those grim thoughts. A single look at Rala's furious face had everyone chuckling, except for her mate, Muloch. His shoulders slumped, and he sighed heavily, his eyes closing in a long-suffering expression. Confused, Belle's gaze flicked between the two.

Coming to stand in front of her husband, Rala went off in a long tirade in Zamorian, berating Muloch over a task he'd neglected to do.

"We're having an assembly, female! It can wait!" Muloch said, giving his wife an annoyed look.

"I've been waiting for a week now, and you haven't done anything!" Rala shouted, her main arms crossed over her chest, while her fisted secondary hands rested on her hips.

"I started it!" Muloch exclaimed.

"Started isn't finished. Get your lazy self home and fix it!" Rala said, pointing an angry finger at the doors.

"Argh! You're impossible. I'll get to it after the assembly," he replied, clearly aggravated.

"That's it," Rala said with that ominous tone females took when they'd had it.

Without a word, Rala leaned forward, grabbed Muloch's braid, and yanked as she walked away. We collectively roared with laughter, burying his pained grunt as he jumped to his feet. He followed his mate while cursing under his breath.

"What the heck just happened?" Belle asked, flabbergasted.

"The leash has spoken," my father said, still laughing. "When a male cannot be reasoned with, that's how our females put an end to the discussion."

Belle's eyes widened, then her face took on a speculating expression as she glanced at my braid.

"Do not get weird ideas, woman," I ground through my teeth in a menacing fashion.

Utterly unimpressed, my mate held my gaze unwaveringly with an overly sweet expression that made no mystery that, if needed, she'd shamelessly use my leash to bend me to her will.

Wretched female…

CHAPTER 12
ANNABELLE

The next few days went by in a flash. With our impending departure on a trip that would last at least a couple of months, Bayron had me traipsing all over Xoccoris. Between the guided tours, shopping, and attending various events held locally or in neighboring clan compounds, I was getting a good sense of my new people.

The Zamorians were not the barbaric people often described by off-worlders. What others perceived as ruthlessness and lack of honor was merely a cultural clash. As an off-worlder myself, I struggled with some of their philosophies; their views of what I considered cheating being chief among them. Still, they had earned my respect and gratitude for allowing me to freely speak my dissenting opinion without attacking me for not siding with them in the end.

However, I had no issues with their games of wit right here on Xoccoris. Everyone played with this same understanding of the rules. Watching one of them getting screwed out of what they believed to be certain victory by some clever ploy by a rival that no one saw coming actually proved to be quite hilarious. The

Zamorians were freaking smart. And for all their down-talking runner ups, they nonetheless acknowledged and gave proper praise to the 'losers' who had come up with a brilliant tactic that simply got outwitted by another.

Among other challenges, as much as my monster lover self had been eager to be immersed in an alien culture, living it wasn't all flowers and rainbows. I innocently did so many inappropriate things, I stopped counting. When each face giving you 'the look' did so with two pairs of eyes, you quickly started feeling tiny in your shoes.

My first few blunders had triggered outraged reactions until they realized I was merely clueless. Thankfully, the word spread quickly within the clan. Every time I screwed up thereafter, people kindly set me straight with a chuckle. To my utter annoyance, some clanmates would lurk around whenever they saw me, just to see what my next fuck up would be. The most aggravating ones actually took bets.

Still, I had learned the hard way not to wink with my right eye at anyone, and especially not in response to a kid making a cute face at me. A right eye wink was essentially a sexual advance. Needless to say the kid's mom went apeshit and probably would have brutally whooped my ass had Bayron not interfered to find out the source of the female's ire.

My hopelessly fidgety self also discovered that absent-mindedly tapping your bottom lip with a pen or a finger in public was a no-no. Basically, it meant that you thought whoever was talking—whether to you or someone else—was lying or full of shit.

Even politeness had a completely different meaning here. Females opened the door and let the males in first. If there were no males with the females, the weakest female opened the door for the strongest one to enter. At first, I thought it was some messed up display of submission. Turns out that, as you didn't know what threat may lurk in the new area you were entering, the better protector was to enter first to secure it if needed. Me going in ahead of Bayron came down not only to emasculating him, but also implying I'd do a better job of protecting both of us if things got ugly.

As if…

For all that, I was loving my new people and how whole-heartedly they embraced me, quirkiness, blunders, and all.

But this morning was special. Four days had gone by since we'd brought Ferach to Krogal. I'd named the stone wolf with the Zamorian word for a warrior unbroken by adversity. In light of the severity of his injuries, Ferach had required longer than the two days Krogal had initially estimated. A series of complications had arisen due to the pup being in such an early stage of his development.

Bayron and I entered the clinic where we'd finally get the verdict. We nodded at Dhalgal, who gestured for us to go into the examination room where Krogal would join us shortly. I'd visited Ferach every day to check up on him. He would zone in and out of consciousness during that time. But the minute he saw me, his four glowing eyes would lock on me, and he would attempt to move towards me.

Being too weak and groggy, he systematically failed. Anyway, he couldn't have reached me as the glass dome of his medical pod remained closed to maintain a sterile environment while he healed. Still, his apparent desire for contact with me touched me deeply. Krogal believed Ferach had bonded with me as his new mother. However, he'd been quick to douse the joy that had stirred within me by reminding me stone wolves weren't domesticated pets.

Both Krogal and Bayron had warned me from day one that I wouldn't be able to keep him, but I wasn't ready to let go. Ferach had captured my heart the moment I saw him fighting to cling to life. That he had four blue eyes like my husband—although the pup's glowed—felt even more like a sign that this was meant to be.

Today, they had moved Ferach to a cage. As soon as he noticed us, he stood up, his overly long and pointy pink tongue hanging while he wagged his tail. He didn't do so in the fast and frantic way dogs did to express their happiness. The movement was slow, almost hypnotic, reminding me of a snake slowly gliding through grass to avoid alerting its prey of its presence, but without the ominous vibe.

The glow in Ferach's eyes intensified. I'd figured out that strong, positive emotions prompted the bright glow, while negative emotions either dimmed the glow or gave it a darker hue.

"He looks a lot better," Bayron said, as we stopped in front of the cage.

"He does," I said with excitement. "Krogal did an amazing job. I don't even see a scar where the ocaih had bitten him and broken his leg."

Bayron grunted in a non-committal fashion. I didn't need to read minds to know he was worrying about me being too optimistic.

"He seems happy to see me," I said as Ferach pressed his face to the cage.

"No!" Bayron exclaimed, startling me when I lifted a hand to scratch the pup's ear through the bars. "He's no longer sedated or groggy. He could bite you."

"He won't," Krogal said behind us, making me nearly jump out of my skin.

How the hell does such a big man move so quietly?

"At least, not her or me," Krogal amended with a teasing expression as he eyed his cousin.

I giggled while Bayron gave him a playfully baleful glare.

However, all amusement faded in favor of anticipation when Krogal opened Ferach's cage. As soon as the veterinarian picked him up, the pup wiggled and jiggled, reaching with his small paws for me. My heart swelled with affection for the young wolf, and I extended my own eager hands towards him.

Despite Bayron's obvious concern, Krogal gave me the pup. Ferach didn't lick my face like a dog would. Instead, he rubbed his face against mine, and especially the fluffy fur that covered his forehead, nape, and back. I wanted to squish him with love.

"Please, give me good news," I told Krogal while petting the pup.

He leaned against the counter upon which the cage rested and crossed his primary arms over his broad chest, a serious expression on his face.

"The infection is gone, and the bones of his legs are stitched. It required some surgery and multiple passes of reconstruction, but it looks like I was successful," Krogal said in a factual tone, devoid of the usual boasting of the Zamorians. "He shouldn't limp or have any lingering effect from it. But I can't guarantee it. Only time will tell."

"That's wonderful!! I knew you could do it!" I exclaimed, beaming at him before I gave Ferach another squeeze and a kiss on top of his furry head.

"But his adrenal glands are still a mess," Krogal said in an apologetic tone. "I can't fix that. I have reached out to all my contacts, and none of them could help. The only solution would have been to grow new glands from the stem cells of a compatible donor, which we don't have."

"No…" I breathed out, crestfallen. "So, what does that mean for Ferach?"

"It means that he will need to live in a controlled environment where his chances of injury and infection are slim to none," Krogal said. "It also means that any time he gets injured, you will need to give him antibiotic treatments to compensate for his nearly non-existent immune system."

"I can do that," I said firmly.

"Belle, I don't know how viable this will be in the long-term," Krogal cautioned. "He's still a pup. Getting him to run around your vessel will suffice for now. But as he grows older and bigger, he will need vaster space, the wilderness to hunt in, and territory to claim as his. If deprived of that, he may become restless, and maybe even violent."

"For the time being, the holodeck on my vessel should give him that wilderness feeling, as well as a realistic but safe hunting experience," Bayron interjected.

I perked up, my eyes widening in wonder upon hearing those words. I hadn't even thought of that. Indeed, Ferach could have a full hunting experience with the most savage and wildest creatures without risk of injury or poisoning. I cast a hopeful glance at Krogal.

He pursed his lips then slowly nodded. "That should work, at least in the short-term. But you will need to keep a close eye on him as he grows older for any sign of restlessness. Again, he's not meant to be domesticated."

"There might be someone else who could help with his glands," Bayron said in a careful tone. "Do not get your hopes too high, my mate. I delayed bringing this up because I had hoped Krogal could have found a miraculous solution. There's no guarantee they will be able to help, but they can have a look and see if anything can be done."

"Oh, my God! Really?" I asked. "Who?"

Krogal's face reflected the same curiosity.

"The Ordosians," Bayron said calmly.

My jaw dropped, and then my heart sank. "The Ordosians? They don't want to mingle with off-worlders, and nobody is allowed anywhere near their cities."

I kept out the part that he was likely persona non grata with them. So the odds of them providing us with any kind of assistance were likely non-existent.

"True, but they are also extremely devoted to the protection of the flora and fauna. Granted, their focus is on those of their homeworld, but they wouldn't deny a pup. When it comes to veterinary knowledge, few can rival or exceed their expertise."

"Okay, but how do we convince them to look at Ferach?" I asked, a sliver of hope wanting to take root in my heart.

"I reached out to Kayog two days ago and explained the situation. He contacted them," Bayron said smugly. "They've agreed to examine the pup when we reach Trangor for the hunt in two weeks."

The squeal that escaped me frightened the wolf. He yelped, his claws coming out to cling to me. Had Krogal not clipped them when he first arrived at the clinic, I'd have some pretty nasty lacerations right now. I would have to remember to keep them short.

But I quickly dismissed that thought as I gazed at my husband with awe, my eyes misting with emotion. I pressed myself against him, careful not to squish the pup. He wrapped an arm around me.

"You're so fucking amazing," I said in a shaky voice. "I can't believe you did this."

"Of course, my mate. It is my duty to anticipate and fulfill your needs, remember?" he said in that rumbling voice that always gave me shivers. "Whatever I can do to make you happy, I will."

"I don't know what I did to deserve you, but I'm so glad I married you," I said, choked by emotion.

Rising to my tippy toes, I lifted my face towards his. Bayron bent down and captured my lips in a tender kiss. Although it was far too early for me to already be in love with this male, the feeling that had my heart on the verge of bursting made it clear I was well on the way there.

Krogal clearing his throat snapped us out of that tender

moment. In my joy and awe at my husband, I had completely forgotten his cousin's presence. Judging by the way Bayron's face darkened and his mortified expression, he had also forgotten. I almost felt sorry for 'tricking' him into this public display of affection. Where I had no qualms holding his hand and sitting on him in public, I normally spared him the kissing part.

I smiled at Krogal. "Sorry," I said without any remorse or genuine guilt.

He snorted and shook his head at me. "I'd been considering contacting Kayog about finding me a mate. I'm starting to reconsider."

I laughed. "You must! You're built to marry a cuddler. Don't knock it until you've tried it!"

He grunted in a non-committal fashion while Bayron chuckled.

"Keep me informed of what happens with the Ordosians," Krogal told my husband. "In the meantime, I will show you how to feed him, care for him, and the exercises he will need to do daily."

We nodded and spent the next little while following his instructions.

~

Our last two days on Xoccoris went by too fast and yet not quickly enough. A part of me hated leaving my new family, and the other couldn't wait to finally visit Trangor. It was not only because I had secretly wished to be paired with an Ordosian, but also because I was hoping they would be able to fix Ferach.

Our departure met the same apparent indifference as our arrival had. No one escorted us to the ship. We didn't get a single hug, wishes of safe travels, or any other such thing. You'd think we were just off to run some errands instead of a long trip that would last at least a couple of months.

As he settled in the pilot's chair and I sat next to him in the copilot's chair, I couldn't stop wondering about it. I bent down and absentmindedly petted Ferach, busy destroying a chew toy.

"Why did no one see us off?" I finally asked as Bayron initiated our flight. "You're clearly close to your family, and your clanmates all seem to like you. Do they not care that you are leaving?"

Bayron smiled. "Of course, they do. However, what you consider a proper send off or welcoming, we consider as inviting bad luck."

I recoiled, having expected any kind of answer *but that*. "How the heck is that bad luck? The whole point of a sendoff is to wish you good luck. And the welcome is showing our happiness that you're back, safe and sound."

"You answered your own question, my mate. If you have to wish someone good luck and rejoice that they returned safely, it implies that you think there's a good chance something bad will happen," he answered matter-of-factly. "By trying to chase away evil, you bring its attention to you. By ignoring it, you deprive it of its power over you. They do not make a fuss about my departure because they are confident I will return safe and sound."

"Wow… I never thought of it that way," I said pensively. For a superstitious person like me, that struck a chord. "Still, I like how goodbyes are a way of reminding the person you care about them and that you'll miss them."

"Those are things that should be regularly communicated, Belle, and not only when the person leaves. It's not when people step out of your life that you should let them know you care. It's while they're by your side that it matters."

"Well, you haven't told me you cared," I said, only half joking. "Does that mean you don't?"

"I claimed you, silly female. Of course, I care."

"Good, because I really like you, Bayron." I couldn't wipe off the stupid grin off my face. I hadn't been fishing for compliments. My mouth just always ran away with me.

"Naturally, you do. What is there not to like about me?"

I burst out laughing and shook my head at him, which had Ferach looking curiously at me, then at Bayron before going back to obliterate his toy. It was a good thing I'd stockpiled a bunch of them. Worse case, I could create more with safe materials for him using the fabulous 3D sculptor Kayog gifted me.

"You're hopeless," I said, amused, even though I knew he'd only said it to make me laugh.

For all his grumpiness, Bayron had started loosening up around me, including making jokes, which I absolutely loved. Some people would likely find some of them lame, but I had a silly sense of humor and always genuinely giggled. His jokes were all the funnier that he was only making them to make me laugh—not out of some newfound sense of humor. Bayron liked the sound of my laughter.

"That, we agree about, my mate."

We chatted amiably for a while before I headed to my studio to start working on full-size paintings of the many sketches I had done on Xoccoris. This was shaping up to be my best work. While Bayron had clearly expressed he preferred a housewife—mainly so that she could follow him wherever his hunts took him—he didn't have a problem with me pursuing a career of my own. He'd been extremely supportive of my art, going so far as offering to fully pay for an exhibit for me once I had completed a collection.

He'd greeted my initial protests with his usual "don't argue with me, woman" look, laced with outrage. I constantly needed to remind myself that, to him, providing for all my needs was far more than a duty but a great source of pride. He gave me total access to his money, which he rarely spent as he didn't need anything. His considerable wealth helped dampen my guilt. Still,

I wanted to earn some credits of my own, if only so I could buy him a birthday present without using his own cash to do it.

In the two weeks of our journey to Trangor, we settled into a comfortable routine. Ferach would hang around me while I painted and join Bayron when he trained or did some hunting simulations. We evenly split the tasks of caring for the pup, from potty training, feeding, bathing—which Ferach surprisingly loved—and making him do the various exercises Krogal had instructed.

I absolutely loved the firm but gentle way he handled Ferach, even when he disciplined him. It gave me a wonderful glimpse into the kind of father he would be the day we had kids. While I wanted many of them, I wasn't in a hurry to start popping them out. Bayron and I had a lot of getting to know each other to do first and just enjoying some couple time together before rugrats became our entire focus. Caring for Ferach was already a lot of work.

That didn't stop us from getting plenty of baby-making practice. We just had to be careful and make sure we had the pup locked up in a safe place when we bumped uglies. At first, I'd thought Ferach was merely jealous, but the menacing stance he'd taken towards Bayron while acting protectively towards me indicated he thought my husband was attacking me.

Some research revealed how canines in general strongly disliked kisses, especially to their face, which they perceived as a biting threat. To think I'd always missed the signs of their discomfort before reading those articles. Now they seemed so obvious.

We ended up having to also train him not to perceive light intimacy between Bayron and me as a menace. However, considering how loud we got during sex, there would be no teaching him that my husband wasn't quite literally rearranging my insides as he pounded into me.

For all that, Ferach was thriving and appeared pretty happy.

Looking at him, no one would guess he'd just survived a very close brush with death or that he was so vulnerable to the slightest scratch or infection.

With the silhouette of Trangor looming in the distance, I could feel another wind of change was about to sweep through my life.

CHAPTER 13
BAYRON

Anger coursed through me as we descended the shuttle into the immense hangar of the Galactic Hunters Federation's base camp on Trangor. This was my fourth year here. I knew most of the hunters and had vaguely heard about the new faces. But today, for the first time, the contempt or obvious dislike they expressed looking at me got under my skin.

I'd never cared how they felt about me. In truth, I'd been rather amused by their annoyance. To me, their resentment of the fact I kept besting them through a mix of skills and wits, while remaining within the very edge of the rule constraints, had been the greatest compliment they could have given me. I had reveled in their bitterness.

But now, my mate—my *human* mate—bearing witness to this contempt gave it a completely different edge… an edge that cut me to the core.

A Zamorian female would have laughed at them and proudly caressed her mate's braid to display her approval. She might even have taunted them about becoming smarter, rather than whining about being outwitted. But Belle felt embarrassed by what she considered public rejection. She tried to put on a brave front, lifting her chin and plastering a neutral expression on her face. But deep down, I knew better.

My wife feels ashamed because of me.

I wanted to bash every one of these *kahbra*'s heads in for causing her distress, and for making her think poorly of me over things I still failed to consider as wrong. Since the first time we'd discussed Serena and the First Hunt, I'd suspected that my participation in hunts—especially here on Trangor—could cause problems in our union. Never in a million years did I expect it would cut so deeply.

The looks filled with sympathy—even pity—the other hunters cast Belle's way infuriated me the most. How dared they imply my wife should be pitied for having married one such as I? How dared they insinuate I was an unfit husband?

Repressing the growl choking me, I led my mate out of the hangar—which also served as a pre-hunt gathering room—and down the long hallway to our quarters in the base camp. For a moment, I considered getting back on the shuttle and returning to the orbital station so that we could live on our ship during the hunt.

However, I immediately dismissed that thought. Not only would it come down to letting our would-be bullies win, but it would also greatly inconvenience us. With Trangor not being a tourist planet, the space station served only as a spaceport for larger vessels to dock so their crews could take a shuttle to the surface. There was no entertainment to be had there. Belle would essentially be alone and a prisoner in our ship. And I'd have to part with her extra early every morning to fly down to the surface in time for the beginning of the hunt.

Furthermore, the Federation base camp constituted only one of three off-worlder buildings the Ordosians had allowed to be built on their homeworld. Therefore, renting a hotel room or another dwelling on the surface wasn't an option. We had no other choice than to 'suck it up' as my Belle loved to say whenever I used to complain about her need to cuddle or do romantic stuff.

We walked in silence, each of us lost in our own thoughts. As I had already been here before, they had preprogrammed the lock of our quarters to my biometric signature. I swiftly added Belle to the lock so that she could come and go freely when I would be out hunting. We then entered our quarters.

As with all Federation events, the accommodations provided far more space and comfort than most smaller hunt venues. Still, compared to my vessel, and even more so our dwelling on Xoccoris, the room would qualify as modest. A single oversized bed—provided as a courtesy to fit my much bigger size—ate up a quarter of the room. A leather loveseat, small wooden center table and large screen made up the living area, and a table for two occupied the space across the bed, next to the door leading to the ensuite hygiene room.

The white and light gray colors of the walls and furniture made it feel more spacious, and the large window onto the wilderness of Trangor kept it from feeling confining.

I put our bags and Ferach's cage down on the floor, then released him. He immediately went off exploring his new temporary domain. In the three weeks since we'd rescued him, the pup had considerably grown. He was already half a meter tall. At full maturity, he'd be slightly over a meter and half tall and weigh about two-hundred and thirty pounds, more with his stone skin.

Belle observed him with a motherly smile before turning her beautiful blue eyes towards me. Despite her neutral expression, devoid of any condemnation or tension, an undeniable awkwardness hung between us.

"I'm sorry you had to face this," I said, breaking the silence, my back stiff with anger and a sense of guilt I couldn't quite reconcile with.

"You don't have to apologize for the opinions and actions of others," she said in a gentle voice. "They don't understand your way of thinking and of approaching competition."

"Do you?" I challenged.

"Yes. Now that I've spent some time with your people, I understand your customs and mentality," Belle answered.

"But you don't agree with them," I insisted.

I held my breath while Belle took a moment to carefully think about her answer. As impatient as I felt, I loved that, no matter how impulsive my mate tended to be, when it came to serious conversations, she always gave thoughtful and honest answers.

"Actually, this is not black and white," my female said pensively. "I don't have a problem with your ways. Those games of wits on Xoccoris entertained the heck out of me. I just think there is a time and place for it. As we say on Earth, when in Rome, do as the Romans do."

"Meaning when participating in a galactic hunt, do as the galactic hunters do?" It was more a statement than a question.

Belle nodded.

I hated that prospect, but simply out of principle. With my massive ego—based on proven skills—I felt confident I could win the hunt their way. But this would come down to them bending me to their will. They would win this psychological war and convince themselves they'd shamed me into obedience.

Is such a loss so bad if it makes my mate happy?

"And what if I don't, Belle? What if I stick to my ways? Will you resent me?" I asked, proud that my voice remained non-confrontational.

To both my shock and relief, my wife shook her head without hesitation. "I knew the deal when I married you, even though I didn't quite understand your mentality back then. I have no right to *demand* that you change now. Would I prefer you played by galactic rules? Yes. There's no doubt in my mind that you will find it far more rewarding than you can imagine. And then people could truly see what a formidable hunter you are, instead of remaining hung up on your different approach to competition. But whatever you choose, I'm your wife, and I'll stand by you."

My hearts filled to bursting with an emotion that was far too early to name or speak out loud. But my face undoubtedly spelled it for me. Belle shivered, a powerful emotion settling on her own lovely face as her eyes filled with hope. I drew her gently into my embrace, and my secondary arms wrapped around her while my primary hands cupped her cheeks.

I studied her features, still unable to believe this delicate female—this human—was stealing my hearts.

"I am so glad I married you, Belle. The Temern was right. You truly are my soulmate," I whispered before leaning down and claiming her mouth.

Just as I was deepening the kiss, my com chimed, startling us both. I glanced at it, and an odd mix of tension and excitement warred within me.

"The Ordosians are on their way," I said in response to Belle's inquisitive look. "They'll be here in ten minutes to look at the pup."

"Oh wow! Already? How do they know we landed?" she exclaimed, excited.

I smiled. "I messaged them after we docked with the space station."

"You're freaking awesome! I knew you were a keeper," Belle said, giving me her version of a bone-crushing hug, not that it would ever crush anything.

I chuckled and returned her embrace, pleased that she couldn't see my underlying unease.

We quickly prepared a bag with a few of Ferach's favorite chew toys and treats, before making our way to the infirmary where we were to meet with the Ordosians once they arrived. As soon as we entered, Dr. Ahmad—the human female physician that always came to provide medical care during the hunts—

greeted us. She led us straight to a large examination room, usually reserved for veterinary treatment of the mounts hunters occasionally chose to ride on instead of using speeders.

I placed Ferach's cage on the off-white tiled floor of the room. As soon as I opened the door, the pup made a beeline for the examination table and, with an impressive leap, jumped on top. You'd think he was a feline rather than a canine. As soon as he landed, he lay down on his left side, extending his right leg so we could tend to it.

I snorted.

"No, sweetie, we're not treating your leg," Belle said with a chuckle. "We have really nice people coming to look at your adrenal glands so that you can do your stone skin stuff and be the fiercest stone wolf hunter out there."

She grabbed his paw and playfully shook it. Ferach emitted a purring growl followed by a half-bark while he gently whipped her hand with his tail. As much as I always worried when the pup played with my mate for fear he would accidentally maim her with his sharp teeth, I couldn't help melting at the sight of the growing bond between them. I especially couldn't resist imagining it was our son or daughter Belle was playing with.

My mate would be a wonderful mother. We hadn't discussed offspring yet. I doubted that we would until after the six-month trial period imposed by the Prime Mating Agency. Even then, the timing wouldn't necessarily be ideal. Belle had been painting up a storm during our journey here. Her pieces were quite stunning. Granted, I was biased as I featured in quite a few of them, and yet the flame her previous work initially lacked shone brightly in these ones. I suspected she would want to devote her energy to her blossoming career for a while.

As for me, I would never be an absentee father, but I wasn't quite ready to cut down on my hunts. However, constantly traipsing around space also wasn't ideal for growing younglings. They needed the stability of the clan and to be surrounded by family and friends. Still, the day would eventually come, and I looked forward to gazing upon her doting over our child.

Seconds before my heightened hearing could perceive anyone approaching, Ferach abruptly stopped playing with Belle. Jumping on all fours, he tensed and bared his teeth, the glow of his four eyes taking on a darker shade. And then I heard the slight slithering sound right before the door opened.

I knew all too well the Ordosian that entered the room. I'd hoped they would have sent someone else, but he usually handled most dealings with off-worlders. Seeing his human mate next to him hit me hard. I had not spoken to Serena since our unpleasant 'confrontation' when I'd been unjustly suspected of having murdered countless innocent creatures for poaching purposes. Although Serena visited the base camp on the few occasions that hunts had been held on Trangor over the past three years, we hadn't exactly sought out each other's company.

"Great Hunter Szaro," I said in greeting as he slithered towards us, then turned to his mate. "Serena."

Szaro didn't respond or otherwise react. His face was cold, the black slits of his green reptilian eyes looking narrower than ever. Having a long snake tail in lieu of legs, the Ordosian glided towards us in a slow and graceful movement that still felt menacing.

As the apex predator of his species, Szaro was a lethal enemy I would think twice about dueling against. We matched in height, size, and strength. While very fast myself, I believed the Ordosian to be slightly faster. I remembered all too well how he had obliterated the Nazhrals who had poached during the hunt.

The supernatural ability of his serpentine spine to bend and dodge out of harm's way, the way his tail had effortlessly shattered every bone in Djomoug's body, and the virulent poison he'd used against Tholya, all made anyone think twice about crossing this male. To think that the mere rattling of his tail had exponentially accelerated the effect of his venom still made me shudder. What other lethal abilities did he possess?

Although she also didn't speak to me, Serena gave me a stiff nod, her face revealing none of her emotions. At least, until she turned to my mate, whom she then eyed with blatant curiosity.

"This is my mate, Annabelle Skortheatis," I continued, as if they weren't giving me the silent treatment. "Belle, this is the Great Hunter Szaro Kota, and his mate Serena Bello."

"It is a great honor to meet you in person," Belle said, her eyes lighting up with a kind of awe far too similar to the one she had cast on me when we first met. "I've read so much about the two of you. And you, Serena… errr, Ms. Bello, you're like a mega superstar throughout the galaxy. I'm kind of pinching myself right now," she added with a nervous giggle.

Although Serena's brown skin was too dark to show her blushing, her embarrassed expression gave her away. Szaro's stern expression melted as he cast a proud sideways glance at his wife before turning to my mate. Despite knowing better than to think the Ordosian might disrespect Belle over his dislike of me, I nonetheless felt relieved when he gently smiled at her.

"Your kind words honor us, Annabelle," Szaro said. "We do not really follow galactic news."

"Well, you two have become the new modern fairy tale," Belle replied excitedly. "A fearless heroine puts her life on the line to save the weak and innocent. Condemned to death for that selfless action, the heroine is saved by one of the terrifying males of a planet deemed savage, if not primitive, who sacrifices his own freedom so she can be spared. And from this most improbable pairing emerged the most romantic love story, overcoming cultural clashes and adversity."

Serena laughed, in part to hide how even more embarrassed she was. "While I did get my happily ever after, I think people are exaggerating a bit."

"Hardly! Every woman wants to be you and wished they could be married to your husband," my mate countered.

This time, it was Szaro's turn to laugh. "I did tell Serena that once you've been with an Ordosian, you would have no time for any other male."

As he smugly spoke those words, he cast a teasing glance at his mate. Serena playfully elbowed him in response.

In that instant, I hated how excluded I felt from their friendly banter. And yet, I took heart in the fact that any friendship that blossomed between them would facilitate whatever care they could provide Ferach.

Szaro flicked his forked tongue at my mate and me. That was another thing I hated. Ordosians could gather a lot of information just from the scent they captured with their tongue. This included the distance of a target, their gender, health status, emotions from fear, to joy, to arousal, and even if someone was pregnant. You couldn't keep too many secrets from them.

He tilted his head to the side with a wistful expression, the slits that served him as nostrils on his reptilian face flaring. "You are not what I expected as a mate for a Zamorian."

"For a Zamorian or for Bayron?" my mate asked with a bit of a challenge in her voice.

Szaro raised an eyebrow, surprised by the question. "Both."

Belle shrugged. "You're not the only one who thinks that way. But that's because none of you know the real Bayron. And most people really do not understand the Zamorians."

She turned to look at me with a tender expression that moved me deeply. Once again, my mate was standing up for me against those who would speak ill of me or insinuate negative things about me. Beyond her words, the underlying conviction and sincerity in her tone touched me even more.

Stretching a hand towards me, Belle gently caressed my braid with a possessiveness that made me want to purr. Had we been on Xoccoris, I would have done it. Here, and especially before these two, I swallowed it down.

"Kayog deemed us soulmates, which I don't doubt for a minute," Belle said in a soft voice, looking tenderly at me before looking back at the other couple. "In time, I hope that you—and everyone else—will get to see what a good male he is."

Szaro and Serena gave me a strange look laced with confusion. They clearly didn't know how to answer my mate's comment. Frankly, in their stead, I wouldn't have known what to say either. Thankfully, Ferach—likely annoyed at being so utterly ignored—made a half-bark, half-growling sound, drawing our collective attention.

"No, love, we haven't forgotten about you," Belle said softly while scratching the back of Ferach's right ear.

"So this is our patient," Szaro said, seeming as relieved as I felt to steer the conversation away from my likeability level.

As soon as he began to approach him, Ferach tensed. He lowered his head in, his body tensing as he bared his teeth with a low warning growl.

"No, Ferach. This is a friend!" Belle said, caressing his head gently.

"Do not worry," Szaro said to my mate in a reassuring voice.

He didn't stop his advance, raising the tip of his tail instead and started rattling it. In seconds, the same deep sense of peace that washed over me appeared to affect Ferach. The pup's menacing stance faded, and he almost looked groggy when, moments later, Szaro gently reached for him with both hands.

He didn't pick him up, proceeding to manually examine him instead. I had heard of the appeasing—almost hypnotic—effect of the Ordosian's rattle but had never experienced it before. From my understanding, they could use their rattle to create completely different reactions in the people listening, from this soothing effect, to create panic, to enhancing their venom, and even stirring a fierce arousal.

While he examined the pup, Szaro asked us a series of pointed questions. Serena took some blood samples and ran a handheld scanner over the little wolf, who appeared almost sleepy.

Belle slipped her hand into mine as she observed them, worry etched on her face while we awaited their verdict. I wrapped my arm reassuringly around her, my thumb gently caressing her upper arm in a soothing fashion. I didn't miss Serena's baffled expression—though quickly hidden—when she stole a glance our way.

I repressed a snort. Considering our history, she obviously couldn't picture me being tender to anyone, least of all a human female. My mate's words to the effect that few people truly knew the real me replayed in my mind. She couldn't have been more accurate. Yet, I couldn't blame them. Zamorian males always projected a boastful and dominant image. When things didn't go our way, we became loud and threatening. But that didn't mean we would turn into uncontrollable beasts.

"The healer did admirable work on the leg," Szaro said at last. "Based on the images and reports Kayog forwarded to us, we wondered how well it would hold."

"So it's fully healed?" Belle asked, her voice filled with hope.

Szaro shook his head. "No. As was to be expected, once Ferach started moving again, some displacement occurred. But it is nothing we can't fix. I expect the leg to make a full recovery. As far as his glands are concerned, it will require a lot more time and effort."

"But you think you can help?" I asked, tension rising within me at the dreadful prospect of how a negative answer would crush my mate.

Szaro hesitated. "I will not make promises as this stone wolf is a foreign species to us. However, we have mended similar types of defects in other creatures of our world. I am fairly confident that, should we not fully heal him, we will be able to improve his condition enough for him to have a normal life."

"That's wonderful! Thank you so much!" Belle exclaimed.

"Do not thank me yet, human. The work isn't done. But I promise we will do everything in our power to fix him," Szaro said in a gentle, almost brotherly tone.

"I know. But at least, now we have real hope," Belle said, grateful.

"Indeed. We will have to take him with us to Krada, our tribe's village," Szaro continued. "Just be warned that it could take the entire duration of the Great Hunt for us to heal the pup."

"Oh wow, okay," my mate said, sounding a little deflated. "But… hmmm… Will I be able to come visit him?"

"No."

The finality in the Ordosian's tone took my mate aback. I had known what his response would be, but it still rubbed me the wrong way to have him so sternly deny my female.

Serena placed a gentle hand on her husband's forearm before giving Belle an apologetic look. "As you probably know, strangers are not allowed to cross into Ordosian territory. They are considered sacred lands. But I can set up daily vidcoms so that you can see how Ferach fares and that he can see your face and hear your voice. He's clearly bonded with you."

"He has," I confirmed, on Belle's behalf. "Thank you for that offer to my mate. It is generous of you."

"Yes, thank you," Belle echoed.

Serena smiled, once again appearing confused as she looked at me. After giving Ferach a final hug and kissing the top of his head, Belle let the Ordosian take away the pup. Szaro refused to put him in a cage.

We walked them to the exit of the hangar under the watchful eyes of the other hunters milling about. Naturally, seeing that couple interacting with us—or more specifically me—in what seemed to be an amiable fashion would have tongues wagging for a while.

We stood outside the hangar doors as they got on their mounts. We remained there as they rode off the long clearing to the thick forest, and until they vanished from view.

CHAPTER 14
ANNABELLE

The first week on Trangor somewhat dragged on for me. I'd spent the prior three weeks almost constantly by Bayron's side, traipsing around the compound with his mother, or with Ferach near me. Now, with the pup being cared for by the Ordosian over in the Krada village, and Bayron gone throughout the day and most of the evening while hunting, I felt quite lonely.

I shouldn't feel that way. After all, I'd been a loner most of my life. In fact, I suspected the reason I babbled so much when someone finally kept me company was so that I could make up for those many days and hours of silence. But since marrying Bayron, I'd grown quite addicted to that feeling of belonging, to a caring presence around me.

That last thought actually poked at the real issue. Aside from my painting keeping me quite busy, even with the hunters gone chasing after Flayers, the base camp still bustled with activity. A handful of other hunters had brought spouses I could technically hang out with. Plenty of the Hunters Federation staff also hung around. Therefore, I shouldn't have felt isolated. However, they weren't a 'caring presence' but a semi-hostile one.

Their hostility wasn't aimed at me, but at Bayron. As his wife, people acted with me either politely distant or with a commiseration that had first embarrassed me and now pissed me off. I wasn't the victim of an abusive partner. I hadn't been conned into marrying him. And I sure as hell didn't need pity.

I quickly distanced myself from the few people who had shown an interest in talking with me. It hadn't been out of a genuine desire to get to know me, but more to draw out any kind of gossip about Bayron and the Zamorians in general. They didn't respond well when I painted a positive picture of my husband, or they made it a point to try and talk as much shit about him as they could. What was their goal? Try and get me to divorce him or think ill of him?

The one person who would have had grounds to act in such a crappy way didn't. Serena was very much the kickass lady I had imagined her to be. She never had a bad word about my husband —not that either of us ever brought up the topic. She was always friendly and gracious to me and kept her word about daily vidcoms to see how Ferach was doing.

I settled in the loveseat in the seating area and turned on the screen, eagerly waiting for her call. Moments later, she did.

"Hi Serena," I said with a grin when her beautiful face came on the screen. "You look breathtaking! That golden top just makes your scales stand out even more!"

She chuckled and nodded, looking flattered. "Hello, Belle, and thank you. It's actually a short dress. Szaro absolutely loves when I wear this. He can't stop bragging about me bearing some of his scales. The reason you always see me with sleeveless tops is because he's all but forbidden me from covering my scales. You'll also notice most of my outfits are backless for the same reason."

I laughed. "Well, I can't blame him. He's a proud husband. Did it freak you out the day you were told you would develop some physical alien traits from your union with him?"

"Of course!" Serena replied with a snort. "Marrying an alien had never featured too high on my list, least of all one that would cause some physical mutations in me. And yet, I couldn't be happier. I'm head over heels for my Szaro."

"I'm thrilled to hear it. Unlike you, marrying an alien that would possibly change and enhance me had always been a dream of mine. I thought I'd end up with someone with scales, horns, and all kinds of other non-human features," I said wistfully. "When Kayog first told me my perfect match had none of the above, I felt a little bummed out. But in the end, Bayron turned out to be everything I wanted, and more. I'm very happy."

Serena studied my face for a brief instant. "You really care about him, don't you?"

I nodded with a soft smile. "I bet you're shocked."

She shifted in her seat, her wheels spinning as she reflected on a proper response.

"It's okay. Obviously, I know about what happened between you and why you may have a poor opinion of him. I won't be offended if you need to vent," I said in a gentle voice.

Serena smiled with gratitude. "You're very sweet, Belle. I appreciate your offer, but I don't believe in speaking ill of someone behind their backs, and least of all doing so with their spouse."

"So you *do* think ill of him," I insisted.

Serena squirmed, a slight frown settling on her brow. "Ill is too strong a word. I was merely using the common expression. Bayron doesn't rank on the list of my favorite people. Had you asked me the same question three weeks ago, I would have said that I had nothing but contempt for him and left it at that."

"Three weeks ago? Why? What happened?" I asked, confused.

She smiled. "Kayog, of course. He messaged us about your pup. Knowing that he paired you with Bayron changed every-thing. He wouldn't help someone he deemed evil or despicable.

And then meeting you sealed it, especially what you said about the fact that none of us knows the real Bayron. I've spent the past few days reflecting on your words and on the way he acted with you. I didn't think he had it in him to care for someone other than himself. But his affection for you is undeniable. He really wants to make you happy."

My face heated, and it was my turn to squirm in my chair. "Bayron really is a wonderful male. He's so sweet, always pampering me and catering to my needs. I wish more people saw this side of him. I know it's a long shot, but I would love it if the two of you could spend a few minutes talking alone. Zamorians have a much different view on competition. But they are *not* cheaters. To them, it's not just about skills but also wits. It's all about how you can stretch the rules without breaking them."

Serena pursed her lips as she pondered, then slowly nodded. "Yes, I see what you mean. Every one of us tries to come up with the best weapons, tools, traps, and tactics to maximize our number of clean kills in the shortest time possible. I remember being blown away by the method Donovan had used during the First Hunt to ultimately win. I hadn't thought of it. But the difference is, the kills were his, by his own hand."

"I do not dispute that," I conceded. "As a human, I feel the same way."

She gave me a sympathetic smile. "For what it's worth, your husband hasn't ruffled too many feathers since the First Hunt. He's raising a few more eyebrows this year by once again using pheromones to lure Flayers. At least, he's killing them all himself. Sadly, as you well know, it only takes one 'bad' thing to ruin a reputation. But it will take a hundred good ones to restore it."

"And restored, it will be," I said firmly.

Serena chuckled. "I do believe you can pull it off. He's lucky to have someone as loyal as you are."

I shrugged. "We're lucky to have each other. Now, where's

Ferach?" I asked, glad to have finally been able to plant the seed I'd been wanting to.

Instant worry filled me upon seeing Serena's apologetic expression. "Unfortunately, he's unconscious right now, and he will remain so for the next couple of days at least. We're basically giving his endocrine system a shock treatment that we hope will kick-start his adrenal glands and force them to accept regenerative medicine."

"Oh okay," I said, my shoulders slouching. "But he's otherwise doing fine, right?"

"Yes, he absolutely is," Serena said in a reassuring tone. "I'll be sad to see him go, and my sons even more."

I opened my mouth to ask something, then bit my bottom lip to silence myself.

Serena narrowed her eyes on me. "What? What were you going to say?"

I gave her a sheepish grin. "Well, Bayron mentioned you once came to the base camp with your sons. I would absolutely love to draw your entire family. Ideally, it would have been directly in Krada, in front of your house. I've heard that Ordosian males make beautiful carvings on the house's façade to honor the great events of their couple's life. But I know that's not possible. However, if you all dropped by the base camp…"

She burst out laughing at the shameless way I batted my eyelashes at her. "I will not make any promises, but I will talk to Szaro about it. Regarding the house, I think the Elders will be fine with me sending you some pictures, if that can be enough for you."

"That would be amazing!" I exclaimed, clapping my hands, which made her laugh further.

"Very well. I'll see what I can do… regarding all that we've discussed."

"Thank you, Serena. I really appreciate it."

She winked at me. "Goodbye, Belle. Talk to you soon."

~

Ten days after our arrival on Trangor, Bayron finally felt confident that some of the memorable landmarks in the area were safe enough for him to take me on a tour. I'd been dying to do some sightseeing since before we even landed. But with the entire planet being essentially one massive animal sanctuary, the Ordosians put a lot of restrictions on where off-worlders could run around freely.

Our hosts didn't really want us wandering into areas other than where the Flayers were currently stampeding. Those creatures reproduced extremely fast. Once a year, during what the Ordosians called the birthing season, sick, old, or single adult Flayers were cast out of their territory to make room for the newborns. Those outcasts would spread far and wide, rampaging through the land. To protect the vulnerable species also in the process of giving birth, the Ordosians had allowed the Galactic Hunters Federation to come help them eradicate this threat.

At first, I had been baffled as to why the Federation would have gotten involved. Sure, the Flayers made a 'fun' creature to battle for seasoned hunters. After all, they were terrifying critters. But of course, it came down to money. Most of a Flayer's organs had highly sought-after medicinal properties that galactic pharmaceutical companies coveted. Therefore, they paid top credits for any clean kills the hunters made with minimal damage to these precious organs.

Just watching the recordings of my camera following Bayron during his hunt, I'd nearly peed myself. I didn't know how he and the other hunters did it. Flayers freaked me the hell out. You couldn't pay me enough to walk up to one and say what's up.

The lower half of their bodies looked like someone had chopped off the front part of a centipede and only kept four legs on each side. A long torso, which could have belonged to a chubby human, protruded above the front legs. Its razor-sharp, scythe-like arms reminded me of those of a praying mantis on steroids. A round head, that basically came down to a gigantic mouth filled with dagger teeth, dangled at the end of an almost one-meter-long neck. And to complete this sexy picture, at least two dozen eyes surrounded its mouth and the sides of its neck.

Thankfully, Bayron was taking me far from the hotspots. I had wanted to go visit the scogas—a kind of small dragon-bird with a chameleon tail that lived in trees—but they dwelled in the forbidden areas. Nevertheless, I'd be seeing some of Trangor's unusual fauna.

This little outing felt even more special to me that my husband was sacrificing precious hours of hunting to hang out with me instead. Normally, Bayron would hunt daily during every available second of the permitted time. Right now, his rivals would keep scoring more kills, potentially getting ahead of him. Considering his obsession with winning, that he would put my needs and happiness above it meant the world to me.

Arms wrapped around Bayron, I shamelessly groped my man while sitting behind him on his speeder. He'd gotten it into his head to get me to behave. Seriously? How was a girl to keep her hands to herself when she had a scrumptious set of chiseled abs within reach?

"Female, stop! Your distraction will cause an accident!" Bayron grumbled.

"No, it won't," I said shamelessly between two kisses on his back. "Surely your great Zamorian warrior discipline makes you immune to your wife's innocent touch? After all, I'm not grabbing the twins… yet."

I giggled at his menacing growl. As much as my fingers twitched with the desire of reaching between his thighs, I wouldn't push my luck that far. Considering how fast our speeder was racing through the forest, if Bayron did lose control, they'd be scraping our remains off the trees and the forest floor. Still, that didn't mean I couldn't cop a feel.

For all that, I feasted my eyes on our stunning surroundings. Overhead, a bright sun shone in the clear blue sky, slightly tinged with greenish hues. Prehistoric-looking trees towered over us. A few vaguely resembled dragon trees, some were an alien spin of monkey puzzle trees, and others could have been baobabs whose trunks had been carefully wrapped in braided bark.

All kinds of small creatures scurried about too fast for me to get a good look at them. But I didn't care. I was off on a date with my man on a foreign planet very few people could have bragged about having ever set foot on.

"We're here," Bayron said, almost in a whisper as our speeder began slowing down.

We stopped a few seconds later and dismounted. Drawing me closer to him, Bayron activated his stealth shield. It had a four-meter radius, which allowed us some freedom of movement without revealing our presence. It also had a sound dampening effect so that we could speak—still in hushed voices—without being heard by the nearby fauna.

We left the speeder camouflaged next to one of the 'braided baobabs' and walked hand in hand straight ahead. A hundred meters later, the trees parted to reveal the most surreal spectacle. I couldn't decide what fascinated me the most between the small creatures on the vast clearing sprawled before us or the fantastical structures erected in the crystalline river behind them.

I first thought a bunch of alien beavers were holding log sales in their version of a flea market, although their bodies didn't really match that description. All over the riverside, a single creature, standing by a pile of wood, was making all kinds of sounds while striking a variety of strange poses and baring their long front teeth. It took me a second to realize some sort of mating ritual was going on.

Bayron drew me a little closer so that we could have a good look at what was happening without risking discovery. He sat down on the short grass and pulled me into his lap. I snuggled against him, slightly purring with content when he wrapped his strong arms around me. That made him chuckle smugly as he kissed my temple.

God, how I love when he's affectionate like that!

"These are voreas," Bayron said in a soft voice. "Unlike most other creatures that are currently in their birthing season, these ones are in their mating season. All the ones you see standing by the piles of wood are males. They are showing off their physical attributes—especially their teeth—and singing to draw a female."

I gave one male a closer look. After further examination, I had to admit that they were nothing like beavers, except for their long front teeth. Their head resembled far more that of a fennec fox with the pointy face and oversized ears. Their plump body could have belonged to a pacarana, aside from the puffy round tail similar to a bunny's. Although they came in different hues, they all had a base white fur, with stripes of a darker color—blue, brown, or shades of dark gray or black—and a splash of a random bright color on their chest and around their forehead.

They were ridiculously cute.

"What's the wood for?" I asked.

But even as I stated the question, the answer became obvious. Bayron pointed at the same male, with dark brown stripes and turquoise accents, who had caught my attention. Another creature, I guessed to be a female, had stopped in front of him. He grabbed a piece of wood and frantically started chewing on it.

"They sculpt presents for their potential mate," Bayron explained. "He's showing off how strong and sharp his teeth are, how quick and efficient he is at sculpting, and how creative he is. If she likes what she sees, the female may either encourage him to sculpt a few more things or let him court her."

"That's so cool!" I whispered excitedly. "But why wait for her to arrive? Why not have a bunch of things already carved so that the females can just browse like you would at a shop?" I asked.

"Because he needs to prove how fast he is. He must first catch her eye physically, then with his skills."

"Oh no! She's leaving!"

The poor male had still been halfway through whatever he was sculpting when the female started walking away. He tossed the piece of wood on the ground, quickly picked another, and called out after the female. At first, I thought she would ignore him, but then she stopped and glanced over her shoulder at him. He chewed at the log with an even greater frenzy. I almost feared he would hurt himself. However, whatever he was doing this time seemed to retain her attention as she slowly moved back towards him.

All over the riverside, other males were also frantically sculpting.

"For almost one kilometer along the length of the river, the voreas have erected their city with sculpted wood. Although they are fantastic architects, when the storm season comes, between the strong winds and agitated water, the structure is seriously challenged," Bayron said. "Therefore, a female will want a mate who can not only pass on strong genes to their progeny, but who will also be able to keep a roof over their heads, either with excellent construction or ability to fix it quickly."

"It's quite amazing," I said in awe while taking a few pictures. "I wish I could snag one of the little sculptures."

"It should be possible," Bayron said. "The female usually only keeps the one that swayed her. They will discard the rest on the riverside. Over the next few days, I'll drop by here when I finish hunting to see what I can grab for you."

"Have I told you what an awesome husband you are?" I asked, my throat tightening with emotion.

"I'm not sure you have. Maybe you should remind me?" he said teasingly.

I chuckled and turned around in his lap to face him, my legs on either side of his. Bayron's secondary hands immediately settled on my behind. He loved their 'soft plumpness' as he eloquently put it.

"You are the best husband I could have ever hoped for. You make me very happy. And I believe I am falling in love with you," I said.

"As you should," he growled possessively, his primary arms wrapping around my back. "You are mine, Belle, until death do us part. My hearts will not accept any other but you."

I melted against him. I didn't know if Zamorian males—or Bayron specifically—had a thing about saying those special three words. It didn't really matter to me. In his own way, he'd just told me he was also falling in love with me. Anyway, he showed it to me in countless ways.

He leaned down and claimed my lips in that dominant and hungry way that always made my toes curl. A rumbling growl rose from his throat as he deepened the kiss, his hands on me becoming more daring. Immediately aroused, I reciprocated, showing none of the restraint I'd exercised earlier while we rode the speeder here.

I briefly thought this wasn't the right place to get down and dirty, with the voreas doing their mating dance. Bayron and I tended to get very loud, too loud for the sound dampener to make a difference. But my husband slipping a hand between us to lift my skirt, sliding my thong to the side, and beginning to rub my clit silenced any thought of propriety and discretion.

A moan escaped me. Bayron immediately slapped my left butt cheek, hard enough for it to sting, but nowhere near enough to hurt.

"Be quiet, female, or I will punish you," he said against my lips in a dangerously low voice that resonated directly in my core.

My inner walls clenched as he silenced me with his tongue

invading my mouth again, and the movement of his hand sped up. Already wet for him, I swallowed a grateful moan when he finally inserted two fingers inside of me. As always with my mate, the minute he started touching me, I ached to be filled.

I ground on his hand, chasing an orgasm with an eagerness that had him chuckling with an insufferable smugness. Too busy kissing and caressing him over the skin-tight shirt he loved wearing, it took me a moment to register that he had slightly lifted me. When he removed his fingers, and I felt the thick tip of his main cock pressing against my opening, I realized he had freed the twins from their confines.

Impulsive as always, I all but impaled myself on his length. I yelped at the exquisite burn, earning me another stinging slap on the butt. Far from deterring me, that only further fanned the flames of desire raging inside me. I enjoyed a spanking from someone with the right level of control on the strength used. And my mate knew how to do it the perfect way.

He knew I'd never be quiet, even if I genuinely tried to keep it down from my usual banshee screams every time he made me see stars. I believed he actually wanted me to be loud to justify giving me the spanking he knew I enjoyed. Anyway, with the vorea males loudly calling out to potential mates, I doubted they would even hear us through the cacophony of their own making.

I quickly began to crest as Bayron's hands effortlessly moved me up and down his length at a frantic pace. The strength of my man would never cease to amaze me. As his secondary cock rubbed against my backside, I once again almost told him to go ahead and put it in. But this was neither the time nor the place. I definitely needed a bit more preparation before crossing that bridge.

As was his wont, my husband broke the kiss, his hand firmly holding my nape so that he could stare at my face when I toppled over. He loved the way I looked when I climaxed. He called it his reward for a job well done. His free hand slipping between us to rub my clit did me in. Teeth clenched to silence my shout of ecstasy, I ended up making a sound akin to a throaty growl, that still earned me a couple more slaps on my butt.

"Quiet, you naughty, naughty female," Bayron whispered in a menacing voice, his lips a hair's breadth from mine.

The whole time, his fingers continued to work my little nub while the head of his cock relentlessly assaulted my sweet spot. I never had a chance to come down from this first high before another climax began building within me. It struck me like lightning. I would have thrown my head back, but his hand on my nape prevented me from moving backward. Instead, I lunged forward, my teeth digging into the thick muscle at the curve of his neck to silence my cry of bliss.

A half-choked roar escaped Bayron. His arms tightened almost painfully around me as he slammed himself home. His seed exploded inside of me. An endless string of feral grunts rolled out of his throat as he surrendered to his own orgasm.

He remained buried inside of me, holding me close while we slowly came back down to reality. As much as I hated the clothes between us that robbed me of greater intimacy with my husband, I loved how perfectly we always came together. Despite our utterly different appearances, we were indeed made for each other.

Reluctantly pulling away from Bayron, I cast a glance over my shoulder to see how much disturbance we'd caused. The vorea males were still carving their little hearts out to the delight of the females.

I turned back to look at my husband with a smug expression of my own. "I believe you were louder than me. Does that mean I owe *you* a spanking?"

Bayron laughed softly, a tender look in his eyes. "Maybe, but you were loud longer. That evens things out."

I scrunched my face at that evasive answer. "But you were still loud. That means you indeed earned a spanking."

His smile broadened. "You're welcome to try and give me one any time you feel daring," he taunted.

I opened my mouth to reply, but a frightened yelp escaped me instead at the shrill roar that resonated in too short a distance from here. The voreas immediately went silent, scattering back to their floating cities, all thoughts of courting forgotten.

Bayron and I got up. With his secondary hands tucking himself back in, the fingers of his main right hand flew over the interface of his bracer while I fixed my clothes. The tension on his face had my heart pounding into my throat.

"What is it," I whispered at the sight of his shocked expression. "A Flayer?"

He shook his head while casting a confused and disbelieving look in the general direction of the forest to our right.

"My scanner says a Nharmyth. There shouldn't be one anywhere near here. Something must have lured it."

"Something like what?" I insisted.

"Something it wants to eat," Bayron said with a frown. "We should get out of here."

"But…" I bit my bottom lip, torn between the urge to get the hell away from whatever critter could make such a sound and the irrational need to protect whatever could be prey to it. I cast a look towards the voreas' homes. None of the small mammals were visible anymore. "It's birthing season. What if he's after some helpless babies?"

Bayron shook his head. "Nharmyths are huge. They would go after larger prey. And I'm not taking you anywhere near it to find out what it's hunting. I need to get you to safety."

"Oh, but we don't have to go there to know! I have my camera!" I exclaimed, whipping it out of my dress pocket. "We can fly it over there to see what's happening. It won't even know."

"Belle…" Bayron growled in a stern 'Don't be unreasonable' tone.

"Please, sweetie. Please!" I begged with my most pathetic puppy face.

Without even thinking about it, I reached for his braid and caressed it while staring at him with pleading eyes. His head jerked towards my hand on his braid. He bared his teeth, jaw clenched, visibly displeased by the thought of keeping me here longer than he deemed safe.

With an angry growl, he took the camera from me, plugged in some coordinates in the tiny interface, and sent it off. I swiftly removed the bracer from my arm, which allowed us to control its flight path, and handed it to Bayron with a deeply grateful smile.

"You're the best husband ever," I said, before pressing my lips to my mark on his chest over the tight fabric of his shirt.

He grunted in a non-committal fashion, his eyes locked on the interface of my bracer. I squeezed close to him to look at the screen, wondering the whole time if I was indeed putting us in serious jeopardy. But then, as much as Bayron wanted to please me, had he believed us in any type of clear and present danger, he would have tossed me over his shoulder like a potato sac and hauled me the heck out of here.

Flying at high speed, the camera quickly closed in on an even more terrifying creature than the Flayer. It resembled a nightmarish version of a demonic Naga. Its snake-like body measured at least six meters. Black as sin, with a dark-red underbelly, it possessed one huge black snake eye in the middle of its torso and another on top of a head that only had a round mouth filled with sharp teeth, and an oversized set of recurving horns. The odd limbs that served as arms might as well have been a set of giant crowbars. But the scariest part were the tentacles around its arms and shoulders that in fact appeared to be a bunch of snakes.

"God have mercy," I whispered as a shudder coursed through me.

Even with the relatively safe distance between us and the Nharmyth, my flight instincts itched to kick in. Bayron moving the camera away from the creature to focus on its target unnerved me even more. Not being able to see what it was up to had my overflowing imagination picturing the worst.

The camera zeroed in on a large fissure in a tall rock formation. A weak, keening sound came from beyond the narrow opening that the Nharmyth was trying to force his way through with its crowbar hands. Bayron flew the camera through the opening. Seconds later, a string of curses in Zamorian poured out of his lips.

"What is it? What is she?" I breathed out, my heart breaking for the visibly terrified creature inside the cave.

Lying on a huge stone slab, she resembled a giant hybrid of a bee, a moth, and a dragonfly. Countless eggs filled her huge, translucent abdomen, weighing her down. There would be no fleeing for her.

"An Atreall Queen," Bayron ground through his teeth, looking torn.

"But where is her hive? Where are her soldiers?" I asked.

"In her abdomen. She's a new queen. Only one or two are born every generation. Kromor's teeth, why now?!"

He handed me back my bracer, ran a nervous hand over his hair, and looked at me with obvious worry.

"We're going to help her, right?" I asked in a trembling voice.

"*You* are going back to base camp," he said in a tone that brooked no argument.

He grabbed my hand and drew me after him, walking in long strides that had me half jogging next to him to keep up as he headed back towards our hidden speeder.

"But—"

"NO, Belle! You will not argue. This creature is far too dangerous for you to come anywhere near it."

He deactivated the camouflage over our speeder and retrieved some weapons from the storage compartment under the seat. Bayron then made me sit on the hovering bike. His fingers flew over the navigation board as he set the coordinates back to the camp.

"You will hurry back to the camp at a safe speed with the stealth cloak on. You *do not* stop or make *any* detour anywhere. As soon as you arrive, tell the Hunt Master to warn the Ordosians. I do not know if I can defeat that creature, but I can hopefully distract it long enough for them to get here."

"Are you going to be safe?" I asked, feeling almost faint with fear. As much as I wanted to save that young queen, I wasn't ready to be widowed.

"I will be fine, Belle. Go now before I'm too late." He cupped my face in his main hands and gave me a passionate, almost desperate kiss. "I care deeply for you, my mate. Promise you will go straight to the base."

"I promise," I said in a shaky voice.

"Go!"

Blinking back the tears welling in my eyes, I took off while he started running towards the east where the vicious beast continued to scream. After only a few steps, he vanished from view as he reactivated his personal stealth shield.

As I raced back towards the camp, a single prayer played in a loop in my mind.

Please, God. Keep my husband safe.

CHAPTER 15
BAYRON

My innards twisted with worry as I raced towards the Nharmyth. A part of me wanted to turn back and go make sure my mate had safely returned to the camp. I didn't even want to fathom how badly it would destroy me if Belle came to any harm. The little human had buried herself deep in my hearts. Even now, the scent of her lingered on my body. I couldn't picture a future that didn't involve her.

Sure, Belle wasn't a clueless female. On our journey here, and during some of our outings on Xoccoris, she'd proven herself quite capable at what humans called extreme sports— which frankly were nowhere near extreme for us. The path back to the camp should also be totally safe.

But this area also should have been.

Beyond worry for the welfare of my mate, I couldn't deny some concern for myself. The lack of proper hunting armor and weapons left me vulnerable. Although I had read plenty about Nharmyths, I'd only battled them on a holodeck, based on the artificial intelligence's interpretation of what the creature's behavior would be. But reality could be quite different.

By all accounts, its limited intelligence could give me the

edge I needed. Despite its massive size, the beast possessed a tiny brain between the huge horns on each side of its small head. Driven by instinct, the Nharmyth was reputed to become single-minded in its pursuits and relentless until it achieved its goal, even if it killed it. This would explain why it had come so far west of Nharmyth territory.

Had there been an Atreall nest nearby, the Ordosians never would have allowed us to traipse about in this area. Considering the young queen appeared to be three or four days away from laying her first eggs, and in light of the four dead males lying nearby, I presumed she'd completed her mating flight a day or two ago and only recently found this cave to establish her colony in. The Nharmyth had likely spotted her while she was mating and followed her here.

I shouldn't meddle with this at all. Ordosians had made it extremely clear that we weren't to hunt or harm any creature on Trangor other than the Flayers rampaging through the authorized hunting grounds. They only made exceptions for extreme cases of self-defense. Even then, they expected us to try to remove ourselves from the situation without harming the beast.

But Atrealls were extremely rare creatures constantly living on the edge of extinction. Only one or two queens were 'born' every twenty-five to thirty-years once the current queen's eggs neared depletion. Unlike most other similar species, you couldn't feed a larvae special nutrients to turn it into a queen or fertile male. You had to wait and pray for one larva to spontaneously start developing those attributes because the colony needed them to.

The young queen would then leave with a handful of males who would mate with her and escort her to the location of the new colony. They would help with basic setup work in the short time they had left to live. Once the males died, usually within one or two days from mating, the queen would inject them with a preservative so that she could feed on their remains until her first eggs had hatched into workers that could tend to her needs.

That her death at the hands of the Nharmyth could push her species closer to the brink of extinction only played a minor role in my desire to intervene. Zamorians believed in the survival of the fittest. Species came and vanished all the time. Therefore, a part of me merely considered it fate. That Atrealls fed on otherwise untreatable parasites on trees and large plants, and that they secreted a substance used in the cure of various severe infections made saving her important.

However, beyond all of this, the thought of a helpless pregnant female stirred my protective instincts. Moreover, I couldn't bear disappointing my mate. Just like with Ferach, Belle might not have forgiven me for abandoning the young queen.

I just needed to make sure I survived the encounter.

Too focused on trying to break inside the cave to feast on the poor female, the Nharmyth didn't hear my approach. Between two impatient screeches, it savagely used its crowbar hands to tear off chunks of rocks around the opening.

Sneaking up on these creatures could be quite challenging. Aside from the primary eye on its chest, the Nharmyth's top eye on its forehead granted it a 180° view behind it simply by bending its head back. Then again, the countless snake-tentacles around its shoulders and torso gave him additional eyes in every direction, although those had a very short range.

The biggest challenge would remain whether to try to kill it or just delay long enough for the Ordosians to get here. Either would be a difficult feat. Both the back and underbelly of the creature were extremely hard to pierce. Even with my blaster at the highest lethal setting, it would require countless shots at the exact same spot to start making a dent. While the eyes could easily be taken out, bone plates behind them protected the brain and other vital organs. Its vulnerable spots hid right above the armpits, where the shoulders connected to the neck.

The trouble was getting close enough to stab it there and take out its heart. Blaster shots wouldn't work. I had to inflict a piercing wound. But with the longer snakes stretching nearly two meters, coming close enough without getting viciously bitten by their lethal venom would be a miracle.

Standing approximately twenty meters behind it, I dropped my stealth shield and took aim at one of the snake heads hovering around its shoulders, like hair swaying in a soft breeze. I landed a perfect shot, the head exploding in a shower of blood and gore. The creature emitted a strident scream while the other snake heads hissed as they turned in my direction. With me being out of range of their sight, the Nharmyth lifted its head, its mouth pointing towards the sky so that its forehead eye could identify the threat behind it.

The narrow slit of its black eye widened when it spotted me.

Turning around at dizzying speed for such a massive body, the creature slithered towards me faster than I had anticipated. Even as I started running towards a thick outcropping of trees, the Nharmyth opened its mouth impossibly wide before spitting a long stream of acid over at least five meters. Thankfully, I'd kept enough distance between us to be spared.

I weaved my way around the narrow passages between the trees, forcing the creature to slow down to allow its broad shoulders to fit through. While doing so, I threw four bangers in different directions, away from where I was heading. Right before the trees spaced out again, I reactivated my stealth shield. The Nharmyth screeched and slowed down, its head turning this way and that as it looked for me.

Although it helped muffle the sound of my steps, it didn't silence them. I set off one banger, the one furthest away from us. With such a powerful sound, one would expect a huge crater to be left behind. But it was a distraction tool, not meant to cause damage to the nearby flora and fauna. The explosion merely caused some dirt to fly up into the air. The creature stopped, its torso jerking around to look behind it.

Controlling my breathing and keeping my movements as silent as possible, I approached the creature. As soon as it started moving towards the explosion to investigate, I set off the second banger. Taking advantage of the noise, I rushed closer, a blade in both my main and secondary right hands, and my main left forearm raised before my chest, ready to deploy my shield as soon as I struck the beast.

As expected, the second explosion startled the Nharmyth. It stopped and turned its head towards the noise. The long, frustrated scream that poured out of its throat further covered the sound of my approach. I stopped barely a meter away, the shamia essence released by the bangers helping to cover my scent.

Bracing, I waited for the beast to start moving towards the second explosion before launching my attack. In keeping with its slithering movements, the Nharmyth swayed left. As soon as it began swaying right, I lunged, stabbing with all my strength at its armpit. At the same time my main blade sank in, I raised my shield, and slashed at the closest snake heads, lopping off two of them.

Although my main blade caused some damage, it didn't go deep enough to inflict a lethal wound. The angle had been off and struck a bone. The Nharmyth's high-pitched screech nearly deafened me. It whipped its left arm around, bashing the side of my right shoulder, sending me flying back. Despite landing brutally with a thud that partially knocked the wind out of me, I considered this a blessing. The remaining snakes—at least seven of them—had been blindly nipping at me. While my energy shield had blocked a couple of snakes, had I remained in range a few seconds longer, one of them might have caught me.

However, the impact had caused a small glitch in my stealth shield, giving the creature a brief glimpse of my location. I barely had time to roll out of the path of the stream of acid it spit my way. Surging forward, it randomly swiped its vicious claws at the ground and surrounding area where I'd landed moments prior.

I detonated my third banger to cover part of the sound of me moving further away. Although the Nharmyth lifted its head to look behind it with its forehead eye, it didn't turn around this time to look for me. The foul thing was learning. It hesitated, its large chest eye flicking this way and that, seeking signs of my presence.

To my utter annoyance, it dismissed the explosion and slithered forward, swiping at dead air with its crowbar hands, its snake heads also randomly biting in the hopes of a lucky catch. Moving with careful steps, I backed away quietly while reflecting on my next course of action. I didn't have my proper hunting equipment and could no longer fool it with the four bangers I had left.

However, the Nharmyth resuming to spray the area with its acid in a wide arc forced me to take action. As soon as I began running, it emitted a triumphant cry and gave chase. It couldn't see me, but the sound of my feet gave me away. Spitting acid in my general direction, it closed in at an impossible speed. Knowing I'd never outrun it, I made a sharp turn around a large tree to block its line of sight and leapt up to catch one of its lower branches to hoist myself up.

By the time the Nharmyth caught up, it had missed whatever glitch my stealth shield might have had when I climbed the tree. It slowed down, its snakes stopping their hissing so that it could listen for me. I all but held my breath. It resumed spitting acid in the surrounding area. The ground sizzled as the acid ate through whatever organic matter littered it.

I cast a glance at the cave located about fifty meters away. Despite the narrow opening, I would be able to squeeze through it. Within its protection, I could impede the creature's efforts coming in until the Ordosians arrived. The question was whether I could reach it in one piece.

Hearts pounding, I watched the Nharmyth below me slither past the tree I was hiding in. When it abruptly stopped spraying acid, my spirit soared.

Has it depleted its reserves?

That would be a game changer. Without the acid, I'd be able to go toe to toe with it. A new plan quickly formed in my mind. Wanting to test that theory, I threw a banger not too far behind me, then aimed my blaster at the beast. As I'd hoped, as soon as I set it off, the Nharmyth lifted its head to look behind itself. Without missing a beat, I fired, taking out its forehead eye.

The monster wailed, whipping its head back down so fast I believed for a split second that it would faceplant. But it straightened, its arms flailing before it angrily turned towards me. To my shock, a powerful stream of acid shot my way. Seconds before it would hit me, I jumped down onto the opposite side of the tree and ran.

Enraged, the Nharmyth chased after me. Knowing my energy shield wouldn't last very long against the acid, I couldn't afford to have my next move fail. I disabled my stealth shield and turned around to face the creature circling around the tree. Standing my ground as it rapidly closed in on my position, I shot its chest eye.

The way it doubled over, you'd think I'd speared right through him. It fell face down, sliding a short distance on the ground, carried by its momentum. Not giving it a chance to recover while it screamed in agony, I reactivated my stealth shield and rushed forward. Energy shield raised in case it spit at me, I chopped off another snake, missing the other one I'd also tried to decapitate.

To my dismay, the Nharmyth straightened, revealing a still functional chest eye, bleeding though it was. The claws of its right arm nearly eviscerated me, forcing me to throw myself out of reach. I fell on the ground and rolled back onto my feet, only to find myself dodging the creature's massive tail. It whipped that tail around in a swiping motion. I couldn't tell if it was in an attempt to strike me or to wrap around my body and crush it the way Szaro had done to Djomoug a few years ago.

I dove over it just seconds before it would have hit me, going into a forward roll and back onto my feet. Without pausing, I ran as fast as my feet allowed, while throwing my remaining three bangers behind me. I set them off seconds later, skidding to a stop as I spun around. The Nharmyth reared, startled by the three loud explosions in front of it, giving me just the opening I needed. With deadly accuracy, I fired at its chest eye twice in quick succession. Both shots found their mark.

The beast doubled over again, this time keeping its upper body propped up by resting its crooked 'hands' on the ground. As it shouted in pain, bleeding from both its eyes and the severed snake tentacles, I contemplated rushing it again to finish it. But then I reconsidered. I couldn't risk getting caught by a swipe of its tail or by any acid it had remaining.

I dropped my stealth shield and baited it to follow me as I ran to the cave. I needed to end this soon. This wasn't the type of clean kills I liked to perform. There was no honor in needlessly prolonging your prey's suffering. With my proper gear, I usually completed a kill against such a creature in under two minutes.

With the snakes' limited vision range, the Nharmyth relied on sound to catch up to me, which allowed me to enter the cave with time to spare. The Atreall Queen immediately began to squeal, a high-pitched sound that would be barely perceptible for most species. I spared her a glance, only long enough to make sure she wasn't a threat to me, then refocused on the beast.

I stood sideways near the opening, grateful that the wide horns of the Nharmyth prevented its head from getting inside. It still stuck its mouth in to spit more acid while its claws resumed their assault on the rock walls. For a split second, I considered shooting inside its mouth but decided to continue blinding it instead so that it would be completely helpless. I shot at two snakes' heads and grazed a third with my blade just as the creature was pulling away.

Any other beast would have retreated by now, but not a Nharmyth. They were far too single-minded. We repeated that dance a couple more times before I finally went on the offensive. Blinded, weakened by blood loss, and with only two snakes remaining, the creature no longer represented a major threat.

When it pulled back, I squeezed back out of the cave, seizing its arms with my secondary hands to keep them from eviscerating me. Simultaneously, I ripped off the two last snakes with my main hands. Growling in pain and anger, the creature blindly tried to bite my face off. I dodged left before grabbing its neck with my main left hand. I wrapped my legs around its body as it struggled to shake me off. My biceps burned from the effort of attempting to restrain its arms and head. But I ignored them.

Pulling out my dagger, I stabbed at its right armpit, its erratic movements throwing off my aim, once… twice… The fifth time, the blade sank in deep. The Nharmyth stiffened. It emitted a brief, startled gurgling sound before a violent shudder coursed through its body. Then it went limp.

I jumped off it moments before it collapsed to the ground.

With every muscle of my body screaming from the effort, I let myself drop to my knees next to the creature. As I caught my breath and gave myself a minute to recover, I gazed at the stinking corpse of the Nharmyth. Feeling less than impressed by the butchery I'd done instead of my usual clean work, I shook my head in disgust and pushed up to my feet.

I entered the cave to check upon the young queen. She lay half on her side, half on her back in a visibly uncomfortable position, no doubt from having attempted to flee.

I whispered soothingly to her as I carefully approached. Panicked, the Atreall attempted to crawl back again, the weight of her overflowing abdomen keeping her pinned down. She'd also obviously drained most of her energy from her previous efforts to hide from the Nharmyth. Although she tried to claw at me and bite my face with her mandibles, I very easily restrained her. Taking great care, I turned her into a more comfortable position on the stone slab she had selected to lie on.

I didn't immediately move away. Gently caressing the soft fur around her nape, I spoke reassuring words to her until her trembling subsided. Her big, black eyes observed me with curiosity as I moved the Atreall male corpses within her reach so that she could easily feed on them when needed. That task done, I went to sit on a large rock a short distance away from her, hoping it would help make her feel safe.

I tapped a message to Belle on my com. To my relief, she immediately responded.

"Oh, my God, Bayron! I was so scared for you," Belle exclaimed as soon as the communication was established. "I can't believe you jumped on that creature like that!"

My brain froze. "How do you know that?"

"My camera! It was still on that monster. I shifted it to you after you killed it. It recorded everything."

"Right," I said, having forgotten all about it in the heat of battle. My hearts sank to have such a messy kill immortalized.

"Master Bron contacted the Ordosians. They are on their way to you. And so am I. I'm onboard a Federation shuttle with two hunters to bring you back here," Belle added quickly before I could go off on her. "I can't wait to see you. I was so scared."

As much as I disliked her coming back to this area, I also ached to feel her in my embrace. "I'm fine, my mate," I said in a soothing tone.

My gaze locked with the queen, who continued to observe me for a while longer before finally reaching for one of the males. She tore off one of his limbs and started eating.

"Is she all right?" Belle asked.

"Yes. She didn't get hurt. But the Ordosians can properly evaluate her when they arrive."

Even as I finished speaking those words, the queen stretched her arm towards me in what I could only interpret as a beckoning gesture.

"What's going on?" my female asked.

"I'm not sure," I said as I approached the queen.

To my shock, she shoved the last bite into her mouth then slowly started rubbing her clawed hands over my arms and chest, like a mother would to make sure her offspring was unharmed.

"Is she groping you?" Belle asked, sounding more baffled than jealous.

"No. But I'm not sure what—"

I never finished that sentence. The queen's lips parted, and before I could react, she spit a dart at my neck. My throat immediately felt numb, the tingling sensation spreading at an exponential rate as my vision blurred.

I only managed to take one step back before I fell to my knees. Through the com, I vaguely heard Belle screaming my name. My tongue having turned to lead, I never got a chance to tell my mate that I loved her as a veil of darkness descended before my eyes.

The last thing I saw was the queen's face descending towards mine, her mandibles parting and a needle-like protrusion coming out of her mouth.

CHAPTER 16
ANNABELLE

When the queen attacked Bayron, I lost my shit. Bryna, our pilot from the Federation's extraction team, ordered her colleague Tarn to go calm me down. In my despair, I wanted to jump out of the shuttle to run to my husband. How was that even remotely logical? It wasn't. But rational thoughts had left the building the instant my man collapsed.

Tears freely rolled down my cheeks as I watched the Atreall leaning over Bayron. I couldn't see what she was doing. My mate appeared unconscious, his head resting on the stone platform the queen was lying on. As her body lightly heaved, she seemed to be either eating the flesh off his shoulders or drinking his blood.

A million thoughts raced through my mind, from cursing the creature for betraying her savior, to hating myself for inciting Bayron to save her, to berating the Ordosians for not being there already, and to praying to every power in the universe to spare his life.

After what felt like a millennium, the queen finally moved her head away from Bayron. A choked sob escaped me when I saw she hadn't beheaded him. Although my husband remained unconscious, he didn't seem in distress. I could only hope that the red streaks around the bite in his neck weren't signs of a poison or toxin coursing through him.

"How much farther are we?" I asked for the thousandth time.

"We'll be there soon, Belle, I promise," Tarn said in an apologetic voice.

Halfway through him speaking those words, the blessed silhouette of an Ordosian finally appeared on my camera, and he slipped through the opening of the cave.

"Oh thank you, God!" I exclaimed, wiping the tears blurring my vision with the back of my hand.

To my shock, the queen appeared to take a protective stance over Bayron. Szaro, in the lead, rattled his tail to appease her. I watched in confusion as she seemed to want to cling to my husband's arm as two other Ordosians picked up Bayron to lay him down a short distance away while Serena ran a handheld scanner over him.

"We are beginning our descent," Tarn said.

I jerked my head up to look out the window. Not waiting for the shuttle to land, I unclasped my seatbelt and ran to the door. Another reckless move, but I didn't care. Tarn opened his mouth, likely to tell me to return to my seat. However, my expression warned him to leave it the fuck alone. His shoulders slumped in defeat. He closed his mouth and shook his head in disapproval.

As soon as we touched down, I repeatedly slapped my palm against the door to urge it to open. No sooner did it start parting than I squeezed through, shouting Bayron's name. Ignoring the stinky, butchered remains of the Nharmyth still lying in front of the cave, I ran inside, bumping my right shoulder rather painfully against the rock face in my haste. I grunted in pain but didn't slow down.

Serena rose from her crouching position next to my husband when she saw me enter. "It's okay! He's fine!" she said in a reassuring tone.

I all but threw myself on him, kneeling by his side. My hand flew to his neck, but I held back at the last minute, not wanting to further infect the wound. I caressed his face and kissed his lips, terrified to find my strong Beast so helpless.

"What did she do to him?" I asked frantically, pointing at his neck. "What is that? Why did she attack him?"

"She did not attack him," Szaro replied behind me in a soothing voice as he slithered close to us. "This mark is her royal seal. She claimed him."

"WHAT?!" My head jerked towards the Atreall Queen, who was looking at me with the oddest look, her small mandibles working as if in a threat to behead me. "What the hell do you mean by 'claimed'?" I asked, fighting between a sense of outrage, disbelief, and the most irrational jealousy.

Despite being a female, the Atreall Queen couldn't be any kind of mate to Bayron. Aside from being a completely incompatible species, she was the size of an eight-year-old child.

Szaro chuckled and wound his long tail behind him to lower himself closer to me, still kneeling on the ground. "It's not what you're thinking. She acknowledged he saved her and thus claimed him as her protector. This is the mark she would give her Queen's Guard."

I glared at the queen, unsure how I felt about this. "He is *my* protector. She needs to find her own," I muttered, which only made Szaro chuckle again and Serena smile. "But why is he unconscious?"

Szaro took on a serious expression that had me freaking out again. "Calm, Belle. There is no cause to panic. This reaction is normal. When an Atreall Queen claims her guards, she doesn't just give them a mark, but she also enhances them. She first gave him an anesthetic, then implanted him with a microorganism that will act like a small gland."

"Oh, my God! Will it hurt him? Can you remove it?" I asked, looking at the wound around Bayron's neck in horror.

Szaro hesitated. "We could remove it, but I would advise against it."

"Why? Will it cause complications?"

He shook his head. "No, not at all. It is safe to remove it. However, this is a tremendous gift from the queen. I am quite envious of that honor."

Some of the tension stiffening my back faded as I looked at him in surprise. "Really? Why? What does it do?"

"It is the same type of gland that allows Atrealls to feed on the parasites who choke our flora. Its secretions will cleanse his system from most toxins and make him immune to a vast array of poisons, toxins, and bacteria."

"Whoa! Okay, that's actually cool," I conceded, looking at the wound with new eyes. "How long is he going to remain unconscious? And how do we know that his body isn't having a negative reaction to this foreign body inside him?"

"Assimilating the graft can be painful, which is why the queen sedates her chosen ones first. Atreall Guards usually remain unconscious for a couple of days, but they are much smaller," Szaro said pensively. "Considering the size and mass of your mate, I wouldn't be surprised if it lasted longer. She injected him with a significant amount of anesthetic. While we have no reason to suspect adverse reactions from him, we will keep him under observation until he has recovered."

"What do you mean?" I asked, my back stiffening again.

"He means that we have contacted the Elders and explained the situation to them. Under the circumstances, they have agreed to allow us to take Bayron back to Krada so that we can care for him," Serena said in a soft voice.

"I will *not* separate from my husband while he's injured!" I exclaimed, ready to fight.

Serena smiled. "We'd never dream of asking that of you. Of course, you can come as well. Salha—my sister-in-law—is currently preparing a guest house for the two of you."

The excited squeal that began to rise in my throat at the prospect of setting foot in Krada died almost instantly as a somber thought filled my mind.

"Hmmm, Bayron is Zamorian," I said, casting a nervous sideways glance at Szaro. "Are you sure you can handle his medical needs?"

"Yes, Belle, we can," Szaro replied in a reassuring tone. "When I bonded with my Serena, Kayog sent us the most advanced medical pod in the galaxy to make sure her needs would be catered to while our healers learned of human biology. It has access to all the medical databases to care for a Zamorian."

"Okay then. Yeah, I'm totally down for a recovery stint in Krada," I said while caressing Bayron's face, my chest constricting with a love I could no longer deny for my beast.

After a brief discussion, the Ordosians once more blew me away by agreeing to let the extraction team of the Hunters Federation fly Bayron to Krada, as he would be a lot more comfortable on a hover stretcher than bound to one of their strange drayshan mounts.

When they carried my husband out of the cave, the piteous keening sound the queen emitted nearly broke my heart. In a way, I could relate to the despair she felt at the thought of her protector being taken away from her. One Ordosian once more soothed her with the rattling of his tail, but her gaze lingered on the opening of the cave long after Bayron had vanished from view. With an apologetic glance her way, I exited the cave as well.

To my pleasant surprise, Bryna and Tarn had already recovered the remains of the Nharmyth, securing it in the cold room at the back of the shuttle. As much as I hated knowing we'd travel with the wretched thing aboard, I was glad not to have to lay eyes on it again.

After settling Bayron inside the shuttle, I rejoiced at Serena deciding to fly with us as we headed for Krada. We passed the

Ordosians that had already left on the back of their mounts. Well, most of them anyway. Two had remained with the queen to watch over her until some workers and guards had hatched and grown enough to care for her.

Despite knowing that my husband was fine, I failed to enjoy the stunning view of Trangor during the twenty-minute flight to the village. My gaze remained locked on his face, looking for any sign of pain or discomfort. However, as we began our descent, Krada's stunning beauty demanded my attention.

A ring of mountains enclosed the sprawling village. While they had carved most of the dwellings directly into the mountain, countless one-story houses surrounded the town square. The pale stone they'd been built with gave the village a tropical feel, seamlessly blending modern and high-tech elements to the houses. A great deal of vegetation surrounded them, from colorful flowers to exotic trees. An elegant stone pavement marked the walkways connecting the streets of the village.

At the left and right edges of the town square and residential area, a series of buildings gave off commercial or industrial vibes. They weren't massive like our shopping malls, just a much bigger version of the pale stone residences. The one exception was a vast atrium or interior garden to the left of the village.

We settled on the landing pad near the clearing next to the town square. Looking as intimidated as I felt, Bryna and Tarn took Bayron's hover stretcher outside of the shuttle. Three older Ordosians stood in the center of the square, waiting for us. All around, more Ordosians than I could count stood quietly, observing us, a few more joining the crowd to witness our arrival.

To my dismay, the Federation employees no sooner left the stretcher in the square than they respectfully nodded at the Elders, gave me a sheepish smile, then got back inside the shuttle. I watched them take off in disbelief before turning back to the Ordosians. If not for Serena by my side, I would have been a total wreck. Swallowing hard, I set the stretcher to follow and nervously approached the Elders, walking a step behind Serena.

"Welcome to Krada, Annabelle Parker. I am Elder Krathi. This is Elder Jyotha," the older female said, pointing at the other mature female to her right. "And this is Elder Iskal," she added, gesturing at the male to her left.

"Thank you, Elder Krathi. Thanks to all of you for generously offering to care for my husband while he recovers," I said with a firmer voice than I expected, my gratitude plain to hear. "It is a great honor, especially considering how protective you are of your lands."

The older female smiled, her alien features softening. "He saved an Atreall Queen in a time when she was desperately in need. A debt is owed. Serena will take you to the dwelling that has been appointed for you and your mate. During your stay, she will be your point of contact."

I nodded and gave Serena a shy smile. She winked in response. I barely repressed a nervous laugh, remembering how the Zamorian female had almost kicked my butt, thinking I was coming on to her child when I'd winked at him.

"You are not a prisoner, but a guest. Therefore, you are free to come and go within the village. Do not go into the forest or beyond without an escort. This is for your own safety," Elder Krathi warned.

"I won't. Thank you so much for your hospitality," I said, moved beyond words.

The Elders smiled, then Serena gestured for me to follow her. I initially thought she'd go to the dwelling in question. To my relief, she first took us to their clinic. My jaw nearly dropped when Serena and the Ordosian female healer named Teichi lifted Bayron off the stretcher to place him inside the medical pod. I'd heard that bonding with Szaro had enhanced Serena, but I never expected it would make her this strong.

After a string of tests, during which I undoubtedly tried the two females' patience with my constant fidgeting, they reassured me that everything looked good. We only had to bide our time while waiting for Bayron to finish assimilating the queen's gift and waking up on his own. To my delight, the medical pod cleaned all the remaining blood and gore off Bayron that I hadn't managed to remove on our journey here.

Once again, the two females effortlessly moved my giant of a husband back onto the hover stretcher. Serena set it to follow, then took me to the guest house that had been prepared for us.

"You will find it rather barren and with very minimalistic furnishing," Serena said apologetically. "Ordosians only decorate their houses once mated."

"Oh, don't worry about that. I don't need much, as long as I have a cushioned place to sleep, and the roof isn't leaking, I'm good!" I said with enthusiasm.

She smiled. "We can do a bit better than that. We adapted it to cater to basic human needs, with a proper hygiene room and kitchen."

I blinked, confused that she felt the need to specify that. Serena explained her cultural shock when she first arrived in Krada and found out Ordosians didn't normally have those two rooms in their houses as they shared communal showers and public latrine-style hygiene rooms. Since they only ate once every couple of weeks, sometimes even up to a month, using space in their houses for a kitchen made no sense. Anyway, they ate their food raw, and usually swallowed their still living prey whole.

I'd suspected as much. Having it confirmed somewhat made me shudder. Although I still thought the Ordosians' sexiness levels were off the charts, I doubted I'd enjoy watching their faces get unnaturally distended as they tried to swallow something bigger than their heads.

"When my parents visit—which really isn't all that often—

they stay here," Serena explained as she opened the door to the dwelling.

Unlike the other entrances, this one lacked any intricate carvings adorning its façade. That was to be expected, as only mated males carved those decorations to honor the story, milestones, and achievements in their union.

She gave me a quick tour of the very simple three-bedroom dwelling. Although clean, there truly was nothing memorable about it. They had roughly carved the pale stones of the walls. The chairs around the table were extremely basic but seemed to have a plush cushion, just like the couch in the living area. A large vidscreen hung on the wall across from the couch. While practical, I had no plans to watch it as I wanted to make the most of my short stay in Krada. The bedrooms each contained a large bed with divine mattresses, a vast wardrobe, and a dresser.

The larger one also contained a massive cushion that I immediately recognized as a dog bed. Serena chuckled when my face lit up.

"Yes, Ferach will come live with you during your stay. As soon as we've got you settled in, we'll go get him," she said.

It took every ounce of my willpower not to pull her into a bone-crushing hug.

To my relief, Szaro arrived just as we were preparing to move Bayron from the hover stretcher onto the master bedroom bed. But my gratitude at being spared the embarrassment of showing how weak I was compared to them, gave way to an almost irrational joy when I noticed Ferach padding alongside the Ordosian.

His four eyes immediately glowed with great intensity. He emitted a deep, guttural half growl, half whine as he ran towards me. The stone wolf jumped on me, knocking me to the floor. Winded by the impact, it took me a moment to regain my bearings while Ferach was frantically rubbing his face against mine. I liked that he didn't lick, which wasn't very hygienic, not to mention how I hated the stickiness. I chuckled, closing my arms around him, shocked to see how big he'd grown.

"Wow, sweetie! You're massive!" I said, still giggling.

"And he will grow even bigger," Szaro said. "At full maturity, he will be big enough that you could, in theory, ride him like a mount."

I looked at Ferach with round eyes, while getting him to calm down a little. "Well that sounds impressive. But you're not a mount. You're a tough cookie and an amazing wolf."

That earned me another rubbing of his face against mine, not that he had understood a thing I'd said. He finally let me up to go sniff at Bayron.

"How is he doing?" I asked, gesturing with my chin at the pup.

"He's faring better than we had hoped," Szaro responded. "His leg is fully healed. It should not pain him going forward. We've been able to mostly mend his adrenal glands. They are a little atrophied but steadily growing. I can't promise that they will ever grow to be 100% functional, but he's now able to turn his skin to stone. It's not as thick as it should be. However, it should be enough for him to hunt in relative safety. With time, we have faith it will improve."

"Thank you so much for everything you did," I said, my throat constricting.

Szaro's face melted into the kindest expression as he smiled. "His treatment is not over, but caring for him has been an honor. Thank *you* for making us discover this new to us species and for allowing us to take part in his journey towards recovery. We are the guardians of our world. To be able to bring a healing touch beyond our frontiers is a true blessing."

I grimaced to hide how emotional I was getting. "I can see how you charmed Serena. You sure have a way with words."

Serena laughed, a tender expression on her face as she gazed upon her husband. "He sure does."

The couple stayed with me a short while longer before taking their leave. That evening, Serena came back to invite me to have dinner with them. At the same time, she brought plenty of changes of clothes for me and drawing material normally used by the Ordosian artists. Initially, I almost took her up on her offer of going to fetch some of my personal stuff back at the base camp but decided against it. They had given me a unique opportunity to experience life in Krada for a short time. I would live their way while it lasted.

Over the next three days, Serena and I spent quite a bit of time together. It felt surreal to get to hang out with someone I'd been fangirling over for so long. I finally got to draw her and her family, first directly in front of the stunning façade of their house that Szaro had so lovingly carved in her honor, and then on their breathtaking terrace at the back.

The damn thing overlooked a hidden valley that served as a sanctuary for countless unique creatures. Naturally, I sketched the heck out of them, too. I'd taken the hover platform down into the valley and settled on the grass near the river that ran through that former volcano to draw. Between two brush strokes, I had to monitor Ferach so he wouldn't go chasing after the local fauna. Halfway through my current piece, Serena dropped by with some refreshments. She settled on the grass next to me.

"Oh wow! That's really amazing!" Serena said, staring at the image I was drawing. "You're really talented."

"Thank you," I said with a silly grin, my cheeks flushing with pleasure. "I've been so inspired since I married Bayron. Until now, I'd never been exposed to such amazingly exotic subjects. And Trangor certainly is a treasure trove of unique and fantastic creatures. I wish I had four hands like my husband to draw multiple things at once. There are so many wonders and so little time."

Serena gave me an odd, assessing look. "I didn't realize you enjoyed drawing creatures. I thought you were only about people."

"Oh no, I love to draw everything," I said enthusiastically. I flicked the pages on the drawing pad Serena had given me to use during my stay here. "See? Here's the Atreall Queen, that dreadful Nharmyth, the adorable Voreas, and even Scogas! My camera is busy recording every creature in this sanctuary so that I can make large scale illustrations of them on canvas once I get back to my studio. But as you can see, I've also been drawing people. You and your family, obviously, but also lots of my husband in battle, not to mention all the ones of his clan on our ship."

Serena pursed her lips as she flipped the pages, looking at dynamic poses of Bayron battling the Nharmyth, others of him fighting Flayers, and even one where he was helping the Atreall Queen back into a more comfortable position.

"What? What are you thinking?" I asked, feeling nervous at the sight of her pensive expression.

"I'm thinking that these are insanely good. You've really captured the spirit and the intensity of the hunt with those drawings of Bayron in battle," Serena mused out loud. "I bet you anything the Federation would kill to have such images as marketing and promotional material. You should show them your work. Hunt Master Bron Kflen will be all over them."

I shifted on the grass, a warm, fuzzy feeling spreading through me at such an avalanche of compliments. "You think so?" I asked timidly. "I really love what I've been putting out lately. I'm just not sure where to go from here. Bayron was telling me to put together a collection for a showing but..."

"Absolutely! If you put together a collection, and all the pieces are even just half as good as these ones, you'll be an overnight sensation," Serena said.

I snorted, flattered but also realistic about it. "Nobody knows me. Aside from Bayron's family likely showing up to support me, it would otherwise be crickets."

Serena waved a dismissive hand. "Oh no, sweetie. It will be packed. Your husband is now a major celebrity for saving the Queen, *and* you have me as a friend. While I never liked the socialite lifestyle of my parents, that didn't stop me from making a lot of contacts. My mother will demand to organize the debut showing of an up-and-coming new artist. And she only mingles with people with deep pockets. You paint, we'll take care of the rest."

"Oh, my God! Are you serious?!" I asked in disbelief.

She nodded. "Very much so. This is really good. In fact, when you are not busy becoming the next big name in art, what would you say about a collaboration with me? As you know, I've been writing a detailed encyclopedia of the flora and fauna of Trangor. While I have included pictures of the plants and creatures, I would love some dynamic illustrations like these."

"Oh wow! This is wicked cool! Yes, absolutely! I'd love to."

Ever the incorrigible impulsive, I pulled her into a bone crushing hug. Before I could freak out at my own boldness, Serena burst out laughing and returned my embrace.

Jealous as always, Ferach pushed his head in between us to force us to release each other. We snorted and included him in the hug.

My roots were spreading deeper.

CHAPTER 17
BAYRON

My eyelids fluttered open. For a second, I stared at the ceiling, roughly carved into pale stone, without quite seeing it. My brain felt foggy, like after a night of overindulgence with Strovia wine, but without the headache that normally accompanied it.

Usually instantly alert when I woke, I struggled to focus for a moment. However, the absence of my mate's soft body wrapped around mine snapped me out of my daze. Belle *always* slept in, not even stirring when I untangled myself from her to get up in the morning.

I shot up into a sitting position, my mind registering a billion bits of information about my strange surroundings while parsing through the flood of memories.

Where in Khivolt's name am I? Where's my mate?

Even as I jumped out of the small—but insanely comfortable—bed, my hand flew to my neck, touching where the queen had stabbed me with her dart. My fingers rubbed over an oddly shaped scar. Judging by its feel and the absence of pain, it seemed to be a properly healed wound. I couldn't perceive any ache or other discomfort in my body, aside from a slight stiffness —the kind one got from extended immobility.

I was naked but for tight black shorts. Considering my last memory was of the queen attacking me, someone had rescued me. But where was I? Although clean, this roughly carved room didn't belong to the Hunters Federation's base camp. This could only mean…

"No way," I whispered to myself.

And yet, the lingering scent of my mate in the room was unmistakable. The padded cushion in the corner of the room, clearly a dog bed, could only belong to Ferach.

As if called by that thought, I heard the distant whine of the stone wolf, followed by his quickly approaching steps. I walked up to the bedroom door and opened it. Down the large corridor, Ferach broke into a run when he saw me. While I braced for the inevitable impact of the surprisingly large pup jumping on me, I only had eyes for the female behind him.

"Bayron," Belle whispered, her eyes misting as a glowing smile stretched her lips.

Leaping from two meters away, Ferach jumped into my arms. I caught him, stunned by how much he had grown since he'd gone with the Ordosians. He rubbed his face over mine, the whole time wiggling excitedly in my arms.

But as Belle reached us, I put him down and ignored his whiny growls demanding my attention. I pulled my mate into my embrace. She didn't throw herself into my arms with her usual excessive eagerness. Instead, she gently wrapped her arms around me, her gaze locked with mine. My female looked at me with such adoration and happiness, my hearts ached.

"You came back to me," she whispered.

"Always, my love," I whispered back.

A short laugh filled with joy escaped her while tears ran down her cheeks. "I love you, Bayron," she said before hoisting herself on her tiptoes to kiss me.

I claimed her lips, pouring the depth of the emotions I felt for her into the kiss. Belle melted against me as our tongues mingled. Love, not lust or unbridled passion, stirred us this time. I couldn't tell how long it lasted, but when our lips parted, we locked eyes. My hand gently caressed her cheek as my gaze roamed affectionately over her beautiful face.

"I thought I would never hold you like this again," I whispered in an almost pained voice. "I thought I would never savor the divine taste of your lips, or lay eyes on the perfection that you are. My hearts and my soul are yours, my Belle. I almost died out there without having ever told you that I love you. That is not a mistake I will commit twice."

More tears poured out of Belle's beautiful blue eyes even as she beamed at me.

"I love you, too, Bayron. You are my impossible dream come true. When the queen attacked you, my heart shattered. I thought I would die right there with you from a broken heart."

My chest constricted with guilt and shame that my negligence had caused her such distress. "I'm sorry, my mate. I should have been more careful."

She smiled and shook her head while giving me a gentle squeeze. "You had no reason to expect the queen would do this. I just thank God she had no ill intentions towards you."

"What *did* she do to me? What happened? And where are we?" I asked, once more touching the scar in my neck while casting a confused look at our surroundings.

She smiled and gently patted my chest, her thumb caressing her brand on me. "We should have a seat so that I can update you on all that's happened."

I complied and let her lure me to the couch in the living area. Once again, the extreme simplicity of the dwelling and very minimalistic furniture struck me. I didn't know whether to take this as a slight that they should give us such basic accommodations.

After I sat on the loveseat, Belle settled in my lap and launched into a detailed explanation of the events that took place since the queen stung me.

"Serena and the Ordosians looked after me?" I asked, disbelievingly. "They *offered* to bring *me* here, on their sacred lands?"

Belle chuckled and nodded. "I had a similar reaction. You cannot begin to understand how important what you did was for them and their planet. She's the only new queen born in the past twenty-eight years. Since you rescued her, the Ordosians have been scouting all the areas where Atreall nests have been known to exist in search of a second queen that might need protection. They found none so far. Had she died, entire forests would have followed suit. You're quite the hero right now."

I shrugged to hide my embarrassment. "I'm sure the Ordosians would have found a workaround."

"They have some Atreall DNA that they could use to clone the species in case it became extinct, but it could take many years, if not decades, for it to be viable. And there is never any guarantee that it won't cause some mutations that will deprive the new breed of the current one's abilities," my mate said. "What you did was important to their world and to the galactic alliance as a whole. If there was ever a time for your Zamorian braggadocio to show itself, it would be now!"

I shrugged again, unsure how to handle this. "We brag when we compete and best others with our skills and wits. Here, I just protected a helpless, pregnant female. It was the natural thing to do."

Belle shook her head at me as if I was a hopeless case. I touched my neck, my fingers tracing the scar left by the queen's bite.

"Can their healers remove this mark? I would like it gone as soon as possible. If not, I'll ask Dr. Ahmad at the base camp," I said.

My mate slightly recoiled, and an uncertain look descended

over her features. "Why would you want to remove it? I thought Zamorians considered each scar as a battle trophy?"

"Not this," I said in a clipped tone. "This wasn't a battle. No female but you should ever put her mark on me."

Belle nodded, looking pleased by my words. "I agree, more than you know. But this isn't the same kind of branding. Or rather, her intention in doing so is completely different. In fact, it looks like a sun shining over my tree on your chest."

"I don't care what her intentions were or what it looks like. No female brands me but you. Returning home with her mark on me would be as big a humiliation to you as you cutting my braid would be to me."

She flinched and licked her lips nervously as she glanced at the mark. "I see. Hmm… We will need to ask the Ordosians. She didn't just mark you but implanted you with something that makes you immune to a lot of toxins and poisons. I like knowing that it makes you safer out there."

"No hunting advantage justifies disrespecting my mate," I replied stubbornly.

Belle gave me the most tender of smiles and caressed my cheek. "Well, let's see what the Ordosians will say about it. I would also prefer the mark be removed, but not the benefits. I like knowing you have increased chances of coming back home to me unscathed, rather than having to spend another four days of you in a drug-induced coma."

I stiffened and stared at my mate in horror. "Four days? I was unconscious for four days?!" I exclaimed in shock and disbelief.

Belle nodded with an apologetic expression. "Apparently, it is painful for the host to assimilate the implant the queen gave you. Considering your size, she injected you with tons of anesthetic for it to last long enough."

A string of curses poured out of my mouth. "I need to get back to the hunt. By now, I've certainly lost the lead. I've probably even fallen to the last place. Where's my armband?" I asked, taking my mate off my lap so that I could get up.

"Sweetie, you can't run off to hunt. We need to have the healer examine you to make sure everything is fine," Belle interjected with a worried expression. "Szaro also said he needed to talk to you."

"I do not have time for this, Annabelle," I said, fighting to keep my anger in check. "I have to go back out there."

"But why? What's the hurry? Isn't your health more important than killing a few more critters? You said it yourself, we don't need the credits," she countered, looking both confused and on the verge of getting angry herself.

"I don't give a grummoll's ass about credits," I snapped. "But by Kromor's teeth, I will *not* allow you to be married to the biggest loser of the hunt!"

Belle's jaw dropped. She blinked and stared at me as if I'd grown a second head.

"Bayron, you are *not* the biggest loser. I don't care what the Federation's kill scores say, *you* are the biggest winner of this hunt."

"By finishing last?" I challenged.

"By single handedly defeating one of the most vicious creatures on Trangor without proper hunting equipment," Belle retorted as if it was self-evident. "By saving an extremely rare creature for the benefit of every member of the galactic alliance. By earning the gratitude and the respect of the Ordosians, who are not a very forgiving species. By being the first hunter who has ever been invited to enter and reside in an Ordosian village out of sheer hospitality, thereby making *me* the first hunter spouse to also enjoy this once-in-a-lifetime honor. By being the reason Ferach has a new lease on life. And by being the first non-Atreall being to have received a royal blessing. I don't give two shits about what anyone else thinks. *You* are the biggest winner of this hunt, and I couldn't be prouder to be your wife."

It was my turn to gape at my mate, transfixed. What could I answer to that? I couldn't reconcile the thought of being a winner when I would come in dead last in a competition. And yet, my female's pride in me couldn't be denied.

Belle gently grabbed my braid and caressed its length, her eyes locked with mine and a tender expression on her face.

"I know ranking high is important to you and your people. But you are more important to me. I don't want to hold you back. If only for my peace of mind, please let the healer confirm that you're fine. It will be quick. And then you can go kick ass again. Okay?"

I pursed my lips but grunted my assent.

She beamed at me. "Thank you, my love. But don't kill yourself out there. Don't forget that, as far as I'm concerned, you've already won."

Once again, I grunted in a non-committal fashion, which made her giggle.

As I quickly got dressed, Belle updated me with the wonderful news about Ferach. I would need to find a way to properly thank the Ordosians for what they had done for both the pup and me. When she caught my critical glance at the bedroom's rough walls, my mate explained how an Ordosian male would only polish and decorate a dwelling for his female once he mated. Otherwise, any home had this half-finished, blank canvas look.

I thanked her for that information as we headed out of the house. Silently, I berated myself for my uncharitable assumptions that they'd put us in an unfinished house as an underhanded slight. Why did we always think the worst or look for insults in every single word or action others took?

Ferach tagged along as we headed for the clinic. Not only was he due for another treatment, but he wanted to be with us. Seeing the deeper bond he'd forged with my Belle rekindled the worry in my hearts. If the Ordosians had truly fixed him, he would need to be released to the wild to avoid stifling his nature.

When we entered the clinic, a female named Salha took Ferach to examine him. A different female, the healer named Teichi ran a few quick tests while bombarding me with a billion questions. Belle had been right saying it wouldn't take too much time. They had been closely monitoring me while I'd been unconscious and merely wanted confirmation from me that I didn't feel any discomfort.

I got out of the medical pod and, as I adjusted my clothes, I inquired about removing the queen's mark and smoothing my skin without having to extract the implant.

My relief at having her confirm it could be done turned to my dismay when she requested I wait to talk with Szaro first. Before I could argue further, the Great Hunter entered the room.

"Perfect timing," Belle said.

I grunted while Szaro smiled at my mate. "Teichi warned me of your arrival. I came as swiftly as I could."

The healer smiled, excused herself and left the room.

"Thank you. My husband is restless to go back to hunting," she said apologetically.

However, Szaro's slight frown upon hearing those words had all my senses on high alert. Whatever he would say next would undoubtedly piss me off.

"Just say what you have to say," I bluntly said. "I can already tell I will dislike it."

Szaro snorted and slowly nodded. "You guessed right. In short, we would like you to delay your return to the hunt until you've spent some time with the queen."

I recoiled at the unexpected reply. "Spend time with her? Whatever for?"

"Despite the great care we are giving her, she's still distressed and in a panic mode," Szaro explained. "She should have started laying eggs a couple of days ago. Based on her current hormonal levels, she's deliberately keeping herself from doing so. We believe it's because she is scared."

"But why?" Belle asked, echoing my thoughts.

"We can only speculate, but from experience, it would be because she feels unsafe and questions her own judgment," Szaro said with a frown while scratching the inner side of his hood. "She chose the location of her nest, which was almost immediately attacked by something she couldn't have defeated. She chose a commander of her guard, who was immediately taken away from her. And now, the people who took her protector from her are trying to coax her into laying her offspring. Seeing you safe and back by her side should help appease the queen and to restore her trust in her own judgment."

I heaved an annoyed sigh. "Very well," I grumbled. "I already lost four days. A couple more hours won't make that much difference." The way Szaro grimaced upon hearing my words immediately had me tensing. "What?"

"She will not start laying within minutes of seeing you," the Ordosian said in an apologetic tone. "In these types of situations, the females will generally wait for a few days of stability before they feel safe enough to lay their eggs."

"Surely this is a bad joke?" I hissed.

"I'm afraid not," Serena said in a commiserating tone. "Believe me, we tried to appease her so that we wouldn't have to trouble you further. But she's remained agitated ever since we took you away from her. And the Ordosians using their rattle to calm her only exacerbates her panic. While it does calm her, she's aware it's artificial, that she's technically being forced to be docile."

I clenched my teeth and slowly shook my head in disbelief. This was a conspiracy.

"Look, maybe we can find a compromise," Serena said in a soft voice. "You don't need to be holding her hand around the clock. So long as you're not gone more than an hour before she sees you again, it could work."

"There are no Flayers in that area," I countered. "By the time I fly to the location of a Flayer, I'll barely finish killing it than I'll have to fly back to the Queen. It would be pointless."

"We could lure a few of them to a safe location closer to the cave so that you wouldn't have to travel far," Szaro offered.

"And be once again accused of cheating?" I snarled. "I will not give the other hunters any excuse to shame or disrespect my mate."

"This would be different. We—"

"No!" I said in a tone that brooked no argument, interrupting Szaro. "I will *not* have anyone bring my kills to me. I'm a *hunter*," I added, slamming my main fists against my chest. "If I wanted easy kills, I'd go to a shooting gallery. I stalk prey myself. "

"Right. I understand," Szaro said, his voice neutral and his face devoid of emotion.

I didn't look at Belle. Her stare weighed heavily on me. I already knew what pleading expression I'd find on her features if I glanced her way.

Serena heaved a sigh with a slight air of defeat. "Well, it was worth a try. We'll sort it out."

I emitted an annoyed grunt and waved a dismissive hand. "I'll go babysit your queen," I said in a disgusted tone. "Anyway, I've already lost the hunt. Based on the current scoreboards, even if I killed myself hunting over the next few days, I'd still end up no higher than the twentieth position."

Helpless anger and humiliation burned in my gut at that prospect. I'd never ranked less than the top five. How would I show my face to my clan after this?

"Thank you for that," Serena said in a gentle tone laced with genuine gratitude and a bit of confusion. "But you know, you didn't lose, Bayron. You actually won this hunt. Credit wise, you're leaving here with pretty much double whatever the winner will get."

"That doesn't make sense," I replied. "And anyway, I don't care about credits."

Serena shrugged. "Be that as it may, the Hunters Federation is awarding you a cash prize for saving the queen, and the Pharmaceutical Coalition is also awarding you a cash prize. Beyond that, news of you single-handedly defeating a freaking Nharmyth without hunting gear and saving the last queen of a vital species has spread like wildfire. You're all everyone is talking about."

"See?! I told you!" Belle exclaimed, beaming at me.

"Did you two discuss this?" I asked, giving my mate a suspicious glance.

"Hell no! We didn't," Belle said, vehemently shaking her head. "But I knew people would react that way. You showed them what a hardcore hunter and wonderful protector you are. I'm so fucking proud of you!"

She walked up to me, wrapped her arms around my waist, and kissed her brand on my chest over the thin fabric of my shirt. I scrunched my face, failing to find an appropriate response to her words, yet feeling deeply touched by them.

"You galactic people are weird," I mumbled.

They all chuckled. But I instantly sobered, remembering the main reason I had wanted to talk to Szaro.

"Regarding that mark on my shoulder…" I said.

"It is best you keep it until a few Atrealls have hatched," Szaro said, guessing what I'd been planning on asking him. "If the Queen doesn't see it on you, she might take it as a personal rejection. But we will be able to completely remove it for you before you leave Trangor."

I grunted my assent, still annoyed it would remain on me a while longer.

"Stop being grumpy," Belle said with a chuckle.

I gave her a baleful glare, which only made her laugh harder.

For all that, my hearts still melted for my mate, for the unconditional love and support she always showed me.

"Before we take you to the queen, I have another question for you," Szaro said.

I narrowed my eyes at him, ready to lose it if he made another outrageous demand. "What?" I growled.

Laughing, he raised his palms in an appeasing gesture and looked at me with the type of amused expression I'd never expected an Ordosian would ever give me.

"Peace, Zamorian," he said teasingly. "This is actually about Ferach."

"Oh?" I said, the stiffness in my back shifting from a preemptive anger to concern.

A similar worry descended on my mate's features.

"It's nothing to worry about, quite the opposite," he said in a reassuring tone. "Teichi performed blood tests on you to see how you were reacting to the Atreall implant. She believes she can derive a powerful serum that would make Ferach immune to most infections and help regenerate his glands better than we can."

"Really?" I asked, stunned.

He nodded. "If you consent, she could prepare twelve doses for you to administer to Ferach once a month. Although she suspects that he will only need six of them before he's fully healed, and in fact enhanced."

"That's wonderful!" I exclaimed. "Of course, do it!"

"Didn't I tell you that you were freaking amazing?!" Belle exclaimed. "Every time I think I've seen the peak of your awesomeness, you blow my mind again!"

I scoffed to hide my embarrassment.

"Oh, he hasn't reached the peak yet," Serena said. "As your mate, he'll be passing on some of his new poison resistance and accelerated regeneration to you when you get frisky."

Unable to decide if she wanted to blush at having our sex life brought up or rejoice at learning I'd enhance her, Belle settled for burying her face in my chest while giving me a tight hug. I returned it, my hearts filling to bursting at such wondrous news.

A knock on the door spared her further embarrassment.

"Ah, Salha must be done examining Ferach," Szaro said.

"How about you and Belle go check on him? I'll stay here and draw some blood samples from Bayron for the serum," Serena said to her mate, taking me aback.

"Great idea!" Belle said, with far too much enthusiasm.

The way Szaro nodded and gave his mate an encouraging glance, I realized they were deliberately leaving the two of us alone. As much as I had been wanting to clear the air with her, I hadn't expected it to happen now, and I didn't feel quite ready for it.

While our mates exited the room, Serena went to fetch a syringe and multiple vials. She gestured at the examination table. I complied and sat at its edge while looking for the right words.

"Belle seems very happy," Serena said in a conversational tone while tying an elastic around my upper arm. "She has nothing but praises about you."

"Shocking, isn't it?" I replied, falling back on my comfortable snark.

She snorted. "Yeah, actually. Very…"

"Maybe she tamed the beast, and showed me the error of my ways," I said with a shrug.

Serena pursed her lips while disinfecting the crook of my elbow. "Or maybe she just helped the rest of us see who you truly are."

I opened and closed my mouth twice, my brain failing to seize the opening she was giving me.

"She… Belle sees the true me and helps me look at things from a different perspective," I said carefully. "Our views don't always align, but it is enlightening."

"Yeah, she certainly excels at making people revisit their

assumptions and preconceptions," Serena replied, giving me a pointed look that made clear she meant her assumptions about me.

I swallowed hard and squared my shoulders. "I do not know if the Flayers that forced you to intrude on the Ordosian territory were from the herd I had lured. They shouldn't have been able to wander that far north. But if they were, I want you to know that I'm sorry for the distress and hardship it caused you. I have faults, but I would never deliberately put anyone's life in jeopardy, least of all females and younglings. And although you do not know of our ways, on my honor, I swear I do not cheat."

I was stunned by the gentle way she looked at me. I'd expected her to dismiss my words.

"If you'd told me this back then, I wouldn't have believed a word of it. But now I do," Serena said softly. "Belle told me about the Zamorian culture and some of the ways you view competition. Since marrying Szaro, I've had to rethink a lot of the things I'd taken as being normal or the right way. If anything, I've learned that you shouldn't judge someone unless you truly understand where they're coming from or at least try to look at a situation through their eyes."

"And I have a lot of eyes," I deadpanned.

She snorted. "That, you do…"

I found myself smiling. She smiled back before sticking the needle in my arm.

"I am glad to see you're happy with your mate," I said.

She beamed at me. "I am extremely happy. When that mess went down, I thought my life had just been ruined. But it didn't take long for me to realize it was the greatest blessing I could have ever hoped for. While I also don't know if those Flayers came from the herd you lured, I'm grateful they forced me into the forbidden territory. Without it, I would have finished the hunt and left Trangor without knowing my soulmate was right here."

I nodded. "He clearly adores you. But… Do you miss the hunts?"

She shook her head firmly while sticking a new vial at the end of the needle. "I get the best of both worlds. I still hunt with the tribe when needed, but I always wanted to be a ranger. Caring for the fauna here is a dream come true."

"It warms my hearts to hear it. I… worried that I had involuntarily ruined your life," I admitted in a grumbling tone.

She chuckled and gave me a mischievous look. "I enjoyed letting you think you had. But no, you have not."

I glared at her, which made her laugh further.

"You're all right, Bayrohnziyiek Skortheatis. Take good care of that wife of yours. She's a true gem," Serena said, after pulling the needle out of my arm and putting a small bandage over the invisible wound. "Now, let's get you to that cave. You've got a queen to reassure."

I nodded and got on my feet.

CHAPTER 18
ANNABELLE

I would never forget the reaction of the Atreall Queen when Bayron and I walked inside the cave. The long, high-pitched mouse squeak she emitted upon seeing my husband nearly broke my heart. Even he couldn't remain indifferent to the joy she felt.

The jealousy I expected to feel never came. When Bayron went to stand next to her, the queen pawed at him like she couldn't believe he was truly here, touching the scar on his neck multiple times. My throat constricted watching her cling to him like a frightened child. I didn't even freak out when he wrapped an arm around her, gently caressing the fur around her neck while softly speaking to her in Zamorian.

Although I was still a long way from being fluent in his native language, I'd learned enough in the past couple of months to get the gist of what he was saying. My heart filled with love for him as he spoke words of encouragement, reassuring her she was safe.

After that moving reunion, we decided Bayron would indeed spend most of his days at the cave until the queen was fully appeased. The Federation shuttle brought us all kinds of creature comforts from cushioned chairs, an inflatable bed that we could fold into a loveseat, a small table, and top hunting equipment. They also left us a small personal shuttle so that we could easily travel back-and-forth if needed.

Bayron had wanted me to go back to the camp to be more at ease, but I was having a blast out here in the wild, drawing my little heart out. I especially enjoyed capturing the interactions of the queen with him and the Ordosians who came in rotation to assist.

As was his wont, Bayron went to hunt fresh meat for us for every meal, giving a portion to the queen, another to Ferach, and keeping the rest for us. At first, I freaked out when the pup joined him on those hunts. But with the Nharmyth gone, the other creatures nearby didn't present a threat. Anyway, the serum derived from Bayron's blood had made Ferach all but invincible. Between his stone skin, that enhanced poison and infection resistance, in addition to accelerated regeneration, our little wolf would have nothing to fear.

While the Ordosian's welcome to stay in their village still stood, Bayron and I decided to sleep in the cave. I'd done plenty of camping—both survival and recreational with my dad—and rather enjoyed this improvised getaway with my man and pup. We would bathe in the river, east of the vorea floating city.

On the fifth day, the queen began laying eggs.

Two days later, with the Ordosians' blessing, we returned to the base camp with the understanding that Bayron would drop by at least once or twice a day for at least thirty minutes. As he'd been spending more and more time away from the queen, and with her busy tending her eggs, she wasn't as clingy anymore.

It was our first time back at the camp in over two weeks. As soon as we stepped out of our shuttle, the hunters greeted us with a standing ovation. Startled, Ferach's skin turned to stone as he took a protective stance in front of us. That and this unexpected welcome turned me upside down. Every single hunter, their spouse, and the Hunters Federation staff were present in the hangar, cheering and clapping for Bayron. As I crouched next to Ferach to calm him, I glanced up at my husband. His expression moved me even more.

He was fighting the type of emotion that his people would deem a sign of weakness. I couldn't imagine how this felt for him. Bayron was used to contempt, general dislike, or cold and begrudging politeness—not this hero's welcome. But the image projected on the giant screen behind the dais, from whence Hunt Master Bron addressed the hunters, took my breath away.

The drawing I had made of Bayron holding the frightened queen in his arms, reassuring her when we first returned to the cave, hung on full display. Serena had repeatedly told me how good it was, even convincing me to let her send it to Master Bron. I never expected he would use it this way. And this big, it *was* stunning.

"Welcome back, Bayron," Hunt Master Bron said, waving for us to join him on the dais.

Confused and slightly uneasy at all the noise, Ferach followed quietly, his stone skin still active as he kept watch on all the overly excited people around us.

"Thank you, Hunt Master Bron," Bayron said, sounding slightly baffled as we reached him.

"We will not keep you for too long as you are likely eager to get back to the comfort and privacy of your quarters after such an ordeal," Hunt Master Bron said with enthusiasm. "However, on behalf of the United Planets Organization, the Galactic Hunters Federation, the Pharmaceutical Coalition, and every member of the Galactic Alliance, we thank you for your courage and your selfless sacrifice for the greater good."

By the way Bayron scrunched his face, I immediately knew he was preparing to make a cringe comment like 'I didn't do it for the greater good or for any of those organizations.' I pressed myself against him and gently caressed his braid just as he was opening his mouth. He glanced down at me. I smiled innocently while my eyes gave him the 'Behave' look he'd grown used to from me.

Although he made no sound, I could almost hear the inner grunt of annoyance he'd swallowed back.

"Thank you, Hunt Master Bron. Any of us would have done the same," Bayron mumbled graciously.

Bron shook his head with an approving glimmer in his eyes. "Any of us would have *wanted* to do the same, but *very few* could have achieved what you did, alone, and with such limited equipment. You have once more proven why you have consistently ranked among the top hunters of the galaxy. By putting the greater needs of others and the protection of the flora and fauna we all depend on before your own highly competitive personality and desires, you have also proven that you embody the spirit of the Galactic Hunters Federation."

I blinked, my face no doubt reflecting the shock my husband visibly felt. Beyond the crazy word salad that had just come out of the Hunt Master, the complete one-eighty degree turn on their views of him had to give Bayron whiplash.

"For this reason, I am honored to present you with this plaque of bravery and valor on behalf of the UPO and the Galactic Hunters Federation," Hunt Master Bron said, extending the medium size holo-plaque to him, which Bayron instinctively took. "Both organizations and the Pharmaceutical Coalition have also combined their resources to grant you a reward of five million credits as a thank you."

The cheers and round of applause that greeted Bron's words drowned my shocked gasp. Five freaking million credits?! This was way too much for just doing the right thing. There had to be more at play. Bayron looked just as shocked as I felt. Sure, Serena had mentioned he'd get a cash reward, but this was more than double what the winner would get.

Then I noticed Tarn filming us.

Is this some kind of publicity stunt?

"This is excessively generous," Bayron argued. "I do not hunt for credits. And I certainly do not need to be rewarded for doing the right thing."

"And this is exactly why you are deserving of this acknowledgment. We have already transferred the credits to your account," Hunt Master Bron added quickly when Bayron opened his mouth to argue some more. "And with your permission, Belle, the Federation would love to feature this stunning illustration of your husband caring for the young queen in our next publication."

I gaped at him, then cast a stunned look at Bayron. To my surprise, his shocked expression had given way to pride.

"Of course, she consents," Bayron replied in my stead, his boastful tone and demeanor coming back with a vengeance as he possessively tightened his arm around me. "My mate is the most talented action artist there is. Even Serena Bello has requested a collaboration with her for the Trangor encyclopedia she's been publishing."

My cheeks burning with pleasure, I gave Hunt Master Bron a timid smile as confirmation I was indeed happy to let them use it. What a freaking tremendous honor and insane exposure this would be for me!

"So, I've heard. We will seek a similar collaboration as well," Bron added with a broad grin.

Despite registering his words, my stupid mind got stuck on how handsome smiling made him. Like all Edocits—a dryad-like species—Hunt Master Bron had kept a youthful appearance even now that he had retired from active hunting because of his age. I'd love to draw him and capture the way the flowers in his vine-like hair had blossomed in reaction to his cheerful mood.

"I look forward to such a collaboration," I said with a nervous giggle.

"Excellent. Well, we have held you long enough. A bottle of

Edocit champagne awaits you in your quarters. Enjoy the evening."

We thanked him, still a little frazzled by all of this. As we came down from the dais, still being cheered by the crowd, Dr. Ahmad intercepted us. She offered to look after Ferach for the evening. Taken aback at first, I almost refused. But the mischievous look in her eyes and her knowing smile quickly shut me up. She chuckled at the crimson shade of my cheeks.

"Thank you," I said sheepishly, before casting a sideways glance at Bayron.

The heat in his eyes had my stomach flip-flopping. It had been too long since we'd been able to properly get frisky. As we had left Krada less than two hours after Bayron regaining consciousness, and we had spent the following days roughing it in the cave with the young queen, opportunities had been slim. Granted, we fondled and kissed when we washed in the nearby river and whenever we could steal a moment in private. However, with Ferach's jealous interference, we could never go all out.

In our fairly small quarters, we'd have to lock Ferach in the hygiene room. Once I started shouting my lungs out, he was bound to break down the door, thinking I was getting gutted. A wild night with my husband sounded just like what I needed.

After we pet Ferach goodbye, we made our way to our quarters while the crowd dispersed.

"That was awesome," I said, trying to ignore the flame in the pit of my stomach. "Now everyone finally sees what I saw in you."

He grunted dismissively.

"It's okay to admit that I was right, and that you enjoyed being praised," I added teasingly.

He gave me a strange sideways glance, his wheels clearly spinning. "It is always nice to be acclaimed," he conceded in a serious tone, far from the boasting I expected. "Hunt Master

Bron also isn't wrong in saying that most of the other hunters wouldn't have been able to do it under similar circumstances. However, this is mostly a marketing ploy."

I frowned, disturbed to have him echo some of the thoughts that had crossed my mind. "What do you mean?"

"I believe that the excessive reward is coming from a genuine place," he replied pensively. "The UPO, the Hunters Federation, and the Pharmaceutical Coalition are extremely grateful for this new queen and anything that will strengthen the relationship with the Ordosians. This planet is a treasure trove for medical research and the drugs industry."

"Right. So you think it's encouraging other hunters to act like you did in the hope of such a steep reward?" I asked.

He shook his head. "Not really. Sure, the lower ranked hunters would love getting such a huge stash of credits. But those with the skills to do something like this already have more credits than they need. This is about courting other 'primitive' planets like Trangor, where the locals are reluctant to deal with the UPO and the Hunters Federation. The illustration you did of me caring for the Atreall is quite impactful. I suspect they will ask for more similar pieces from you, showing both the heroic and altruistic faces of our hunts."

"That makes sense," I said as we reached the door, which Bayron opened before entering first. "But whatever the reason, I'm just happy you're the one who made all of this happen. You're my superhero."

"No," Bayron growled, pushing the door closed behind me. "What I am is your husband, who has severely missed his time alone with you."

I chuckled with approval, my stomach quivering as he effort-lessly picked me up. His lips greedily claimed mine as I wrapped my legs around his waist. Even with our lips locked and his hands groping me, Bayron moved around the room with confi-dent steps. He stopped next to the dresser, placing the holographic plaque on top, before proceeding to strip me of my clothes.

My husband didn't fully remove my dress. As soon as it cleared my head, he left it up to me to discard it. His mouth eagerly reclaimed my mouth while his hands frantically worked on my bra. He nearly yanked it off me, tossing it somewhere in the room while bending me backward. Holding me with his secondary hands, he sucked and licked on my right nipple, pausing only long enough for his primary hands to remove his t-shirt.

I felt him stepping out of his shoes, and I kicked my own off, my hands slipping between us to undo the waist clasps of his pants. I gasped against his mouth when he firmly pulled my hands away. Bending them behind my back, he held my wrists with a single massive hand. My toes curled at this imposed help-lessness. I gladly surrendered to Bayron's dominance.

My stomach did another backflip when his fingers brushed against my core. His tongue silenced my frustrated groan once I realized he was merely undoing his leather pants himself. They slipped down his legs with the soft sound of fabric. Bayron broke the kiss as he stepped out of them, his teeth bared in an almost menacing way as he locked gazes with me while removing his bracer.

I freaking loved the famished, almost feral way he always stared at me, like I was the sexiest, most desirable woman in the universe. He looked like he simply couldn't resist the urge to have me, to ravage and defile me in every way possible. And I wanted that.

"I'm going to do unspeakable things to you," he growled, as if he'd heard the thoughts crossing my mind.

He carried me inside the shower. The much smaller size, compared to the ones on his ship and in our dwelling on Xoccoris, forced greater closeness between us, not that I minded. My back stiffened at the cold feel of the white tiles against my back, severely contrasting with the heat of Bayron's skin around me.

He turned on the water, letting it rain over us, while he continued to kiss and touch me. With him still holding my hands behind my back, I could do nothing but accept his control of me. A needy moan escaped me when his fingers brushed over my clit, before dipping inside of me.

Contrary to his usual slow build of my pleasure, interspersed with much teasing, Bayron seemed impatient, as if under too powerful a need of his own for long preliminaries. Instead of scaring me, that turned me on further. My inner walls palpitated around his fingers as they moved in and out of me. They immediately zeroed in on my G-spot. Normally, I had to beg him to stop avoiding it as he subjected me to the most exquisite torture.

If he wanted me to climax quickly, I wouldn't deny him. Gyrating my hips, I shamelessly rode his hand as pleasure built inside me. His teeth nipping at the hard bud of my right nipple had me cresting in no time. To my shock, just as I was about to fall over the edge, Bayron pulled his hand out. My eyes jerked open in outrage.

Any word I might have spoken got swept away by a throaty cry when my mate slammed his lower cock inside me in one powerful thrust. Slipping his secondary arms behind my knees, Bayron propped me up a little higher. His primary right hand still bound my wrists while his left held my nape in that dominant way he always did to stare at my face.

Lips parted, breathing heavily between two moans, I felt on the verge of combusting as Bayron immediately set a punishing pace, pumping in and out of me. With the friction of his main cock rubbing against my clit, I never stood a chance. I cried out, swept away by bliss. The spasms shaking my body were barely noticeable in his tight embrace.

Restrained as I was, I could only take all that he had to give and did he ever. I loved feeling this helpless, like he was using me for his pleasure. And yet, his entire focus was on mine. He wouldn't allow himself to climax until he had made me scream at least a second time. An inferno raged inside of me as his cock relentlessly pounded my sweet spot, sending electric shocks coursing down my legs. His fingers starting to probe my rear further fanned the flames consuming me from within.

My orgasm started as a slow tide that quickly turned into a squall, leaving me boneless in my husband's arms. Only then did Bayron release my wrists and free me from this restrained position.

Still thrusting into me, this time at a much gentler pace, he covered my face with tender kisses as I continued to ride my orgasm.

"Do you have any idea how breathtaking you are when you fall apart for me?" he whispered in a rumbling voice made even deeper by lust. "Do you have any idea how much I love you?"

Still half-dazed from the throes of ecstasy, I looked at him through hooded eyes, my heart filling with love for my Beast. I clasped my shaky hands behind his neck and smiled.

"Hopefully at least half as much as I love you," I slurred, looking at him with adoration.

"My love… My soulmate," he whispered, kissing me.

It was slow and tender, filled with devotion, and none of the previous fury he had unleashed on me. He pulled out of me, carefully inserting his main cock instead. Bayron proceeded to gently make love to me, his lower cock rubbing against the seam of my bum.

We exchanged kisses and caresses, a part of me wishing we were in bed instead so that I could explore all of him. And yet, I wouldn't want the distance it would require for me to do so. I would never tire of being wrapped in my husband's strong embrace. The fresh scent of our lightly perfumed soap tickled my nose as Bayron's hands roamed over me. He wasn't so much using the soap to wash me than for how it made each caress silkier.

I cupped his face with my hands and locked eyes with him, my lips a hair's breadth from his.

"Put the second one in," I whispered.

Bayron stiffened, his eyes widening. "My mate?" he asked, wondering if he had heard me right.

I smiled and nodded. "Put it in. I want to fully be one with you. I want all of you inside me."

"It will hurt, my love," Bayron insisted.

I kissed his lips and rubbed my nose against his. "The first time we made love hurt a little, too, but you quickly made it amazing. And now I can't get enough of you. You have been preparing me for a while. Go on, my husband. I trust you to take care of me, like you always do."

"If it's too much, you tell me, you hear?" he warned in a stern voice.

I smiled and pressed my lips to his, and he immediately took control. His tongue dominated mine as he stepped away from under the water. He didn't start pushing himself in right away. Instead, I felt the familiar tingling effect of his self-lubricant relaxing my muscles.

Despite my desire for him to proceed, I tensed when he removed his main cock. Lifting me slightly higher, he began inserting the tip of his lower cock in my rear. It didn't go in very far before meeting resistance. Ignoring the nagging little voice telling me this had been a bad idea, I focused on the taste of his lips, the feel of his body, and my blind trust in him.

His fingers on my clit further helped to distract from the discomfort. Each time it threatened to become painful, his self-lubricant numbed it, making my muscles relax. With shallow thrusts, he gradually inserted himself, whispering words of love and encouragement. It was a strange sensation, heightened by the string of 'pearls' along the sides of his cock.

"You did it, my mate," Bayron suddenly whispered, his voice laced with awe and wonder.

Shocked, I realized he was indeed fully sheathed, his erect main cock pressing against my clit. "I told you I could trust you to handle me right," I whispered back. "I love you."

"I love you more, my wife," he replied before kissing me again.

He started moving at an exceedingly slow pace, making sure he wasn't hurting me, then gradually accelerated. Soon, the friction of his main cock against my clit had me aching for more. When he finally pushed it inside my vagina, I thought I would burst at the seam. Good heavens! I had never been so full. Thankfully, he paused, giving me a moment to adjust to having both of his cocks inside me.

My inner walls contracting around his main cock gave him the signal I was ready for some action. As soon as he started moving, a tsunami of sensations crashed over me. Between the pearl-shaped ridges of his length, the pivoting head grazing my sweet spot with each stroke, and the aphrodisiac properties of his self-lubricant making me wild with need, I dove head-first into an overwhelming maelstrom of pleasure. Lava coursed through my veins, setting each of my nerve endings ablaze.

One strangled moan after the other rose from my throat as I clawed at my man, needing more and yet fearing my mind would shatter from this excess of bliss.

"So good… So fucking good," Bayron suddenly growled as if under severe strain.

With both of his cocks inside me, doubling his pleasure, I couldn't begin to imagine what he felt. A single look at his face made me fall apart. Eyes closed, features constricted almost with an air of extreme pain, Bayron appeared to be fighting not to lose control. I had seen his blissful expressions before, but never one this intense.

I climaxed with a sharp cry, a blinding white light exploding before my eyes. Bayron roared, his hold painfully tightening around me as something broke inside of him. He gave in to his unbridled passion, taking me hard and fast. The Beast had truly been unleashed as he voiced his ecstasy in grunts halfway between moans and almost feral growls. The knot at the base of his main cock partially swelled, quadrupling the sensation of the ridges around his shafts. I felt like a ragdoll swept away in a whirlwind of pleasure-pain, which wrested one climax after the other from me.

When Bayron finally surrendered to ecstasy, my voice was shot, and my mind was all but gone. After a lengthy embrace during which my husband showered me with words of love and devotion, I vaguely felt him pulling out of me. He washed us, dried us, and took us to bed.

Completely destroyed, I fell asleep in the strong arms of my soulmate, feeling safe and cherished.

EPILOGUE
BAYRON

Two weeks after our return to the base camp, the Great Hunt ended. All the hunters left Trangor, some heading to their next hunt, others going on a well-deserved break. But not Belle and me. Although the Atreall Queen—who Belle had named Maya—had laid hundreds of eggs, they were all still in the pupal stage. It would take another ten to fifteen days before the first Atreall Workers reached maturity.

The Ordosians didn't have to tell me it would be preferable I stick around until the first soldiers could take on their duty in a couple of weeks. Once surrounded by her army, the queen would no longer require my presence to keep feeling safe. Considering my next hunt wasn't due for another thirty days, I didn't mind the delayed departure as it would still leave us with enough time to get there before the start. I had planned on taking my mate shopping on some of the finest pleasure barges along the way, but we could postpone it until after.

As an additional perk, since the base camp was shutting down until the next hunt, we received a second invitation to stay with the Ordosians while I completed my role with the queen. I suspected Serena had played a significant role in making this happen. As I had been unconscious for the duration of our initial stay here, I finally got to experience life in an Ordosian village.

Despite spending years traveling to various worlds and mingling with countless foreign species, for the first time, I truly immersed myself in a different culture. At last, I realized how you could spend a great deal of time working alongside people and know nothing about who they really were. I didn't know my fellow hunters any more than they knew me.

The cultural clash struck me hard. Where Zamorians were extremely social with regular assemblies, frequent communal meals in the gathering hall, and countless competitive activities, Ordosians were the exact opposite. As adults only ate once every two weeks to a month, they didn't gather for meals, not even with their family units. They usually only gathered for specific events, one of them being a rhythmic gymnastics dance Serena performed for us and the entire village. Generally, they kept activities to their family unit, and most of them had careers revolving around the protection of their world.

And I got the honor of experiencing it all by their side. While Serena and my mate seized the opportunity of our sojourn to begin their collaboration, Szaro took Ferach and me scouting with his people. It was a broad term that included assisting creatures injured or in a precarious situation, eliminating or relocating predators that had roamed past their territory, and assessing threats to the local flora. Of course, we also performed some proper hunting of the most insane creatures, some of which I'd never heard of. We fully consumed all kills. What couldn't be eaten, they used to make weapons, crafting material, or medicine.

Aside from opening my eyes to a new way of living—not that it was for me—it also gave Ferach the opportunity to train his impressive skills in a real hunting environment. As he acknowledged me as his alpha, he adapted to me, following my cues. He would crouch down in his stone skin to make himself look like a rock covered in dark-brown moss before leaping on unsuspecting prey coming within range.

It was with heavy hearts that I saw our stay come to an end. While I wouldn't define the evolution of my relationship with Szaro as brotherly friendship, we had developed an honest mutual respect. However, the sisterly affection between our mates moved me deeply. Even leaving the young queen felt strange. But I would drop by to see how she fared in six months when we returned here for another hunt.

On the morning of our departure, while their healer Teichi removed the queen's mark on my neck, Belle collected the countless hair ornaments she'd had the Ordosian crafters make for her—which were technically for me. I couldn't wait to return home and show my braid off to everyone.

As our shuttle left Trangor, a part of me had irrevocably changed.

❧

ANNABELLE

When I met Kayog on Earth in the hopes of being paired, I never imagined just how completely it would change my life and exceed all of my wildest dreams. Any fairy tale paled in comparison to my happily ever after.

First, I'd married the perfect husband, with a body to die for, who made me feel like the most cherished treasure in the world, and who gave me chains of mind-blowing orgasms like he had a quota to maintain. And my girly bits fully approved.

Second, I had seen and experienced in person more worlds, more foreign cultures, and way more insane creatures than most people had ever simply heard of. Before Bayron, my wallet had not permitted me to leave Earth, let alone travel extensively. My Beast made it a point to take me all over creation in-between hunts.

Third, all that traveling further fueled the crazy career I never dreamed possible. My husband had been right about them using my illustration of him tending to the young queen as a marketing ploy. They regularly commissioned more pieces from me, some featuring different hunters, and many with Bayron as the hero.

Initially, I'd worried they hadn't retained me for my talent but to milk the fame that had befallen my husband after him rescuing the queen. People loved a good redemption story. As Bayron had correctly guessed, the UPO and the Hunters Federation were using it to court primitive species reluctant to welcome them on their worlds. Him mending his differences with Serena and the friendship that blossomed between her and me only added to that beautiful narrative.

However, the resounding success of the showing of my personal collections, as organized by Serena's mother, kicked my imposter syndrome to the curb. I remembered the days when I had to almost beg people to commission me, and now I was turning down requests left, right, and center. Between my work on Serena's encyclopedias, my contract with the Federation, and working on my own new collections, I had no time left for free-lance work.

Frankly, I considered ditching the Federation. But on top of the amazing pay and unparalleled exposure I got from that collaboration, Bayron enjoyed far too much being one of the faces of the Hunters Federation. Seeing him strutting like a peacock, puffing out his chest, and bragging to his clan every time they published one of my illustrations featuring him had me in stitches.

But my Beast had much more to boast about.

Thanks to the exotic material and ornaments I acquired in the various worlds we visited, and the ones I created myself,

Bayron's braid became a sensation. In the illustration of him caring for Maya—which I had titled The Queen's Guard—I had included the Ordosian adornments I had woven into his braid. Once the Federation published it, and it went public, adorned braids began trending.

A handful of hair care and hair accessories companies approached Bayron about campaign deals. One even offered to sell my own line of accessories. I seriously considered it but ended up declining. Aside from designing them, the company expected me to hold a blog with how-to videos, quick tips, and life hacks. I had no time for it. That didn't stop fashion bloggers from regularly sharing pictures of my man's latest hairdo. While it became an added pressure for me to stay creative, I loved how proud it made him, and especially the envious looks it earned him every time we returned home. Seeing his clanmates flaunting braid styles similar to some of my previous creations had me strutting just as much as Bayron.

Life was good.

During the first five years of our marriage, we traipsed all over the galaxy, Ferach in tow. On top of making a full recovery, the stone wolf had grown bigger and stronger than most males of his species. From paws to head, he measured five feet and weighed two-hundred and fifty pounds. In stone form, he weighed over three-hundred pounds. While he enjoyed life with us, and now joined Bayron in most of his hunts, we could feel him growing increasingly restless.

At the approach of our sixth wedding anniversary, Bayron radically cut down on his hunts so that we could spend more time at home on Xoccoris and start our family. The minute I removed my contraceptive implant, I immediately became pregnant. With us still going at it like rabbits, it inevitably happened fast.

As Ugrul had forewarned, Zamorian babies were massive. Since I could never go about things the easy way, I ended up with twins. It was all fun and games until I became so big and so swollen, the shortest walk had me out of breath and with serious back pain. Like all Zamorian pregnancies, the gestation lasted ten months. Despite the various physical discomforts I had to deal with, I cherished every moment of that experience.

Bayron pampered me with a zeal that bordered on obsession, seeing to my every need, anticipating most of them, feeding my weirdest cravings, and giving me the most insane massages with those four hands of his. Then the entire clan also stepped in. Their genuine worry and care moved me to the core. I thought I had finally found a family when I married Bayron. I never expected it would extend to an entire clan. My roots had spread wide and deep.

The only dark cloud in that perfect sky was Ferach leaving us. In the last weeks of my pregnancy, every time Bayron took him out hunting for the day's fresh meat, the wolf would vanish in the forest for increasingly long periods of time. When it started dragging into hours of absence, Bayron gave him a loose collar, with a discreet chime that would tell him it was time to come back. It worked a few times, but eventually, Ferach didn't return.

As much as it broke my heart, we had always known that eventually, the call of the wild would be too much for him to resist. We still cherished the years he had spent with us, and the knowledge we had given him a chance at a future.

A month later, I gave birth to our fraternal twins, a beautiful daughter we named Astrasaya—Astra for shorts—and a firstborn son named Rygarsayek—Rygar for shorts, which meant invincible in Zamorian. They were both fully Zamorian, with double of everything, their features a perfect mix of their father's and mine. While Rygar had my undisciplined blonde locks, Astra inherited her father's bluish-black hair.

Born petite by Zamorian standards, with the cutest face, Astra got ridiculously doted on by both her sire and grandfather. Bayron even had to break up some heated arguments between clanmates—both male and female—fighting over who got to play with her and look after her when we needed a babysitter.

Naturally, calling our kids 'the twins' was a hell no. I cringed every time someone referred to them as such, to Bayron's malicious amusement. He called it vindication for having dubbed his cocks at such for years, against his wishes. I called them *dananns*, the Zamorian word for twins.

Standing naked in front of the mirror but for my undies, I was trying to decide what to wear for that evening's assembly. I'd taken to dressing like the Zamorian females with cropped tops and long or short skirts with a high slit on the side. In my years living among them, I'd gotten over feeling self-conscious about my paunch. However, since giving birth to my huge babies then losing that baby fat, those insecurities had come back with exponential acuity. While the scar of the C-section had been smoothed out to where you couldn't even see it, a lot of extra skin had now joined the expanded network of stretch marks that had now tripled.

Bayron entering our bedroom startled me. I instinctively pressed a skirt in front of my stomach, my stupid face heating as if I'd been caught doing something bad.

"Sorry to make you wait. I'm almost ready. Just give me a minute," I said, hurrying towards the hygiene room.

"Belle!" Bayron called, his voice stern and imperative.

I stopped and cast a curious look at him over my shoulder. A deep frown creased his forehead as he stared at me, clearly displeased.

"Enough of this," he said in a chastising tone as he walked towards me.

Taken aback, I turned around to face him. "Enough of what?"

"Put the skirt down," he ordered, ignoring my question.

I immediately squirmed, my brain struggling to produce a

good excuse to deflect. "Why? We're going to be late for the assembly. Let me just go——"

"Belle… Drop. The. Skirt," he repeated in a tone that brooked no argument.

I scrunched my face and tightened my arms around my waist, further pressing the skirt to my front. My eyes pricked with an irrational need to cry. Bayron had never made me feel unattractive. The passion he still showed me proved his desire for me had not waned in any way. But with each passing day, I just kept growing increasingly insecure. Losing my baby fat had only made my stomach look worse.

To my surprise, Bayron's anger dropped just as quickly as it had appeared, replaced by a deeply wounded expression that cut me to the core.

"Do you really doubt my love for you this much?" he asked.

I recoiled, flabbergasted by such a question. "No, of course not! But——"

"But nothing! I love you, Belle. *All* of you; paunch and stretch marks included. You are even more beautiful to me today because of them," he said forcefully.

I gaped at him, too stunned to resist when he gently pulled my arms open with his main hands and took the skirt from me with his secondary ones. I swallowed hard, feeling vulnerable and exposed as he stared at the saggy, stretched skin around my stomach. My brain couldn't process the air of wonder and adoration on his face.

He slowly kneeled in front of me, two of his hands keeping my arms spread on my sides while the other two caressed my stomach.

"These are the reminder that two perfect little beings, *my* offspring, now live thanks to you and are being doted on as we speak by my mother. No one thought you would be able to carry a single Zamorian child to term, let alone two. And yet, here they are, strong and healthy," Bayron said passionately. "These are your battle scars, the trophies that testify of the strength and courage you displayed for ten months carrying my children. Wear them proudly. Show them off to the world. Remind them that you, Annabelle Skortheatis, carried Bayron's twins without faltering."

"*Dananns*, not twins," I corrected in a shaky voice, my throat almost too constricted to speak.

He snorted and smiled tenderly as he looked up at me. "Do not hide your beauty from me, my mate. I love everything about you, and especially these."

Tears of joy rolled down my cheeks as he leaned forward and kissed my stomach before rubbing his face over it. I had no idea what I had done to deserve this male, but I would never be able to thank Kayog and all the powers that be enough for such a blessing.

A high-pitched sound resonated in three quick successions, startling us out of this tender moment. Bayron got up and cast a concerned look at the interface of his bracer. Shock quickly replaced it.

"What is it?" I asked.

"Get dressed, quickly. I have a hunch…" he replied enigmatically.

Baffled, I almost insisted he tell me, but it would be a waste of time and energy. I slipped on the skirt and tank top, stretch marks on full display, and slipped a pair of shoes on. We climbed inside our personal shuttle on our terrace and flew out of the compound. To my utter shock, many of our clan's warriors had gathered outside the city walls in a defensive stance. It took me a moment to realize what had prompted such a response.

Five hundred meters away, standing by the tree line of the forest, a pack of at least two dozen stone wolves stared at the city. My heart leapt in my chest.

"Ferach…" I whispered, easily recognizing him by his collar as he stood in front of the pack.

Of course, he had left us to rejoin his people.

No, not rejoin them, but lead them.

He looked so much bigger than the others, no doubt thanks to the enhancement Bayron's serum had given him. All these years of him hunting with my husband had also made Ferach the ultimate predator. No wonder none of his peers could challenge him as their alpha. The oddest maternal pride warmed my chest.

Bayron landed the shuttle at a relatively safe distance. "Stay inside," he warned me. "Do not come out until I say so."

I nodded. I didn't fear Ferach, but I had no idea how the rest of his pack would react to our presence. Thankfully, their stance wasn't threatening.

As soon as Bayron disembarked, Ferach looked over his shoulder at the pack and emitted a single bark. The other wolves didn't react, remaining still as he started walking towards my mate. Tears welled in my eyes when the two of them embraced. Ferach rubbed his cheek against Bayron's before looking at the shuttle, his eyes glowing a bright blue.

My mate gestured for me to come. I all but ran over, giving Ferach a tight hug.

"Thank you for letting us know you're doing okay," I said in a trembling voice.

He rubbed his cheek against mine before pulling away. I thought he would leave, but he emitted a brief howl in the direction of his pack. My jaw dropped at the sight of a female approaching with three pups in tow.

I pressed a hand to my chest, more tears rolling down my face. Good heavens, I was a pathetic cry baby.

"No wonder you left, my friend," Bayron said in an approving tone. "You have a family to protect."

Ferach introduced us to his mate and offspring. While the female remained a little distant, the young pups came to us with the bold and careless curiosity of the young and innocent. My chest constricted further, feeling like a proud grandma.

Before we parted ways, Bayron gestured at the collar still wrapped around Ferach's neck. The wolf lifted his head, exposing his neck so that Bayron could remove it. To our surprise, Ferach took the collar back, holding it in its mouth.

"You want to keep it?" Bayron asked.

"I think he wants you to be able to call him, should you want to," I said in a soft voice.

"Maybe," Bayron replied.

We gave Ferach a final caress then watched him head back inside the forest, his family and pack following his lead. I pressed myself against Bayron, who wrapped a protective arm around my shoulders.

Yes, my roots had buried deep and wide, even in the wilderness of Xoccoris.

THE END

BAYRON

GRUMMOLL

STONE WOLF

VOREA

NHARMYTH

ATREALL

ALSO BY REGINE ABEL

THE VEREDIAN CHRONICLES
Escaping Fate
Blind Fate
Raising Amalia
Twist of Fate
Hands of Fate
Defying Fate

BRAXIANS
Anton's Grace
Ravik's Mercy
Krygor's Hope

XIAN WARRIORS
Doom
Legion
Raven
Bane
Chaos
Varnog
Reaper
Wrath
Xenon
Nevrik
Rogue

PRIME MATING AGENCY
I Married A Lizardman
I Married A Naga
I Married A Birdman
I Married A Minotaur

ABOUT REGINE

USA Today bestselling author Regine Abel is a fantasy, paranormal and sci-fi junkie. Anything with a bit of magic, a touch of the unusual, and a lot of romance will have her jumping for joy. She loves creating hot alien warriors and no-nonsense, kick-ass heroines that evolve in fantastic new worlds while embarking on action-packed adventures filled with mystery and the twists you never saw coming.

Before devoting herself as a full-time writer, Regine had surrendered to her other passions: music and video games! After a decade working as a Sound Engineer in movie dubbing and live concerts, Regine became a professional Game Designer and Creative Director, a career that has led her from her home in Canada to the US and various countries in Europe and Asia.

Facebook
https://www.facebook.com/regine.abel.author/

Website
https://regineabel.com

Regine's Rebels Reader Group

https://www.facebook.com/groups/ReginesRebels/

Newsletter

http://smarturl.it/RA_Newsletter

Goodreads

http://smarturl.it/RA_Goodreads

Bookbub

https://www.bookbub.com/profile/regine-abel

Amazon

http://smarturl.it/AuthorAMS